JAWBONE

JAW

BONE

Mónica Ojeda

Translated by Sarah Booker

COFFEE HOUSE PRESS
MINNEAPOLIS
2022

First English-language edition published 2022
Copyright © 2017 by Mónica Ojeda
Translation © 2022 by Sarah Booker
Cover design by Zoe Norvell
Book design by Bookmobile
Author photograph © Lisbeth Salas

Cover images: Portrait of a Ballerina © Studio Marmellata stocksy.com
/marmellata; Sober Woman Portraits © Thais Varela stocksy.com
/azulclaritocasiblanco; crocodile © shutterstock.com/g/EmBaSy;
volcano © Jayzel Florendo unsplash.com/@jayzflorendo.

First published in Spanish as *Mandíbula* (Barcelona: Editorial Candaya, 2018);
author represented by Agencia Literaria CBQ (Barcelona).

Coffee House Press books are available to the trade through our primary dis-
tributor, Consortium Book Sales & Distribution, cbsd.com or (800) 283-3572.
For personal orders, catalogs, or other information, write to info@coffeehouse
press.org.

Coffee House Press is a nonprofit literary publishing house. Support from private foundations, corporate giving programs, government programs, and generous individuals helps make the publication of our books possible. We gratefully
acknowledge their support in detail in the back of this book.

LIBRARY OF CONGRESS CATALOGING-IN-PUBLICATION DATA

Names: Ojeda, Mónica, 1988– author. | Booker, Sarah, translator.
Title: Jawbone / Mónica Ojeda ; translated by Sarah Booker.
Other titles: Mandíbula. English
Description: First English-language edition. | Minneapolis : Coffee House
    Press, 2022.
Identifiers: LCCN 2021035312 | ISBN 9781566896214 (trade paperback)
    ISBN 9781566896306 (ebook)
Subjects: GSAFD: Horror fiction. | LCGFT: Horror fiction.
Classification: LCC PQ8220.425.J433 M3613 2022 | DDC 863/.7—dc23
LC record available at https://lccn.loc.gov/2021035312

PRINTED IN THE UNITED STATES OF AMERICA

JAWBONE

A huge crocodile in whose jaws you are—that's the mother.
—JACQUES LACAN, TRANSLATED BY R. GRIGG

The jawbone of death
of the cannibal jawbone of death.
—LEOPOLDO MARÍA PANERO

Everything I write boils down to two or three words
Mother Daughter Sister
A trinity Psychoanalysis failed to foresee.
—VICTORIA GUERRERO, TRANSLATED BY
ANNA GUERCIO ROSENWONG

There is a joy in fear.
—JOANNA BAILLIE

Horror is tied to life like a tree to light.
—GEORGE BATAILLE

Any practice of speech . . . is a language of fear.
—JULIA KRISTEVA, TRANSLATED BY LEON S. ROUDIEZ

And the hue of the skin of the figure was of the perfect
whiteness of the snow.
—EDGAR ALLAN POE

It was the whiteness of the whale that above all things appalled me.
—HERMAN MELVILLE

While beyond it rose the white, ghostlike height of Mt. Terror, ten
thousand, nine hundred feet in altitude, and now extinct as a volcano.
—H. P. LOVECRAFT

There he lies, white and cold in death.
—MARY SHELLEY

I

She fluttered her eyes open, and in rushed all the shadows of the breaking day. Those voluminous stains—"Opacity is the spirit of objects," her therapist said—allowed her to make out some battered furniture and, farther away, a phantomized body scrubbing the floor with a hobbit mop. "Shit." She spat onto the wood against which the uglier side of her 1966-Twiggy-*face* was pressed. "Shit." And her voice sounded like one from a black-and-white Saturday-night cartoon. She pictured herself on the floor but with Twiggy's face, which was actually hers except for the English model's classic-duck-colored eyebrows, rubber-ducky eyebrows that didn't look anything like the unplucked burnt straw above her own eyes. Even though she couldn't see herself, she knew the exact shape her body was lying in and the hardly graceful expression that must have been on her face in that brief moment of lucidity. That total awareness of her image gave her a false sense of control, but it didn't entirely calm her, because, unfortunately, self-awareness doesn't make anyone Wonder Woman, whom she needed to be in order to free herself from the ropes that bound her hands and legs, just like the most glamorous actresses in her favorite thrillers.

According to Hollywood, ninety percent of kidnappings have a happy ending, she thought, surprised that her mind hadn't assumed a more serious attitude in such a moment.

I'm tied up. That statement sounded so unbelievable in her head! Until then, "to be tied" had been a metaphor without substance. "My hands are tied," her mother would say, her hands free. Now, however, thanks to the unfamiliar place and pain in her extremities, she was sure that something very bad was happening to her, something like what happened in the movies she would watch so she could listen, as she touched herself, to a voice like Johnny Depp's saying: "With this candle, I will light your way into darkness"—according to her therapist, that arousal, with her since she was six years old, when she began to masturbate on the toilet seat while repeating lines from movies, was indication of a precocious sexual behavior that they should explore together. She always imagined violence as a crashing of waves that engulfed the rocks until bursting against the flesh of something living, but never as this theater of shadows, nor as the stillness interrupted by the steps of a hunched silhouette. In class, the English teacher made them read a poem that was just as dark and confusing. She still remembered two lines that suddenly, in that possible cabin or bunker of creaking wood, began to make sense:

> *There, the eyes are*
> *Sunlight on a broken column.*

Her eyes had to be that now: sunlight on a broken column—the broken column was, of course, the place of her kidnapping, an unknown and arachnid space that looked like the antithesis of her own house. She had mistakenly opened her eyes, not thinking about how difficult it would be to make out that shadowy rectangle and the kidnapper that cleaned it like any old housewife. She tried not to think about such pointless matters, but she was already outside herself, in the snarled mess of the unknown, forced to confront what she couldn't figure out. To look at the things that make up the world, the darkness and the light weaving together only to unravel again, the accumulation of all that exists and occupies a place within her friend Anne's histrionic composition of the drag-queen God—what would she say when she found out about her disappearance? And Fiore? And Natalia? And Analía? And Xime? Everything in her eyes burning hotter than any fever ever could was all an accident. She didn't want to see and be hurt by what the world was made up of, but how bad was the situation she found herself in? The answer suggested a new inconvenience: an upwelling in the depths of her throat.

The floor-scrubbing figure stopped and looked at her, or that's what she thought she did, though with the backlighting, she couldn't see anything more than a figure that looked like the night.

"If you're awake, sit up."

Fernanda, with the right side of her face pressed against the wood, let out a short, involuntary laugh that she regretted the moment she heard herself, comparing the sound of her instincts to a weasel's cry. With each passing second she better understood what was happening, and her anxiety rose and spread through the dimly lit space as if it were scaling the air. She tried to sit up, but her limited movements were those of a fish convulsing under its own fears. That last failure forced her to recognize the pathetic state of her body, now worming around, and prompted a fit of laughter she couldn't contain.

"What are you laughing at?" the living shadow asked, though without real interest, as she wrung out the hobbit mop into the silhouette of a bucket.

Fernanda gathered all her willpower to hold back the toothy laugh threatening to burst forth, and when she finally regained control, ashamed of how little command she had over her reactions, she remembered that she had been picturing herself on the floor in an electric-blue dress, a modern version of a kidnapped Twiggy, *top-model-always-diva* even in extreme situations, and not the school uniform she was actually wearing: hot, wrinkled, and smelling of softener.

Disappointment took the form of a plaid skirt and a white blouse stained with ketchup.

"*Sorry,* Miss Clara. It's just that I can't move."

The body leaned the mop against a wall and, wiping her hands on her aspirational nun's clothing, walked toward her, emerging from the sharp shadows into bright light that revealed the pink flesh of a plucked pelican. Fernanda fixed her gaze on her teacher's oviparous face as if that instance of scrutiny, during which she identified, for the first time, purple veins on her cheeks, were vital. *Don't cocks only protrude from legs?* she wondered as hands that were too long lifted her from the floor and into a seated position. But for all that she tried to take advantage of her proximity to the *Latin* Madame Bovary, she couldn't make out a single fumbled word in her gestures. There were people who thought with their faces, and it was enough to learn how to read their forehead muscles to figure out what the creases overflowed from, but not just anyone had the ability to elucidate the messages of the flesh. Fernanda believed that Miss Clara spoke a primitive facial language: a code that was sometimes inaccessible, sometimes naked, like a paramo or desert. She didn't dare say a thing when the teacher moved away and the shadows shifted. Seated like that, she could stretch out her legs, tied with a green rope—the same kind they used at school to skip rope during gym class—and see the spotless moccasins that Charo, her nanny, had washed the day before. At the back of the room, two big windows occupied the top part of the wall, allowing her to see exuberant foliage and a snowcapped mountain or volcano that told her they were far from her hometown.

"Where are we?"

But that wasn't the most important question: *Why did you kidnap me, Miss Clara?* she should have said. *Why have you tied me up and taken me out of the city with its puddles of fetid water, slutty motherfucking bitch? Eh, fucking bitch?* Instead, she endured the silence with the resignation of someone upon whom the roof is falling and began to cry. Not because she was scared, but because yet again, her body was doing senseless things, and she couldn't handle all that chaos destroying her consciousness. Her self-awareness had cracked, and now she was a stranger she could picture from the outside but not from within. Shaking, she watched with hatred as her teacher's body moved like a leafless branch, mopping the floor. Locks of long black hair grazed her wide jaw— the only feature of that average face that was out of the ordinary. Sometimes, when she smiled, Miss Clara looked like a shark or a lizard. A face like that, her therapist said, was discreet in its aggressiveness.

"I want to go home."

Fernanda waited for some response that would alleviate her anxiety, but Miss Clara López Valverde, thirty years old, five foot five, 125 pounds, hair hanging down to her tits, arthropod eyes, and the voice of a bird at six in the morning, ignored her like she would in class when she asked how long until the bell rang and she could go out for break to sit on the ground with her legs spread out, say obscene words, or watch the things that made up the world— which, at school, were always smaller and more miserable than they were anywhere else. She should have asked: *How long will I be here, stupid bloody-ass bitch?* But the important questions didn't well up from her guts as easily as the tears and the ire her molars were shredding into her, her molars that were so different from Miss Clara's and from those painted by Francis Bacon, the only artist she remembered from her art appreciation class, which, moreover, made her think of old horror movies, the furious teeth of Jack Nicholson, Michael Rooker, and Christopher Lee. Grinding teeth and jawbones: that force she held in her bones did not inhabit her mouth. Crying the way she was, out of shame and anger, was just like getting naked in the snow of Miss Clara's mind. Or almost.

She swept her eyes over the place where she was locked up and confirmed that the cabin was small and gloomy, the ideal home for the worm she now was, the lair where she'd have to learn to devertebrate herself in order to survive. Suddenly, the cold began to make her hands shake, and she understood that being outside of Guayaquil meant floating within a suspended void where she couldn't project herself. That void, moreover, was suspended in Miss Clara's breath and lacked a future. *What if the superwhore took me out of the country,* she wondered, though she quickly discarded that possibility—it couldn't be that easy to take a teenager without documents, completely knocked out and tied up, abroad. Then she tried to recognize the mountain or volcano she saw through the window, but her knowledge of terrestrial humps in her flea-of-a-South-American-country could be reduced to a few grandiose names and small images from her geography book. The coast with ocher shores, the heat, and a river running with the drama of mascara on a teary cheek were all that her body identified as home, even though she hated it more than any other landscape. "The port is an elephant hide," said a poem Miss Clara had made them read in class and that everyone used to make airplanes that crashed into the big blackboard. What she saw through the window, however, was a different beast. *Damned piece of earth in the clouds*, she thought while hardening like a rock, and then she looked at her teacher with all the disdain she'd been forced to stifle beneath her eyelids.

"You're fucked."

The silhouette stopped mopping and, for a few seconds, looked like a piece of modern art in the middle of the living room. Fernanda patiently waited for a reaction that would kick off the dialogue, a voice that would destabilize the silence, but no word came. Instead, Miss Clara crossed the shadows and walked out the door, which, upon opening, swallowed up all the afternoon glow and lit the cabin's interior. Fernanda heard water splashing against something hard, the noise of the wind tangling the trees, and steps that got louder and louder, but before the light disappeared again, she saw a revolver shining like a skull in the center of the long table.

And her rage recoiled.

"No," Miss Clara said when she was once again a shadow. "You're the one who's fucked."

Fernanda saw her approaching and closed her eyes. That branch-like body was doing something behind her own. A vaporous breath spilled onto her neck as she felt the ropes around her wrists loosen. The pain of freedom arrived with a warmth that ran up her arms at the precise moment she released them to either side of her body. She tried to untie the rope that was wrapped around her ankles, but her hands responded stiffly and clumsily, much like a rusty machine. Meanwhile, the exterior expanded, painfully dilating her pupils. *Why?* she wondered when the rope yielded and she could separate her legs so her school skirt spread out like a fan. *Why the hell am I here?*

Before her, Miss Clara looked on with the authority granted by the revolver behind her.

"Stand up."

But liberated-Fernanda stayed still. She knew it didn't make sense to refuse, yet she couldn't help but react the same way she did when Miss Clara or Mister Alan or Miss Ángela sent her out of class and she, not moving from her seat, looked them in the eyes and dared them to touch her, knowing they never would. That security, now that she had been kidnapped, no longer existed. For the first time, she wasn't invincible, or rather, for the first time she was aware of her own vulnerability. Her mind felt like a boat filling up with water, but the sinking could be a new mindset.

"Stand up. Don't make me say it again."

Obey. Her chest was a rodent fleeing down the drain at daybreak. It was still uncomfortable to bend her fingers, but this time she could press them into the floor and clumsily stand up. She avoided looking at the revolver that lay behind her teacher. *Maybe,* she thought, *if I don't look at it, she'll think I haven't noticed.*

But Miss Clara signaled the chair on the other side of the table with her chin.

"You and I are going to talk about what you did."

II

"Hi, my name is Anne, and my God is a rhinestone-encrusted firefly," Annelise sang, swaying back and forth with one hand on her hip. "He says he's my lover, and he wears stilettos. He puts lipstick on to kiss my neck and dances a red lambada for me when I'm sad. His dress sparkles in the early morning: his nails drag the corpses of crushed insects that he pulled from my head. If you must know, I met him one night on the little stage in my bedroom. He crossed his legs and licked my armpit with his eyelashes. His dress dripped with milk and black diamonds while he clawed insects from deep within my skull. He called me 'Daughter,' and I called him 'Mother,' for that wide-eyed pussy smile. He told me: 'Only broad hips can birth the dimensions of the universe.' His eyelashes lifted all the wet earth from my heart. 'Take note,' he said. 'The father of creation is a mother who wears a wig and smells of Dior.'"

Fiorella and Natalia applauded as their friend recited on tiptoe, stirring up circles of bone-colored dust from the cement, her back to a glassless window where pigeons had nestled until Analía accidentally startled them with her plump, sweaty hand.

"Leave 'em alone," Fernanda said as she shook an aerosol can that reminded her of the Schwarzkopf extra-strong-hold hair spray her mom used on her hair.

"I can't help it. I wanna touch them."

"Analía, stop! That's so nasty!" Natalia screeched.

"Stop scaring them!" Fiorella shouted.

"I do whatever the hell comes out my ass."

"What's coming out? Lift up your skirt and show us."

"Very funny."

"You have a horrible ass."

"Not as bad as yours."

"Stop it! I'm gonna pee my pants!"

The echo of their voices against the walls disturbed the geckos. "Are they reptiles or amphibians?" Natalia asked. "They're lizards that look like toads," Fiorella answered while braiding her hair. There, they shouted louder than they did anywhere else, because with time, they had discovered an enigmatic pleasure in speaking fiercely to each other when no one else was listening, as if deep down they were tired of good manners, as if raw friendship could only materialize among radiant shrieks at four in the afternoon. Annelise was the one who had found the place. "I want to show you something," she said, and from then on, they visited in secret, after school, to paint on the walls, sing, dance, or do nothing, just inhabit it for a few empty hours, with the sensation—sometimes frustrating, sometimes exciting—that they should be doing something there, something they sensed in their joints but were not yet able to explain. It was a three-story unfinished building, a grayish structure with uneven stairs, semicircular arches, and an exposed foundation, and according to Fernanda's father, it now belonged to a bank that had not made a final decision whether to finish or demolish it. They were all drawn to the spirit of ruins that floated around the naked construction. "Our lair," Annelise said. "I like it. It sounds animalistic," said Fernanda. It quickly became their anti-parent, anti-teacher, anti-nanny headquarters, a space of phantasmal sounds that felt both gloomy and romantic. Its beauty resided, as Annelise said, in its insinuated horrors, in how easy it was to flow into an abyss or find brown snakes, iguana corpses, and broken eggshells on the floor. Fernanda liked seeing how nature covered with life what was dead. "Divine chaos devours human order," she told them. "Living nature devours dead nature," Annelise translated, observing the path the ivy forged for itself on the walls of the first floor and the insects that had settled into the corners. There were some afternoons when the building looked like a bombed-out temple, others, a hanging garden, but when the light began to recede and the walls filled with shadows, it adopted the appearance of an infinite dungeon—or a Gothic castle, according to Analía—which sent them home, uncomfortable. Of the group, Fernanda and Annelise had been the first to jump the fence that surrounded the lot. The rest followed, though less convinced, so they wouldn't look bad, and because "being a coward has never been fashionable," Natalia said as she wound a curl around her index finger. At first the idea of trespassing on private property scared them, but it wasn't long before they were infected by Fernanda and Annelise's enthusiasm—they were the inseparables, the dirty-minded sisters, always stripped of fear and ready to invent adventures that would help them avoid boredom. That first afternoon, once inside the off-limits area, the six girls felt reckless and rebellious, that their lives were worthy of being filmed and discussed in a reality show or portrayed on a TV series. Suddenly— they knew it instantly—they had a true secret. Not like those that weren't worth lowering your voice over and that nevertheless kept them speaking softly for a long time, murmuring Mom's recipe, forming snail shells around someone's ear because the occasional whisper was chic and because everyone at that age wanted to feel like they owned something precious enough to hide, something that could only be shared with a limited number of people: a private world, complicated, full of nuances and abrupt plot twists. That was why, when they crossed over the fence and felt the adrenaline pumping behind their eyes and knees, they were sure that the richness of the true secret resided in how interesting it would make them: they would no longer just be elite students at an Opus Dei school, but also explorers, violators of the unknown, "enfants terribles," as Ximena's mother had called them ever since she signed up for the French class she took in the garden of one of her badminton friends while sipping mojitos and caipirinhas. From that very day on, they sensed that taking over that place was the prologue to something, but they didn't discuss it because they didn't have a clear idea how they would use it. They occupied themselves instead with examining every corner, finding shoes, needles, and scraps of sheets from beggars who once made the building an improvised home. For a few days, they were afraid that someone was living there—"a street person," Fiorella said as if she were referring to a rat under her pillow—but after several weeks of visiting and examining every last corner of the building, they concluded that they were the new and only tenants.

"The place is ours, *bitches*," Fernanda said after blowing a kiss that ricocheted off all the walls.

On each floor, there was nothing but climbing plants, dust, insects, shit from the fat gray pigeons—"aerial rats," Ximena called them, "sky cockroaches," "cloud frogs"—little lizards that came from the mangroves, and bricks. The stairs were dangerous, imprecise, and twisted, with unexpected dips in the landings, but on the top floor was a terrace with columns and rebar where you could watch the sunset. They spent the first month doing the same thing they did anywhere, only in there, surrounded by the flora and fauna that grew in their gardens. "We aren't going to adopt this place, we're going to be part of its neglect," Annelise said, determined to find a spectacular plot to match the spirit of her new castle-stage from *The Rocky Horror Picture Show*. That's why they talked, played with the insects, the geckos, the eggs they enjoyed smashing against the walls. They smelled their hair, watched the sky get dark, eyelashes heavy with sweat, and later went home to sleep for the night. They liked dedicating their afternoons to the nothing the building offered them: to the silence plagued with animal noises, to the postapocalyptic atmosphere that breathed its residue into every ruined-apartment-of-the-world; but with the passing of days, twilights, and lizards, they recognized a scaly frustration rubbing against their stomachs, a dissatisfaction of not having found the climax to their adventure. It was as if their minds faltered before the ambiguous, and their desire grew, though they could find no concrete way to satisfy it. Shortly after that first month of imprecision and dalliance, they began to explore other possibilities: clumsy experiments destined not to catch on but that forged a path to a coordinated inquiry that tried to stretch the limits of what they could do to themselves in a place without adults and without rules. That's how they stopped sharing rooms so as to take ownership of spaces that they claimed as individuals. The game began by marking the borders of each territory: Fernanda took over the top floor, Annelise the first-floor atrium, and the others the rooms on the second floor. For two or three hours, they split up and, alone in their respective spaces, talked to themselves. Fernanda proposed the exercise, though not everyone was able to carry it out. Fiorella and Natalia ended up tiring of it and secretly meeting up after the fourth day, while Analía, instead of talking out loud to herself—which seemed to her like something a crazy person would do—decided to sing songs from Taylor Swift's new album; Ximena, in a nearby room, sometimes sang Calle 13 songs. "I don't like listening to myself. It scares me," she confessed to Fernanda. "It doesn't scare me, but I don't have anything to say to myself, and I get bored," Fiorella said. "I, on the other hand, have terrible things to say to myself, and I say them," Annelise said to encourage her friend.

"My therapist says when you talk out loud without stopping for a long time, and you really listen to yourself, the mysteries end up coming out of the tangle of your subconscious," Fernanda explained the day before changing the exercise.

Fernanda talked to herself out loud as much as possible: when she showered; when she went to bed; when her father's chauffeur drove her to school; when she ate lunch alone at a table with eight chairs; when Charo helped her put her tights and shoes on in the mornings; when she shut herself up in her room; when she brushed her hair; when she trimmed her long pubic hair with her mother's nail scissors; when she went to the bathroom at school and sat staring at the tiles and door number five, covered with testimonials: Hugo-&-Lucía-4ever, Salsa-is-not-dead, Daniela-Gómez-is-a-lesbian, I-will-love-you-X-siempre-Ramón, Bea-&-Vivi-BF, We-don't-need-no-education, God-loves-us-but-not-you, Miss-Amparo-zorra, Mister-Alan-cabrón; when she pretended to do her homework; when she intentionally dirtied her clothes so Charo would have to wash them; when she swam in the pool and peed in it right before getting out; when she watched movies alone or with other people—her parents, who never watched movies with her, weren't bothered by her solipsistic rambling, because they believed it was part of an exercise proposed by Dr. Aguilar, the psychoanalyst Fernanda had been seeing since she was a little girl and who had a lazy, almost-blind eye that he covered with a pirate eye patch for aesthetic reasons. She talked to herself because she wanted to, and even though it wasn't part of her therapy, she had discovered that there was someone more scurrilous inhabiting her body and sharing her thoughts; a girl who was her and, at the same time, wasn't. "What's important is that this someone always has things to tell me," she said. "My therapist assured me that we all have a voice like this banging around in our heads." Fernanda wanted her friends to start listening to themselves so she could find out if what they said was anything like what she said. She wondered if their hidden voices were more or less like hers, the one that shouted at her to do things, like hit her mother, kiss her father, or touch Annelise's underwear and bite her tongue. To her, the building seemed like a perfect place to conduct the joint therapy, but Annelise wasn't convinced that was what they needed to do. In any case, to placate Fernanda, they bought various colors of spray paint and brushes with the idea of writing on the walls. "My therapist says writing is a space of revelation," she told them. "I hate writing. I'm going to draw," Analía said before making a strange version of Cardcaptor Sakura on the wall. Ximena, Fiorella, and Natalia wrote out their desires as epigrams, and Annelise drew her drag-queen God on the first floor: a doll with hair on its chest, boomerang eyebrows, a cancan dress, and a curly beard. Of all of them, Annelise was the only one who shared in Fernanda's quest, if not in her methods. The building encouraged the disembowelment of a revelation beating within them. "Here, we have to be other people. I mean, the people we truly are," Annelise explained to them. And for several weeks they didn't return to the subject, perhaps because—though they understood that to squeeze all they could from the experience, they had to get naked and open their minds—they didn't have the faintest idea how to go about it, much less how to contend with the shame of doing things they wouldn't do in front of anyone else. "It's not about doing just anything either," Fernanda was saying while Annelise nodded at every one of her words. "We have to do something we can't do in any other corner of this world." They knew that whatever it was, it had to be something that made sense, something that shook up their insides and provoked something close to a fever, but also connected and united them in a special way. A hardly simple matter that for months they couldn't resolve, but that inspired them to persist in spite of how difficult it was to keep the adults from finding out where they were spending their afternoons. The excuses had to change every now and then out of necessity, and they also had to reduce their visits to the building to three days a week. "Your parents are so annoying," Ximena told Fiorella and Natalia, whose parents had asked too many questions even though they were almost never home, since they were the owners of an advertising agency that every year came close to winning El Ojo de Iberoamérica. "What if we assign a different activity to each floor and room?" Analía suggested one day. "Yeah, but what activities, dummy?" Natalia asked her. "Let's tell horror stories!" Fernanda blurted out, inspired by Nickelodeon's *Are You Afraid of the Dark?*, a program from the nineties that she had found on YouTube in which a group of teenagers gathered around a campfire to tell scary stories. "That's good, we can try it," Annelise said. "But we need some rules." The first was that the stories had to be told on the second floor, in a windowless room that Fernanda had painted white; the second, that the recitations would take place once a week; the third, that in each meeting, only one story would be told; the fourth, that the order would be determined at random; and the fifth—perhaps the most important— that whoever told a story that didn't scare the others had to complete a challenge set by the group. The activity began with a certain apathy on Annelise's part, since she didn't have much confidence in her friends' storytelling abilities. Analía was the first to tell a story and, of course, the first to find herself obliged to accept a dare. The others hotly debated before assigning her the task of lifting her skirt and showing her ass to Miss Clara, aka *Latin Madame Bovary* (because she looked like the drawing on the cover of Flaubert's novel). "I'm not doing that. Are you crazy? She'll call my parents!" Analía shrieked. "You have to do it without her seeing you," Annelise explained. "If you succeed, no one will call your parents. If you don't, well, you deserve it for being stupid." That afternoon they fought, insulted one another, and Analía went home early, crying out of rage. "Maybe we should change the challenge," Fiorella said, but Annelise refused outright: "If we do that, this will never be fun again." Fernanda agreed and suggested they not talk to Analía until she completed her punishment.

"I'm starting to like this game," Ximena said.

After two days of the silent treatment, Analía took advantage of a moment when Miss *Latin* Madame Bovary was writing something about genre on the board to lift her skirt and wiggle her ass behind the teacher's back. The class held back their laughter, and even though the murmurs made Miss Clara turn around, she didn't do so in time to see what had happened. Soon, the afternoons telling horror stories became an excuse to come up with challenges that were at first meant to entertain them and make them laugh, but that slowly evolved until settling into what Fernanda called "tightrope-walker exercises." They consisted of carrying out small feats: things of a certain degree of difficulty for the person who would execute them, almost always on the corporeal level—the first exercise was a duel of hot hands between Annelise and Fernanda in which both wore their mother's rings and withstood, for an hour, each other's slaps; for the second, Fiorella screamed in the shouting room until she lost her voice; for the third, Natalia jumped from the second floor to the first without using the stairs. There was something in those childish games of resistance that filled the group with a hard-to-conceal emotion, a sensation of power and control that outweighed the physical pain. They were games they had all played—or seen others play—at some point in their lives, like Russian roulette or slaps, and that at fifteen years old, they would never admit to playing for the simple fact that they were for kids and implied a disconcerting physicality, but there, inside, they seemed to have taken on new dimensions, become unique events, ruptures in time that made them feel strangely on fire. In a little over a month, they opted to separate the tightrope-walker exercises from the afternoons dedicated to telling horror stories and established the game as one step closer to what they were looking for: a new and unifying sensation, an excess of experience. "I think we should have different names here," Fernanda said a few days before Mister Alan, aka Cosmic Ass, found Ximena's notebook with a sketch of Annelise's drag-queen God. The scandal was immediate: not only did he call her parents, he brought the matter to the rector. "I imagine you know how serious it is to play with the name and image of God, especially like this, transvesting him as if he were a monster," they told her. "Explain to us what was going through your head when you sat down to draw such a thing." Wrinkled foreheads, contorted lips, Ximena's mother's shrill voice rising on all the *a*'s, the rector pounding her heel into the floor, the Bible on the table, a crucified Jesus bleeding next to a forged Guayasamín, and Mister Alan, aka Cosmic Ass, looking at her like the lost sheep he was. Ximena, of course, couldn't resist the pressure and ended up ratting out Annelise. "I don't even know how to draw!" she said. After that, she distanced herself from the group, unable to show her face, and Annelise was exposed to numerous sermons and punished with extra language and literature classes every Friday.

"One day she'll have to come back," Fernanda said, graffitiing a wall.

"Who? Ximena?" Natalia asked.

"Who else?" She continued: "We need new names. And a manifesto or something."

"Why?" Fiorella asked.

"Because. I read that's what you do."

"Oh? Where'd you read that?"

"What's it to you?"

And indeed, one day Ximena returned. She showed up at the building with a fresh outlook and a stained uniform, from when

Fernanda had tripped her that morning in PE and she had fallen
to the wet earth. Less ashamed than resigned, she apologized and
promised to never again rat on anyone. "From now on, I would
rather cut out my tongue than tell them about any of our business," she said, and Annelise looked at her for a long time without saying a word, which was overwhelming for them all because
even though the new, unifying feeling they'd been looking for was
weaving together at that very moment under their tongues, each
one was waiting for someone else to take the step, the move the
group needed to close the vacillation phase and to begin the period
of true experimentation. That's why when Annelise said what
she said, more than excitement, the group felt relief, freed from
the burden of articulating what was in each of their heads, even
Ximena, who seemed to anticipate and desire it, and who had to
confront the first real challenge—the one that started it all—with
admirable stoicism.

That afternoon they were all themselves, and no one was
ashamed.

III

If she had to be honest during her job interview, Clara López Valverde would find herself in the awkward position of having to admit that she was a language and literature teacher without any calling whatsoever to teach. It wasn't that she was bad at her job, at least not much worse than those who showed a true enthusiasm for education, who plunged into long diatribes in the teachers' lounges or hallways on meaningful learning, pedagogical methodologies, cognitivism, and all the other problems, but she was missing a particular inclination—what others called "passion," for lack of a better word—for what went on in a room full of adolescents. Her mother, dead for five years but more alive than ever in her thoughts—even more so when she was nervous and sweaty and picked at the delicate skin between the fingers of her left hand—had warned her that to teach, you had to believe in yourself; that education was much like religion in that the teacher is the priest, the minister, the pastor, and that with no faith, there is no meaning, and with no meaning, there's nothing worth reading—her mother liked being sententious and rhyming, because the sound of repetition, especially of consonant rhyme, made her feel like a medium through which a sort of immortal, classical wisdom spoke. That's what she energetically told herself, spouting rhymes in a tiger-striped armchair while smoking her therapeutic joint of the day, when Clara was just beginning to study for her master's in education and was already wearing skirts and dresses that fell below the knee, hair spray in her hair, and blouses with buttons the shape of pearls—not out of modesty, discretion, or any of those pruderies unsuitable for someone with legs like a pelican's, breasts like two atrophied lemons, and the coarse hair of a gorilla, but because they made her look like her mother in the eighties, which is to say, very *vintage*, and feel more professorial than she did wearing anything else. The maternal maxims—she remembered as she switched seats to avoid the jet of cold air from the vent blowing three loose hairs against her nose—were usually meant to discourage her. After all, that's what her mother was best at when it came to her motherly role, along with highlighting—always in a condescending tone—how uncomfortable she was with 90 percent of the decisions her becerra-daughter made. "Golden Calf," she called Clara until she was ten years old, when during arguments it became just "Becerra," stretching out the double r's if she was mad, shortening them if she was in a good mood. Elena Valverde, that is, the mother who Clara, as a consequence of nearly forty-five minutes of boredom in the reception of the Delta Bilingual Academy, was now thinking about, had been a middle school teacher for thirty years, until the state of her neuromuscular scoliosis impeded her ability to continue in the profession, and she had to hand it over reluctantly—because what did her daughter know about real teaching, uninspired snot-nosed narcissist that she was, sick in the head—to Clara, the most tiresome girl in the universe—that's what she told her shortly before dying: "You are the most tiresome girl in the universe." Another time, when she still believed it was possible to convince her to stop usurping her life, she also told her that teaching was not meant for tropical nihilists. But Clara, the becerra-daughter, didn't consider herself a nihilist, but a woman from the tropics with flexible beliefs and multiple convictions, like the politicians—or like those people with low self-esteem who were never entirely sure what they thought—and all she opposed with real defiance were her mother's beliefs. Such that after several years of study, she became a language and literature teacher without faith, though she was attracted to etymologies, alliteration, grammar, free-verse poems—rhymes, to her, seemed as artificial as natural makeup or flesh-colored nylons—orthography, volcanoes, and Gothic horror novels—which she was especially proud of but would abstain from mentioning during her interview, because she didn't see how it would help her obtain her principal objective: to be hired (as soon as possible) by the Delta Bilingual Academy, *High-School-for-Girls*.

Her mother, she remembered, as she brushed from her knee a fat mosquito filled with someone else's blood, liked to reproach her for having chosen a profession she considered her own, as she withered away with her spine in the shape of an *s*, barely corrected by a thoracolumbar corset she had baptized "Frida Kahlo." Of all the things her daughter had snatched from her identity, it was this, her lost profession, that reinforced her filial resentment. Clara didn't know precisely, not even at that moment, as she watched the secretary-hostesses of the Delta Bilingual Academy, *High-School-for-Girls*, offer visitors tea in porcelain cups and animal crackers—panda bears crunched, elephants crunched—when her obsession with becoming an exact replica of her mother had begun. That imperfect imitation, nevertheless, had split the earth between them until the end, such that Clara was only now able to recognize—picking at the delicate skin between the fingers of her left hand while to her right zebras crunched, rhinoceroses crunched—the crafty violence her attitude had imposed, unconsciously but prolongedly, over someone—the mother—who had no choice but to die while she—the daughter—grew like a tree over her death, because children accentuate the mortality of their parents, she had concluded, turning them into compost and embodying Yorick's skull, rocking with laughter every morning (something that, nevertheless, Clara would never say in her interview, because it might make her look like she didn't like parent-child relationships). Her being a daughter, she understood with time, had led to the death of her mother—everyone engenders their murderers, she thought, but only women give birth to them—a death she carried like a seed in her profession, her hairstyle, the way she dressed, even her gestures, but not in her beliefs or her way of speaking. To describe something as one's "calling," for example, she found unpleasant, the word like an old, stinky shoe next to the bed, but she'd surely repeat it several times in her interview, because the rectors loved to hear it (as much as or more than her mother had).

There were things she couldn't say if she wanted the Delta Bilingual Academy, *High-School-for-Girls*, to hire her, and she went over them in her mind while the secretary-hostesses in reception answered the phones, spoke with some parents crunching horses and camels, greeted her possible competitors, and seated them very close to her. Dull things, though potentially irritating for the rectors, like her true interests, hobbies, or life goals—"They'll see you in a moment," a secretary with a voice like a five-year-old girl told her while a housewife bit the head off a giraffe. What really held her attention about teaching—and what she was sure she couldn't talk about during her interview—was what took place outside of class hours. She saw herself as an aficionado of reading and linguistics and orthography, or, as she liked to call them, matters "of form"; she enjoyed various and disparate literary traditions— from Aeschylus to Parra, from Woolf to Dante . . . (though at the moment, she was occupied by a translation exercise that kept her reading only English)—and detecting errors in newspapers, magazines, books, advertisements, graffiti, etc.—she had learned that from her mother, who liked to use Flaubert's (or Warburg's, or Voltaire's, or surely Mies van der Rohe's) famous phrase, "God is in the details," for almost everything, despite being atheist and having once spit on a Jehovah's Witness who knocked on the door before she had smoked her therapeutic joint of the day (very important for alleviating the unbearable pain of her advanced neuromuscular scoliosis). Perhaps, in fairness to her job, Clara would have to admit that the only thing she liked about teaching was correcting her students' writing—though she would never say that in the interview, because, beyond not being very flattering, it brought on memories of her mother reproaching her for her nonexistent pedagogical vision so as not to reproach her for other things (like having chosen her profession or dressing and talking exactly like her, but twenty-eight years younger and without a Frida Kahlo embracing her spinal column). By the end of every school year, Clara had always managed to improve the writing of a few students. Teachers older than her, by contrast, let the problems in their students' written expression pass as if they were minor issues, or as if they couldn't detect them, she sometimes thought. On various occasions, she entertained herself by identifying errors in the exams designed by her colleagues, who, for the most part, were disciples of Paulo Freire—during discussions on pedagogies of the oppressed and pop-culture methodologies, they were Sarmiento, and she, preferring to talk about the adequate usage of orthography and grammar, was a disciple of Bello and her own mother. Many of the teachers she had met in her four years on the job were sloppy, and they defended their lack of care, their distaste for details, by diminishing the importance of the formal aspects of writing. "What's important isn't the how, but the what," they would say, but Clara was incapable of understanding them, even less so when they spoke of the power of orality in the ancestral traditions of Andean countries, relegating writing to a technology of epistemological colonization—a position that always seemed to her mother (the implacable middle school teacher) to be reductionist and which she protested by painting Walter Mignolo's face blue and hiding Cornejo Polar in a cardboard box. Clara, for her part, was convinced that it was possible to know a person through their writing. She liked to think that deep down, her work made it possible for others to discover and show their true character—her mother's, for example, was rhythmic, definitive, sibylline; hers, disorganized, digressive, populated by subordinate clauses and parenthetical remarks. Once, because she had graded a student's assignment "insufficient"—six points out of ten—for its clear mechanical problems, a debate erupted among full-time teachers: one group, the larger, argued that the grade should be a seven out of ten—"sufficient," "acceptable," "achieves the required objectives"—because the content developed across the pages was argued creatively, while a small group, of which she was a part, held that content and form were inseparable and that the arguments, by not being well expressed, lost their effect and resulted in fallacies, while also lacking logic. The debate—which was really about the precision of the language of the standardized evaluation—ended with both sides becoming enemies, as often happens with that kind of discussion, since everyone believed they had the final word on true education and the pedagogical avant-garde (although her opinion on her colleagues' egos she would not share, under any circumstance, during her interview, because the rector of Delta Bilingual Academy, *High-School-for-Girls*, could interpret it as a hostility both unjustified and unappealing for the working and learning environment).

Her mother—before she found out her spinal column was becoming a serpent—very much enjoyed engaging her students with reading but hardly concerned herself with the correct use of language. "All that matters is art, Becerra. Art gives us heart," she told her once, when she had already begun to exaggerate the state of her myopia in order to feel more oracular as she delivered her rhymed sentences. Clara, in contrast, was irritated by how little love high schools showed for Rimbaud—*A Season in Hell*, for out-of-date reasons, generally disgusted high school rectors—and facing the scarce freedom she had to select materials for her courses—and the absence of commitment she felt to motivate reading (convincing her students that reading was pleasant seemed to her to be just as absurd as not loving Rimbaud)—she decided to concentrate on encouraging the development of writing among her pupils. It made her feel satisfied: enclosing in circles the poorly used words, in triangles the orthography errors, and in rectangles those of syntax; covering the paper in red and later asking for the essay to be rewritten to cover it in red again, though a little less, until the page was finally free of her own geometry. She didn't achieve it with all of them, but by the end of the year, two or three of her students always learned to write better. Creating lovers of literature, on the contrary, seemed, to her, like a pipe dream—not for her mother, but for teachers like herself. After all, she had never been good at transmitting her own passions to others, though that, definitively, she would not say in the interview, because if there was something that made the hair (sometimes long and bleached) on the arms of high school rectors stand on end, it was that teachers were infectious and passionate (but with the curriculum).

In short, she wasn't convinced that she was a teacher who instilled in her students an interest in the literary arts, but at least she was a decent proofreader.

"You're a decent proofreader and an indecent teacher," her mother told her two days before they went to the hospital and saw, for the first time, the X-ray of her spine snaking through her flesh, curving it, twisting it like a predatory monster from which Clara would have to feed. She left the gray X-ray hanging on the living room wall like the portrait of a fetus—her mother put it there so she could look at it in the moments when she forgot to feign her symbolic oracular blindness. It was evidence of the bone creature that had managed to vanquish the only person Clara had truly loved. When Elena Valverde died, Clara adopted all her things, even her undergarments (which she now slept in, because unfortunately, they were too big for her to wear during the day, under her high-waisted skirts and nineties-maternal-style satin blouses). Even in that instant, surrounded by strangers who didn't have the faintest idea that her headband was the same design as her mother's from the eighties, she recalled how the few family members who attended the wake—and who noticed she was wearing Frida Kahlo under her black 2010-maternal-style blouse—looked at her with the same indifference and repugnance as Elena had up until her final moment, when she could no longer even get out of bed, and Clara fed her, bathed her, combed her hair, emptied her bedpan, and in her free moments perfected the art of walking with her spine twisted slightly to the left. Clara had learned that, for some reason that was totally incomprehensible to her, they found her imitation of her mother's physical appearance obscene, as if in her amorous mimesis there were something abject that forced them to screw up their faces and shoot her suspicious glances. Sometimes she noticed, on the part of the few living family members left (with whom she no longer maintained contact), an open disdain caused by the discomfort they felt when she not only pretended to be her mother, but actually became her (on those occasions when her interpretation reached its zenith, Clara saw herself dissolving into the maternal character like a drop of blood into another drop of blood). Picking at the delicate skin between the fingers of her left hand, for example, was something that came to her naturally when she was anxious, but it had taken seven months to adopt her mother's body language—two years to sweat like her, a year and a half to go to the bathroom the same number of times a day. All this had irritated Elena Valverde, who cried, screamed, and talked about her hair but never dared broach the subject with her daughter; she never asked "Why are you my shadow?" nor did she confess that it scared her to see herself in another, a damaged reflection or doppelgänger about to disappear so her double could exist. Only later, when her mother began to stare into space when she talked and conclude that her feigned blindness allowed her to see metaphysical matters with greater clarity—and use as a cane the handle of an old mop with the intention of looking like Martha Graham's Tiresias—did Clara understand that behind the maternal ire, there was an arcane horror, a blatant rejection of an imitation that had perhaps been perceived as a challenge or a joke rather than what it was: an act of love. Nevertheless, and contrary to what Elena Valverde believed up until the very end, Clara hadn't decided to become a language and literature teacher just to imitate her, but because it was the kind of work that fit best with the personality she wanted. She didn't feel guilty—she realized it as she read a phrase attributed to Gabriela Mistral on the bulletin board, sometimes eclipsed by one father's skunk hair: "The worst teacher is the one who is afraid"—about having chosen a profession loaded with a quasi-religious discourse of abnegation, sacrifice, and the success of others as recompense, in exchange for personal comfort—not monetary, but attitudinal. After all (during her four years working at a public high school, she had seen it with her own eyes), the majority of the shapers-of-tomorrow-teachers took pleasure in the images of martyrdom they projected onto the world— their exhaustion and dedication were the emblems for which they puffed out their chests, but Clara perceived, behind that pride, a colossal effort to hide from themselves and from others; they were teachers who were afraid (her mother, though she would never have admitted it, was also a teacher who was afraid, just like her [but the rector of the Delta Bilingual Academy, *High-School-for-Girls*, with her international degree, didn't need to know that]). The teaching sector—her experience told her, as did that of her armadillo-backed-mother—was the garbage dump of overestimated mediocrity: everyone saw themselves as essential and indescribably valuable, but almost no one really was. Clara admitted to herself—though not to the high school rectors—that she had little to contribute and that for her, teaching was just an excuse to read and solve redaction problems like Sunday crossword puzzles. If she looked at it from that angle—she thought, while beside her, cows and deer crunched—her lack of calling affected no one. Her students, with some exceptions, respected her—this, she would subtly drop in the interview, because high school rectors loved teachers who inspired respect. Furthermore, she still hadn't met a high school language and literature teacher who managed the subject materials better than she did; she had inherited (or perhaps adopted) her mother's voracity for reading, which the professors aged fifty and up, disillusioned and tired ("the dinosaurs," she called them into her pillow), had lost following the Pleistocene. Despite being so young, Clara had achieved, as she understood it, two qualities indispensable for a teacher: command of the material and command of the classroom. *Without the first, a teacher can hold her position until the end of time, but without the second, the administration will soon lose confidence in her capacities*, she thought, seated with her knees together, the skin between the fingers of her left hand a deep magenta.

Education, she'd had to learn right away, was a matter of strength.

"No one likes to say it, Becerra, but the education system is made for lion tamers, not teachers," her mother once told her, placated by her therapeutic joint of the day, before she had baptized her thoracolumbar corset Frida Kahlo, and when she still believed the pain would be temporary. But the true challenge, she thought, was to be a tamer of tamers, which is what she became upon adopting her discarded mother's identity while she was frozen in time like a mollusk, chiseled for years by the illness in the very tiger-striped armchair where later—fifty-seven months later, to be exact—two students would tie Clara up with the intention of stealing the qualifying exams. The memory of that day slipped before her eyes and compelled her to scratch the delicate skin between the index finger and thumb of her left hand. Her kidnapping—or, as they preferred to call it: "the exam-theft event"—was one of the many topics she had decided to avoid during her job interview, though she had of course considered the possible scenario in which the rector of the Delta Bilingual Academy, *High-School-for-Girls*, with a theater holding 250 seats and a red velvet curtain, would ask about her recovery and would request a psychological report, in addition to a medical one (and she, who had inherited [or adopted] from her mother the talent for having your excuses ready, had both reports in her blue maternal-design-from-the-year-1976 bag). Furthermore, she had stood before the mirror and practiced—just in case the rector asked her about it—her version of what happened during the thirteen hours and fifty-seven minutes in which the students kept her tied to the tiger-striped armchair; she would say: "It was a very difficult experience that nevertheless reaffirmed my calling to teach," and she would carefully pronounce the word "calling" to satisfy the pedagogical-institutional ears of the rector at the high school with the largest library in the city. It might also happen—and this was the scenario that worked best for Clara—that the rector of the Delta Bilingual Academy, *High-School-for-Girls*, would not be interested in asking her about something that occurred three months, two days, and eleven hours ago, because in spite of having appeared in all the newspapers in the country—and even some regional ones—and being the cause of her temporary distance from the classroom—as well as her obligatory attendance at meetings with people who wore expensive wristwatches—the incident had nothing to do with her professional performance. Clara wanted to be positive and think it possible—though not likely—that the rector of the only high school in the country with a covered Olympic-size pool would not be interested in the details of her experience with Malena Goya and Michelle Gomezcoello—aka the *M&M's*, according to their classmates, aka the *Hard Candies*, according to the tabloids, aka Those Girls, according to the directors of the high school where she had previously worked and where she had quit without any remorse. But the fact was, few people existed who, knowing what happened three months, two days, and eleven hours ago, would not want to hear from the mouth of the victim a story that promised to be intense—though perhaps a bit morbid—so Clara knew it would be difficult to escape from the question "And how do you feel after what happened with Those Girls?" A question that—now that she thought about it, as two mothers with supernaturally white teeth blew each other a kiss—she hadn't practiced responding to but dodging, because the narrative elaboration of the thirteen hours and fifty-seven minutes she spent tied to her mother's tiger-striped armchair—with her students running around her house, eating her food, playing with her things, and above all, mocking her fear—was too complicated, even for her. And perhaps because of that—she thought as she looked at the horrible portrait of Josemaría Escrivá de Balaguer (sometimes hidden behind a grandmother's prominent hunch)—because she'd refused to tell them the details of what really happened, the teachers and administrators at the school where she previously worked—who at first had expressed their unconditional support before the "barbaric" and "savage" behavior of Those Girls—ended up thinking she must have done something as a teacher—and human being—to make two fourteen-year-old girls want to kidnap her in her own home. It wasn't that they excused what Those Girls did to her—Clara concluded, smoothing her skirt while, to her left, a mother won a game of Candy Crush—but that, as her colleagues and superiors understood it, there had to be motives behind an act that violent and disconcerting; motives like the girls' home lives, their friendships outside of school, their consumption of narcotics, and of course, their relationship with Clara—after all, what they did, they did to her, not to another teacher at the school, and that had to mean something; maybe Clara was, in reality, a bad teacher (a despot or a pushover), maybe she'd earned their hatred. They never told her they thought as much, but it was obvious—in the way they looked at her, in their gestures—that they blamed her in part for what happened with the *M&M's* and were at the same time ashamed for doing so: they knew that terrible experience could have happened to them, and deep down, they were rabidly happy it hadn't.

Clara understood the kind of happiness fed by the disgrace of those around you. It was a guilty but powerful feeling the majority tried to hide when it stirred inside them in the form of "I'm glad it didn't happen to me!"—*I'm glad I was your daughter and not your mother!* she had thought when she buried Elena Valverde in a grave without an epitaph. She was sure her colleagues had felt that miserly delight, and she didn't hold it against them, but sometimes—as in that moment, for example, with the sea lions crunching and the father blowing his nose into a tissue—she wondered if she might have misinterpreted them, if in reality they hadn't felt happy or guilty, but frightened—"The worst teacher is the one who is afraid," she read again as the secretary-hostess who smelled like nail polish refilled the plates with new animals. For Clara, fear had a very specific smell, as recognizable as the smell of that room and of every person waiting in it—her mother, for example (she remembered, taking a whale from the plate and cracking it between her molars), had smelled of the antiperspirant she used to avoid the profuse sweating of her feet ("I like how it smells," Elena would say, spritzing the antiperspirant-spray-for-feet on her neck as if it were perfume). Fear smelled like a body: like hot urine soaking moon-and-star pajamas. Clara knew that none of the adults surrounding her in that reception area—part chapel, part zoo—wore children's pajamas, nor did they wet themselves, but they had once, and whether they knew it or not, they could do it again; because if there was anything she'd learned from her time as a becerra-daughter—and an obstinate carbon copy of her mother—it was that you could wet yourself from fear at any age—Elena Valverde had, lying in agony in her hospital bed, and so had she, three months, two days, and eleven hours ago, tied to the tiger-striped armchair. Perhaps—she thought while looking around the space, luminous and decorated with indoor plants— her ex-colleagues were afraid to accept that what happened with the *M&M's* had been arbitrary—like anything that really terrorizes people—and to avoid the vertigo—and because at least that way there existed one certainty, one reasonable explanation to prevail over the unknown—they preferred to conclude that part of the blame for the incident was on her, the kidnapped, but above all, the only adult in the triangle, the one who wasn't supposed to wet herself and who, even so, threatened to soak the moon-and-star pajamas of their minds. Clara believed that at that point— when she tried not to dwell on the details of what happened during the thirteen hours and fifty-seven minutes she spent tied to the tiger-striped armchair—her ex-companions protected themselves from their fear of the unknown as adults always did: by way of reason, and because of that—because that apparent judgment, that phantom of common sense, might have protected them from accepting that maybe there was no cause for the violence other than violence—she ended up forgiving them several times a week, including in moments like the present one, as she chewed a tortoise shell and performed the exercise of inventing explanations for the enthusiasm with which the *M&M's* tickled her belly. That excessive and involuntary analysis of uncomfortable situations— beyond strengthening the undeniable symptoms of her anxiety disorder—helped her remain aware of everything happening in her immediate environment and created an illusion—false but necessary—of control. She had an enormous capacity—that's what her mother used to say, when she was little—for mulling over possible reactions and deducing, in broad strokes, how people felt and thought about her and others. "Girls who imagine too much end up sick in the head," her mother had told her when she heard for the first time what Clara believed her teachers thought of the way she wrote, drew, ran, spelled, chewed, and sneezed. It was an unhealthy habit and, at the same time, a talent that served to calm her nerves, but—in spite of not feeling ashamed—she had resolved to hide it during her interview because the rector of the Delta Bilingual Academy, *High-School-for-Girls*, might not like the way she interpreted—or overinterpreted—her ex-companions' feelings or thoughts following an incident that did not define her as a person or as a high school teacher.

"Your brain is a cockroach nest," her mother had told her when she explained what she believed her teachers thought of the way she pronounced her *rr*'s and obsessively washed her hands during recess.

Clara's biggest problem was the unwanted thoughts that—like cockroaches—laid eggs inside her head. But the anxiety climbing up her heels like an invisible tarantula while lions crunched, seagulls crunched—and while she discreetly sucked on a drop of blood from the delicate skin between the index finger and thumb of her left hand—was the result not only of the inevitable mental rehearsal of what she could say during her interview, but of never having been in a private school before, much less in the most expensive—and therefore exclusive—one in an underdeveloped, though increasingly aristocratic in spirit, city. Her mother, who had worked her whole life in public education, would have said she'd "sold out" if she saw her there, about to drink from a porcelain cup in the only school in the city with a chess club and an artistic gymnastics room. The staging of the reception also increased her anguish because it forced her to rehearse a situation she had already exhaustively studied at home—alone and in front of the mirror—but which now—with new elements in the landscape—became much denser. For example—she concluded, rubbing her elbows—the parents of the girls at that school paid a monthly tuition that doubled her previous salary and that was visible in every detail of the furniture, infrastructure, gorgeous uniforms, and tiny security cameras, though not in the quality of the writing—while she waited, she detected eight errors in the brochures, posters, and texts that hung on the walls and rested on the table in the center of the reception (her anxiety [she confirmed in that instant] had an important orthographic component). Elena Valverde, the implacable middle school teacher, would have thrown up her hands in response to the endless paraphernalia from the Delta Bilingual Academy, *High-School-for-Girls*, who, in their brochures, defined themselves as "a cutting-edge center" whose objective was to "empower young women to respond to the political, economic, and social demands of their surroundings." But she was not her mother—even though she yearned to be—and there was something seductive in the floral perfume of the indoor plants, the sound of high heels, the voices at lowered decibels, docile, and the freshness of the cooled air that made her forget she was surrounded by mangroves.

Here, she thought, *I won't sweat*, and she scrunched up her nose as she watched a mosquito penetrate the capillary forest of a mother yawning with her mouth closed.

Clara had made the decision—and she reaffirmed it upon discovering a new portrait of Josemaría Escrivá de Balaguer looming beyond the partly open door of the rector's office—not to allude to religion during the interview and instead to mention matters that would stand in for them, like the humanities crisis—which (according to the mother who inhabited her mind) was the topic high school rectors preferred. Because of that, in the plans she had meticulously rehearsed—and reinvented—in front of the mirror, Clara would show an interest in the future of the humanities in secondary education while the rector of the Delta Bilingual Academy, *High-School-for-Girls*, tapped on the varnished wooden desk with her enormous rings—above all in those areas that were important to the rector—to avoid mentioning, for example, the translations she was doing of poems about volcanoes—an exercise that wouldn't do much to help her obtain the desired position of language and literature teacher, in spite of the fact that (in her opinion) it said a lot about her personality and emphasized her creative streak (an essential attribute in a good teacher, according to the conventional wisdom of modern pedagogy). "My spine looks like the chimney of an ice volcano," her mother had told her one night, looking at the X-ray of her vertebrae as if it were a landscape petrified on the wall. Clara didn't think the high school rectors would like volcanoes or literature—given they didn't love Rimbaud—so, according to her meticulously designed plan, practiced and reinvented in front of the mirror, she would talk for two minutes—maximum three—about learning outcomes and pedagogical methodologies, even if the rector didn't ask about them, because in her opinion (and in that of the mother who inhabited her mind), it would make her more hirable than any of her competitors. She would also try to not get too distracted by the titles, medals, certificates, and diplomas, among other accolades, that would surely fill the office of the high school rector with the strongest teaching record in the country. "Those are the royal titles of teaching: the caste system of the Western episteme," her mother would say if she were alive. Because education, she had learned very quickly, was a matter of status, even though no one would say it out loud, not even Clara—who was repelled by the teacherly resistance to things that cannot be changed (for example, the fact that [like it or not] they were part of an elite). In the Opus Dei schools, that status was built upon a foundation of authority and order—which Clara adhered to with relief, out of not a religious but a psychological affinity (an ordered life that responded to a fixed system was the only thing that calmed the cockroaches of her mind)—but she knew that to be hired on as the language and literature teacher at the Delta Bilingual Academy, *High-School-for-Girls*, she would have to avoid uttering those words. If she managed to withhold her interpretations—or overinterpretations—and control the sometimes unruly symptoms of her anxiety disorder, it was very probable that she would get the job offer; after all—she began to convince herself, watching a mother leave the rector's office—she was young, and she had the profile, the experience, and a recommendation straight from the director of the high school where she'd worked until the incident with the *M&M's*. Her worries about the difficulties of adapting to a new—and unknown—environment were irrational, she thought: her work in large classrooms with a maximum of twenty students would be the same as she had done in small classrooms with forty sweaty and overexcited ones, but in comfortable and favorable conditions for learning that—according to the brochures of the only high school in the city with a private chapel—"aspired to educate capable and emotionally mature women through the cultivation of the doctrines of the church"—an objective that was irrelevant to her since her subject had less grandiloquent aspirations. Therefore—she thought as she counted twelve indoor plants, eight pairs of high heels, and fifteen animal species in the form of sweet cookies—neither the staging of the reception area nor the office of the rector at the high school with more than five national youth-debate medals—nor the memory of her mother's dead eyes like two jellyfish sinking into water—could make her forget the lines she had practiced so many times in front of the mirror: "I'd like to work here because it's one of the few places equipped with everything a teacher needs to do an exceptional job," she would say to the rector. And even though the light that came in through the windows gave a strange air of irreality to the space—part tearoom, part travel agency—and that unsettled her and produced an immense desire to run away, she wouldn't run away; she wouldn't say a word about the missing accent marks or diaereses, the poorly placed commas or the incorrect use of uppercase letters—or about how much her mother hated indoor plants because they breathed at night (just like the robbers or murderers on TV). She would control her tongue: she would suppress her wildest muscle as she should have done before, when it tried to enter—without permission—her mother's mouth with a kiss that was rejected with a punch to her forehead. She would keep her legs still, knees together, shoulders relaxed, and she'd say—she decided as a secretary-hostess hung up the phone and gave her a tight-lipped smile—that a teacher called to the profession adapts to all kinds of situations, and she would do it without thinking about the taste of the eyelashes she had ripped from her mother's cadaver like a bouquet of flowers, or the father who, right then, stood up and pulled the fabric of his pants out from between his butt cheeks, or the pallid green of the indoor plants that trembled almost imperceptibly in the air conditioner's breeze, or the insufferable Clorox stain on the skirt of the secretary-hostess now walking toward her.

"Let's be scrupulous about paperwork," she read on a notice next to a foggy window; "GODS PHILOSOPHY," she read on another, next to the watercooler. "Just because a word is written entirely in capital letters doesn't mean it's exempt from apostrophe rules," she had explained hundreds of times to her poor students—or "humble students," in the words of those who, more than scrupulous with paperwork, were scrupulous with language. If they hired her, she would have wealthy students, and she would explain the same thing to them, because it was all she felt capable of teaching: when and where to place accent marks, apostrophes, periods, and commas; how to read a poem; how to analyze a text; how to write different kinds of papers; Romanticism, literary genres, Shakespeare, science fiction, Cervantes. . . . She would explain—cannibalizing her mother—that rules existed to be followed, at least the rules of language and of her classroom—because education, she had learned early on, was a matter of form.

Two steps away from her seat, the secretary-hostess showed her teeth.

All the indoor plants were made of plastic.

IV

A: I want to tell you the story of the day I killed my imaginary friend.

F: That's my story.

A: His name was Martín, like my dead brother.

F: Martín is my dead brother.

A: We'd gone to the beach, but it wasn't sunny.

F: It was sunny. We were at the hotel pool, and it was really hot.

A: We started to build a house like ours next to the waves.

F: My therapist says it's normal that my imaginary friend's name is Martín.

A: It was impossible to see the sky, and Martín's face went gray.

F: Martín was an ugly boy.

A: Martín was a really ugly boy.

F: My therapist says it's normal that my imaginary friend's name is Martín.

A: I asked him what was happening, but he couldn't answer, because imaginary beings don't talk.

F: He told me he was dead.

A: He was so gray he looked dead.

F: My therapist says it's normal that my imaginary friend's name is Martín.

A: That's when I realized I wished he were dead.

F: That's when I realized I wanted to show him what it was like to be dead.

A: I grabbed him by the hair and dragged him toward the waves.

F: And I said to myself: "I'm going to give me a dead body."

A: I told him: "I'm going to give you a dead body," and I plunged his head into the current.

F: His head was as small as a mango, and I smashed it against the side of the pool so his sweetness would spill out.

A: Since he didn't stop moving, I squeezed his neck under the water.

F: My therapist says it's normal.

A: I dug my thumbnails into his cottony throat. His peachy throat.

F: My therapist says it's very normal.

V

Fernanda woke up with her goose neck stiff and her saliva growing into a salty puddle on the table. Was it already tomorrow, today, the future-present? Why was she still there? Why hadn't anyone rescued her yet? She moved slowly so her numb muscles and joints wouldn't crack after hours of playing the calm role of Sleeping Beauty, but her body filled with tremors and despair much worse than any sickness. Worse than the stomatitis that had filled her mouth with sores years ago. Worse than the fever caused by the stomatitis and the blood that ran from the corners of her mouth whenever she tried to eat something Charo prepared for her. Her parents had been very worried then—her parents must be dying of worry now. She was disgusted with herself: saliva seemed to spill from her mouth every time she closed her eyes, drool reeking of eggs and tuna—the last thing she ate at the cafeteria before her kidnapping. How many hours had passed since she ate or drank anything? *A lot,* she answered herself, and she was dying of hunger just like the coyote who chased the roadrunner while her mother cried in the next room—her mother must be crying now. She painfully straightened up and glued her spine to the back of the chair. She needed to pee, brush her teeth, wash her hair. It seemed absurd that personal hygiene, seemingly irrelevant under those circumstances, took the same precedence as before. To scrub toothpaste into her gums, to spit her bad breath out in the sink, to let the water and the pipes carry away the grease from her Mia-Farrow-in-*Rosemary's-Baby*-hair; she would have given anything to clean the prison of her soul, as Mister Alan, her theology teacher, would say. Anything but her hare brain. Her freedom, yes, but not her brain. With her brain, she could obtain other freedoms and even recover the losses. That's why Mister Alan was an idiot whose only real distinction was having a giant ass: because he talked about the soul and not the mind, and because, like Descartes but without his sharpness, he believed the human being was made up of two substances operated by God. "The body is the prison of the soul," he would say. "The soul is the prison of the body," she had once told him, just to watch him swell up like a puffer fish. "Why did God prefer Abel's offering if Cain had worked just as hard as his brother? What's the point of an injustice like that?" "God revokes his threats; he's unstable. Jonah knows it, and that's why he doesn't want to go to Nineveh." "If it's thanks to Christ that God knows what it means to be a man, to suffer as we do, and to forgive us, then it's not true that he knew everything from the beginning. God was, at one point, ignorant." The mind is corporeal, and the body is mental; that's why she needed to clean even her soul, shake off the sensation of disaster, feel light again. She would have given anything, aside from her consciousness, to laugh at Mister Alan, aka Cosmic Ass, with her friends again: his pants up to his waist, his lumberjack shirts, his checkerboard socks. She had even read parts of a book by Hume, *The Natural History of Religion*, just so she could contradict him in class and watch him ignite and go red like a forest fire. "Hume says we shouldn't turn to religion to establish morality, but to society and ourselves, because otherwise morality would be based on dogma and superstition, and not on reason." "God doesn't want Adam and Eve to know the difference between good and evil; he doesn't want them to move beyond ignorance." "Don't you think God is a machista?" She wanted to clean her body in order to clean her mind, but she was kidnapped, and the knowledge of God was more dangerous than that revolver breathing a meter away from her. *I'm sure Cosmic Ass has never seen a real gun*, she thought with strange satisfaction. *If he were here, he'd shit himself.*

The light washed out the inside of the cabin: two cabinets, a table, a revolver, two chairs, a stove, and a stone countertop. There was something sinister in the transparent whiteness that lit the semi-empty space; she could see now that it was broad and deep, like the inside of a whale must be. Miss Clara had made them read the chapter "The Whiteness of the Whale" from *Moby Dick*, and though she remembered little of its content, she had a clear sense of the meaning: there was something unnamable and unsettling in whiteness—after all, that's what inspired Annelise's story about the white age and the White God. Fernanda, of course, accepted it as true; that's why that foamy morning light that discolored the objects tormented her, made her recoil into her chair. Outside the songs from beaks and antennae multiplied, while inside it seemed that a thin fish membrane covered everything and nothing moved. The room was a still-life landscape that she hated immediately because it made her think about death. *They'll definitely find me soon*, she told herself, rhythmically pounding her heels against the ground, a symptom of her full bladder. In the movies, no one died without a reason: everything was arranged to somehow serve the development of a plot. That's why she had never given death much serious thought, her breath catching in her slight Keira-Knightley chest. "At some point, we've all dreamed of killing someone or dying," her therapist had told her. "Not me," she said, but she was lying. Her parents' room was the only place in the house where there were photos of Martín, the little brother she barely remembered, who had lived for only a year. "Being alive for one year is ridiculous," she told her therapist. "It would have been better not to be born at all." Her lips were dry, and she started to chew them with gusto. "How do you feel when you have those kinds of thoughts?" "Normal, *why*? Should I feel something in particular?" A metallic flavor told her she had done damage, and she swore under her breath. "No, Fernanda. What's important is that you know what happened with Martín was not your fault." And she listened and felt a strange discomfort in response to his lie, because it had been her fault, even though her parents had explained it to her differently, holding hands, looking at her with compassion, and then making weekly appointments with an expert in human behavior who sat like a girl and held up his pants with suspenders. She was five when the stuff with Martín happened. She should have been able to remember, and nevertheless, her memories were just that: white depths, milky depths.

Why am I thinking about Martín now? she wondered as she looked at her purplish wrists. *I'm not going to die, let's not even talk about that.* It was decided. She breathed deeply with the intention of calming herself but only managed to draw in all the snot caused by the cold air. She sighed. That's how it felt to sleep handcuffed to a table: as if your bones and your flesh were two creatures fighting with open jaws to get at the roofs of each other's mouths. The elegance she'd imagined the day before had vanished when Miss Clara, instead of talking to her—which is what she had said she'd do—handcuffed her to a table screwed into the ground, went up the spiral staircase, and never returned. *Is she asleep, peacefully clutching her pillow, that big sack of shit?* Through the windows, she saw the foliage and, farther off, the volcano—now she was sure it wasn't a mountain and sure she wasn't Twiggy, but Mia Farrow playing the lead in a B horror movie. The cabin had to be in a forest because she couldn't make out the sound of a highway or anything else, besides creatures dragging themselves along the ground or swarming in the trees. That natural silence was also the color white, and it made her hair stand on end, above all because yesterday, after shouting for hours into the void, she had been able to confirm that the cabin of her kidnapping was far from any town. Miss Clara, *fucking cheap whore*, didn't even bother to stop her from flinging out bestial screams for hours, scrunching up her throat and throwing herself on the table in an effort to grab, with her teeth, a revolver that looked like a firefly in the dead of the night. Only a few animals responded to the shrieking and howling of her shredded voice, and even though it didn't make any sense, she believed they were also desperate, deprived of a future in their own worlds of chaos, and at least in that, she wasn't alone.

Demented slut, she thought. *Piece-of-shit crackpot.* Why her? Why had she taken her there? To ask her family for money? Had she done it for revenge? Didn't she know the police would lock her up? Or did she think they would let her off after what she did to her, Fernanda Montero Oliva, daughter of a minister and of a well-known lawyer and pro-life activist? Their faces, hers and her teacher's, must be all over social media, national and international TV, print and online media . . . *What was this crazy bitch thinking when she decided to ruin her life by kidnapping one of her students?* she thought. Her heels were pounding the floor because of the cold and her overwhelming need to urinate. She tried to stretch her legs, to stand up, but her knees shook as if her patellae were on the verge of dislocating—the fragility of the body: "True humiliation only exists in the flesh," her therapist said. She went back to fighting against the table, but it was impossible to lift it off the ground: its legs had dark bases that were screwed into the wood. With each movement she attempted, her wrists rubbed against the metal of the handcuffs, and her skin burned and threatened to bleed. The revolver, completely out of her reach, was aimed at her like her mother's finger in the nightmares she frequently analyzed with Dr. Aguilar, aka Interpreter of Dreams, aka Decoder of Minds, aka Lacan's Seminar Z. Miss Clara had left that revolver there in an obvious attempt to intimidate her. *Or maybe she just wants to mess with me,* she reflected. Nothing could be ruled out, but she had to calm down before her teacher's intentions became the object of increasingly convoluted fabulations.

Fucking bitch.

Her swollen bladder began to ache like a slashing bolt of lightning. She needed to distract herself, to think of something else. She could think instead about the *exploitation fiction* comic she had started, but hadn't finished, with Annelise. It was a project titled *Sor Juana: Zombies, Vampires, and Lesbians* and featured the poet as the protagonist and was set in a convent of lesbian dominatrix nuns, where, thanks to a Chacmool and an ancestral ritual, a zombie-Nahuatl virus is spreading. The story is narrated from the future by an Arabic researcher at UNAM who, while investigating the true history of the Phoenix of Mexico, found an aleph in a urinal marked out-of-order by a blind, etymology-loving custodian. Thanks to that aleph, the researcher was able to draw connections between his vision and the various historical facts gathered up until then; it was a revelation that allowed him, in turn, to narrate the true history of Sor Juana Inés de la Cruz. She and Annelise had the idea for the comic during a language and literature class. In their comic, the vampires appear in the second chapter through a character physically similar to Miss Clara and based on Sor Gertrudis de San Ildefonso, a Quiteña nun and writer of *The Mystic Pearl Hidden in the Conch of Humility*—a title they thought sounded sexual when an excited Mister Alan noted it on the board in a class on the writer-nuns of Ecuador. She and Annelise hoped the project would make them famous. Recognition, after all, was the one thing their parents' money couldn't buy.

She's doing it for money, she thought. *Nothing is going to happen to me.* The sound of her handcuffs reminded her of the jangling of her mother's bracelets. *My parents will pay whatever she asks. Nothing that bad could happen.*

Her mind quieted as she remembered the comic, the characters, and Annelise's freckles, but then the door swung open with a bang, and the wind, for a few brief seconds, snapped at her vertebrae. Miss Clara, who she thought was sleeping upstairs, went over to the kitchen countertop and threw a big gray rabbit—perhaps a hare—onto the stone. Its bulging eyes, infused with blood, made Fernanda look away: toward the window, toward the volcano. *What if she doesn't want money?* she wondered, wary again. Everything around her started to smell like herbs and sweat, but she kept quiet, her chin pointing toward the light. There was fog behind the windowpanes: a white, curdled thickness, like spit-up. Clarity: the clothing of grace. She felt a particular agitation when an uncontrollable bead of snot trickled across her lips. She thought her body, stripped of cleanliness, bore a baffling resemblance to that of the rabbit on the countertop.

A natural enigma.

A landscape of claws.

She wanted to ask her teacher questions: Why her and not Annelise, Fiorella, Natalia, Ximena, Analía, or anyone else? But something strange stopped her, something like fear, but also like the certainty that sooner or later, she'd find out, and it didn't make much sense to rush the moment. Meanwhile, she listened, not daring to peel her gaze away from outside, to the sound of the rabbit being skinned. She couldn't pinpoint the moment when her indignation gave way to that interior trembling twisting up her intestines. Perhaps it was the revolver, the dead animal, the silence: metaphors of uncertainty, enigmatic scenes out of a film by Polanski.

She wiped her mouth on the shoulder of her blouse before saying:

"I need to go to the bathroom."

Miss Clara stopped what she was doing, and Fernanda heard squawks near the cabin, but there was no movement, no attempt to shorten the distance and free her, at least momentarily, to give her a bucket, or to resolve her need in any way. Now her gaze was glued to the stairs, but she could picture her teacher watching her, like in any normal class, when she lectured them about Ecuadorian, Latin American, or universal literature, jumping around in the textbook or leaving unintelligible scribbles on the board.

The sudden sound of a knife being sharpened, the whack of the blade against flesh, told her that this time, she wouldn't be getting a "Go to the bathroom, but come right back." As if she hadn't said a word, Miss Clara resumed her activity, leaving her an invisible piece of knowledge: what she said or desired had no importance anymore, and it wouldn't until she, her kidnapper, decided to sit down, look at her, talk to her. Only then would the gift of language—that hedgehog so soft, its barbs so black—be returned to her; only then would she glimpse the intentions lurking behind the night-rock her teacher had for a face.

She squeezed her thighs and tensed her vaginal muscles. In *Sor Juana: Zombies, Vampires, and Lesbians*, Sister Gertrudis seduces the nuns at the convent and turns them into dominatrix vampires, and she does it by whispering poems in Nahuatl into their ears. She dies in chapter eight, when one nun drives a stake into her heart just like Nina Dobrev in *The Vampire Diaries*. "Lacan was

right when he said truth is always structured as fiction," her therapist had told her one afternoon when they talked about memory. She carefully looked at Miss Clara, disheveled and covered in
sweat, cutting open an animal that wouldn't stop spurting blood.
Someone should tell that bitch she needs therapy.

VI

They dragged their chairs. Miss Ángela, aka Baldomera, asked that they pick them up, but they dragged their chairs over her golden Angelus Novus voice: the sleeping-angel-of-history voice dictating the past, though inevitably pushed along—like the chairs—by the present, toward the promise of a future with twenty-three skirts, five smiles with braces, three Tory Burch watches, twenty-one iPhones, three iPads, and a rosary. The pack of metal barking across the floor tiles woke up Ivanna Romero, aka Full Ride, who jumped to carry hers forward. Fernanda shoved her chair against Annelise Van Isschot's, aka Freckles. It had been a long time since there were bumper cars in the city. *It's so fun to crash into everything that matters,* she thought, recalling the childhood that roused her fangs. Fiorella and Natalia Barcos stood at the back of the classroom, behind Ximena Sandoval and Analía Raad, their *best-friends-4ever*-never-change-baby, and pulled their ponytails tight, grinning with their incisors. Ximena and Analía turned around: they stuck their clitoris-tongues out to their chins. The others' chairs taunted the floor while Baldomera asked again, this time more emphatically, that they carry them, but no one listened to her. Then she banged her Muhammad Ali fist on the table, and the scraping metal quieted only to be replaced by the sound of chairs thudding to the ground. A wave of minute giggles and exchanged glances made Baldomera regret disrupting the rows of the auditorium layout in favor of that of an amphitheater: a beautiful, pedagogical half circle that would position the girls as her equals. Equity. Democracy. Parity. *Vile snot-nosed girls.* How could those rats starved for desire ever bear any resemblance to her? Lucía Otero undid the top buttons of her blouse. María Aguayo adjusted the skirt that, made to measure by some tailor, accentuated her

Nicki-Minaj-booty. Renata Medina gave it a squeeze, her hands opening like umbrellas. Cascading cackles. They didn't have male classmates, but the most popular ones got invited to college parties. Fernanda and Annelise got invited. Sometimes they went; sometimes they brought along the Barcos sisters, Ximena, and Analía. They were the most perfect group in the class. That's what they thought: *We're the most perfect group in our class.* They arranged their chairs together in the back. Miss Baldomera gave them a skeptical look, as if they were frogs about to jump into a puddle of mud and splash everyone around them. Valeria Méndez pulled a Hello Kitty nail file from her pencil case. Full Ride sharpened her pencil over Bolívar's face. Raquel Castro watched her with disdain and then made fun of her nose with Blanca Mackenzie. *Pinocchio. Beak face.* More than a half circle, the shape formed by the chairs looked like an irregular pentagon. Miss Angelus Novus opened the book to page fifty-six: "Today we're going to talk about the abolition of slavery in Ecuador," she said. Fernanda caressed Annelise's elbow, and Annelise blew her a kiss with her eyes closed. Analía and Ximena smiled and opened their notebooks. The Barcos sisters yawned. Full Ride took notes even though everything Miss Sleeping Angel of History said was in the book. She was writing, everyone knew, so she wouldn't have to see Raquel Castro and Blanca Mackenzie making fun of her nose. Fernanda put a stick of gum in her mouth. Chewing gum in class was not allowed. Dyeing your hair blue or getting a tattoo wasn't allowed either. "Your bodies are temples for honoring God," Mister Alan always said. They had talked about a lot of things in history class, but never about why the past was important. "Why is the past important?" Fernanda asked after pressing the gum to the roof of her mouth. María Aguayo uncrossed her legs and revealed her blood-stained underwear. The Barcos sisters pursed their lips. "Because it's essential that we learn from our decisions, good and bad, and also because it's how we understand who we are today," Miss Baldomera answered. Red is a pungent color. Fernanda didn't understand why the past, the ruins, the casualties she neither knew nor loved, were any of her concern. The teacher talked about racial segregation while Analía passed a piece of paper to Ximena, and Ximena passed it to the Barcos sisters, and the Barcos sisters passed it to Annelise, and Annelise passed it to Fernanda. There were no Indigenous or Black people at the school, except Miss Black Angel of History and the women who cleaned the bathrooms. Fernanda wrote in her notebook: "Why is the past important?" Miss Clara, aka *Latin* Madame Bovary, came into the classroom and put Miss Baldomera's histrionics on hold. The Barcos sisters watched her, two sets of eyebrows almost touching. She had given them both a five on their last papers. "Terrible redaction," Bovary had written in red marker. "It's like she grades with her period blood," Ximena had said. Miss *Latin* Madame Bovary always wore dress pants or skirts that fell below the knee. "She's the Anti–Cosmic Ass," Annelise said when Miss Clara bent to whisper something in Miss Angelus Novus's ear. "That's how they get through the boredom: from one ear to another," she said to Fernanda, and they both shrugged. "What's boredom?" Miss *Latin* Madame Bovary's hands shook; Miss Big Angel knit her brow. "Knowledge of the world and everything else that exists." Fernanda took Annelise's hand and spit the gum into the middle of her snowy palm. "I want to be wise. I'd hate to be as ignorant as most people," Ximena said. Annelise brought the wet blue gum, like the brain of a Smurf, to her mouth. "If you were uneducated, you'd have to work jobs for people without a brain, and you'd be poor," Analía said. The Barcos sisters shuddered. Poverty was ugly, and they loved beauty. "The history of aesthetics is the history of class struggle," the off-screen voice had said in a documentary they watched in art appreciation. Fernanda thought, watching the teachers speak very softly, that knowledge of the world and everything else that exists couldn't possibly be contained in a classroom but outside, day to day in the gardens; or in the experience of intensity, burning as fast as a match; or in her heart, going up in a cruel smoke when a college guy who looked like a young Johnny Depp put his hand down her pants. The sublime: the vertigo of what's unexplored, that drive toward sensations that launched her desire into the darkness. "What would it feel like to kill someone?" Annelise suddenly asked. Too many questions to live through: What will it feel like to die? Will it hurt a lot the first time? What will we do when our parents die? What will it be like ruining other people's lives? What about our own? Will it be enjoyable or overwhelming? Will the mountains break first, or our spirit? Will we be afraid of horses? *Yes, we will be afraid of horses*, thought Fernanda. "I'll go, what does it matter / let the dark horse / reign," went the lines they'd read in *Latin* Madame Bovary's class, from a poem by Roy Sigüenza—"that faggot poet," Mister Alan called him. "Here, the horse symbolizes desire: breaking free, the Dionysian," she had told them, strangling their imagination. Once, Miss Lidia, aka Caravaggio's Medusa, showed them Fuseli's *The Nightmare*, a painting in which a woman who has fainted or is sleeping appears on a bed with a devil-gargoyle on top of her and the head of a ghostly horse emerging from a red curtain. Was desire something like being possessed by a nightmare? Full Ride dropped her pencils on the ground, and Raquel Castro and Blanca Mackenzie laughed, touching their noses. *Bird face. Her nose looks like a limp dick.* "Miss Clara's hands always shake, have you noticed?" Fiorella said. "Excuse me, girls, I'll be right back," said Miss Baldomera, standing to leave with Bovary. Annelise jumped out of her chair and glued herself to the window. Fernanda followed her, and then the Barcos sisters, Analía, Ximena, Full Ride, all the little birds, skirts bouncing and calves tense, standing on tiptoe, looking out over other heads. Out in the schoolyard, the rector was speaking sternly to an eleventh-grade girl. Miss Baldomera, Miss Bovary, and three other teachers were there, standing silently. "What do you think she did?" Ximena asked. Steal something? Plagiarize her homework? Hit someone? Call the teachers names? Set off a stink bomb in the classroom? The possibilities were infinite, but they all screamed the same thing: contempt. "She must have thrown her textbook in the trash, like Diana Rodríguez," Analía said. "She must be pregnant, like Sofía

Bueno," Natalia said. Sofía Bueno had left the school and the country. "Motherhood is your future so that, in caring for your families, you may find God," Cosmic Ass said the week before. "To be a mother is to surrender yourself to your daughter, to be a daughter is to surrender yourself to your mother," Miss Bovary said when they told her, but she seemed to regret saying it. *No one should be forced to care for anyone,* Fernanda thought then, imagining a monstrous woman whose belly was expanding like the universe. The girl outside was crying: her hands hung clasped at the height of her pelvis. Every face in the window wanted to know what she'd done. Fernanda was interested in the profound rage she felt toward the teachers and the rector, aka Moctezuma's Crest, who, crowding around the girl, looked like a group of stupid walruses approaching a wolf cub. *She could bite them,* she thought. *Why doesn't she bite them?* Whatever she may have done, it was justified if they wanted to pull out her teeth. "I've thought about it more," Annelise said. "Boredom is knowledge of the world filtered through a chalkboard." Natalia shoved her shoulder: "Or through a book." *Or through words,* Fernanda thought. "One comes to know the world through the body." Mister Alan emerged, coming down the stairs of the building opposite with a red-faced girl. "Here comes another," the ones on the right said. "What did they do?" the ones on the left wondered aloud. "Maybe they hit each other," Natalia said. "Maybe they found them kissing," Fiorella jeered. Annelise spit her gum discreetly into Raquel Castro's hair and licked Fernanda's cheek. "Now are we lesbian enough to be punished?" The Barcos sisters laughed. On the other side, Full Ride stared fixedly at Miss Baldomera's bag. Fernanda ran her tongue over her teeth. "Careful, it bites," Annelise said, excited. "It looks like the mouth of a crocodile," said Analía, running toward the bag. "At any moment, BAM, it rips off your arm." Makeup, pens, dry-erase markers, a notebook, a wallet, a cell phone. Yawn. "Let's write something in the notebook!" Ximena said. Fernanda opened it, but Annelise tore it from her hands and took off running to the other side of the room. "You have gum in your hair!" screamed

Valeria Méndez. They all turned toward Raquel Castro's head, and she began to shriek. Annelise leaned against Blanca Mackenzie's desk and wrote something on the last page of Miss Baldomera's notebook. Fernanda watched her from afar and thought about how beautiful her panther hair was. "It was you, wasn't it?" Raquel Castro said to Full Ride. "You're not going to forget me for the rest of your nasty life." Fernanda thought, too, about how much she would have liked to be Annelise. "One day you'll be on your knees, begging me for a job." Not to be *like* Annelise, but to be Annelise. "Because that's what you're going to do: work for people like us." To get up every morning and see the freckles on her cheeks in the mirror splattered with toothpaste, to speak with that wild voice, to have a little brother she could love. "Here she comes!" Ximena yelled, running to her seat. They all launched themselves at their chairs, and Annelise put the notebook back in Angelus Novus's bag. To smell of new toys at the nape of her neck; to dance, eyes closed, on other people's mattresses; to believe in a drag-queen God and draw it in the corners of the Bible. "What did you write to her?" Analía asked when Miss Baldomera entered the classroom like nothing had happened. "Tell us what you wrote!" Fiorella said. To have the most beautiful toenails imaginable. "It's a secret," Annelise said, and then winked at Fernanda.

And class started again.

VII

Clara started working at the Delta Bilingual Academy, *High-School-for-Girls*, one month before the start of classes. They gave her a cubicle in the teachers' lounge, the key to her desk drawer, a code to log in on a Mac, the Wi-Fi password, a card for checking out books from the library, notebooks and pens with the name of the institution—as well as a mug with the school logo—and a permit for the private parking lot. On her first day, she toured the facilities with the dean of student life, a sixty-year-old woman with greenish-yellow hair and a puckered expression, as if she'd just tasted something tart. "My name is Patricia, but everyone calls me Patty," she said listlessly. Clara learned that Patty was the kind of person who was accustomed to talking out of obligation. She approved of her policeman-like air and the order, neat and minimalist, that she noticed in the dean's office when they went to pick up her class schedule and the corresponding lists with the names of her future students. Nevertheless, she found the extreme organization of the place inconsistent with the clothing Patricia was wearing that afternoon, excessively loose and resembling pajamas, as well as the little care given to her feet—her mother would have said, if she were alive and could see them, that exposing long, dirty toenails was something that only animals did, or people who weren't ashamed of their own ugliness (perhaps, Clara thought, aging meant losing the shame of one's own unpleasantness). Weeks later, when the students began to arrive, Patricia Flores—she could never call her Patty—swapped her pajamas for the dean's uniform, but she still wore the orthopedic sandals in which her long toes brushed the ground, and that—though it was difficult for her to admit it to herself (she didn't want to be superficial)—deeply bothered Clara, to the degree that she was uncomfortable every time she was near her, since she had to make such an effort not to look at her feet, and, in spite of her attempts, she always ended up looking, then feeling a mixture of disgust and rage toward that woman with the vinegary face who didn't know how to maintain her toenails or heels.

Her aversion to Patricia-the-dean was one of the first annoyances she experienced at the school—she couldn't believe the same person who organized the dry-erase markers by color would choose a hair dye à la Beetlejuice, but that didn't happen until later. On the first day, Clara ignored Patricia's pajamas and sandals and concentrated instead on what was hanging around her neck: a red whistle on a fine chain that swayed between her saggy, ample boobs. It was that whistle, and her disproportionately large breasts, that made her think Patricia—in spite of her disregard for personal hygiene—must be a good dean, that she would take care to monitor the students and support her in controlling them, strictly if necessary, any time she asked. That's why she was grateful, almost relieved, that it was Patricia-the-dean who walked her through the school and showed her the classrooms, library, dining hall, cafeteria, Olympic-size pool, theater, media lab, chapel, artistic gymnastics room, gymnasium, auditorium, soccer fields, basketball and volleyball courts, nurse's office, science lab, computer labs, kitchen, garden, and skating rink, and also because she was old and only spoke when she had to and didn't bother to initiate casual conversation—her mother had also been a woman of few (though judgmental) words, and Clara (who knew that her evermore-severe anxiety disorder tended to worsen during imposed social situations) preferred to follow her example.

That day, as they walked in silence, Clara felt content, or perhaps overexcited at the prospect of resuming the life she had led before the *M&M's*. Her feverish energy—"Stay still, Becerra!" her mother would say when she was six years old and got so worked up that she hugged her mother with a stifling insistence—caused slight tremors and covered her body in a thin layer of sweat, which she attributed, during her uniform fitting, to her good mood and not her nerves. There were rules that required the teachers at Delta Bilingual Academy, *High-School-for-Girls*, to wear the institutional shirt, pants, and jacket on the days when public-facing activities took place. She enthusiastically cooperated with the tailor, who had the delicacy to touch her as little as possible, and surprised herself by accepting the fact that two or three days a month, she wouldn't be able to dress like her mother. The rest of the time, however, she would wear her long 1989-maternal-style skirts and blouses with pearl-shaped buttons.

Two or three days a month is nothing, she consoled herself, and even though the uniform depersonalized her and set her at a dangerous distance from her dead mother, she thought she'd be able · to bear it.

At one point during the tour, she tried to imagine the school—then almost empty—full of girls with skirts and bows and acne and new teeth, and she felt sick, on the verge of tachycardia—the anticipation of a possible panic attack stopped her in her tracks, as always happened when the fear of being afraid triggered her worst crises ("You have cockroaches in your head, you sick little girl," her mother would say, sitting in the tiger-striped armchair, every time Clara asked her for help breathing). Patricia, saying the words without really seeming to mean them, asked if she wanted to sit down, but Clara said no and was able to recover a sense of calm by dampening her forehead with a splash from a nearby water fountain.

The dean didn't ask any more questions.

Even though her anxiety disorder had intensified since what happened with the *M&M's*—now not even the pills could calm all the symptoms afflicting her—Clara had little fear of the pain in the delicate skin between the fingers of her left hand, or of her heel pounding the floor like a hammer for hours, or her gnawed fingernails, or her excessive perspiration, or the way she organized the fruits and vegetables in the kitchen, or the interminable cleaning of the bathroom, or the way her thighs burned when she scratched herself until she bled at night, but she did very much fear the recurrence of her panic attacks; they had reappeared with force in recent months, stiffening her muscles and making her heart race, leaving her incapable of relaxing. Before her first interview with the rector of the Delta Bilingual Academy, *High-School-for-Girls*, Clara had convinced herself that her panic attacks were lessening—she hadn't had one for several weeks—and that the trauma she'd incurred after what happened with Malena Goya and Michelle Gomezcoello would disappear as her life returned to normal. Returning to the classroom was her only escape: the best way to recuperate what little was left of her dignity.

She had never been able to stand the chaos and lack of discipline at public high schools, which is why she was pleased to confirm that Delta functioned like clockwork. The academic calendar for the year was finished months before the beginning of the semester, and when she arrived, the teachers were already holding meetings by subject area and grade, as well as polishing curricular designs and quarterly activities. The distribution of tasks was equitable and fair: every teacher had the same number of student-break and after-school shifts; they also had enough time to prepare materials and produce reports and projects, because no one could teach for more than ten hours per week. There were manuals and informational pamphlets for everything, from how to create an environment conducive to collaboration with "fellow defenders of education," to how to ensure that each subject corresponded to the institutional mission and Opus Dei doctrines—the mission, vision, and learning outcomes were tacked to the bulletin boards in every lounge, classroom, and office.

Religion played a central role at the Delta Bilingual Academy, *High-School-for-Girls*, which included a special schedule for spiritual events that students and staff were required to attend. The person who organized said activities—and scheduled the use of the chapel—was Alan Cabrera, theology teacher, a sickly-looking man who hiked up his pants as far as they would go and had the ass of a broad-hipped woman. Clara talked to him on her second day of work, and he seemed to her, among other things, like someone who tried too hard to please everyone else—he smiled when there was no need to smile and opened his eyes lunatically, play-ing the fool. She realized that every time Alan Cabrera made a joke, the teachers laughed out of courtesy, and that was enough for him. Like Patricia, Alan had no living relatives, so his family, he said, were his students and his colleagues—an idea that (in the opinion of the dead mother who inhabited her mind) belonged to a pitiful person. The only one who didn't laugh at his jokes—which were sometimes racist, though he didn't seem to notice—was the history teacher, Ángela Caicedo, a tall forty-something woman, with a deep, almost masculine voice who spoke even less than Clara did—she just barely heard her greet everyone in the morn-ings and say good-bye in the afternoons (every now and then, she also heard her ask for A4 paper for the printer). Without know-ing it, Ángela alleviated the pressure Clara felt to get close to her colleagues—she soon discarded the plan she had designed, which had consisted of casually commenting on something three times a day (the ideal number to be considered reasonably sociable)—since if everyone accepted the history teacher's silence, that meant they wouldn't find hers rude either.

She came away from the first days of her job with the impres-sion that, in general, an environment of cordiality reigned in the teacher's lounge, and everyone took great pains to keep it intact. They talked to each other, smiled, discussed some things, and even made jokes, but the conversations lasted no more than two minutes, and at the end, everyone buried themselves in their work again, not taking any real interest in the others' lives. Because of that, Clara thought for a few days that she would be safe from their broaching the subject of the M&M's, asking how she was doing after having been kidnapped in her own home, attacked by two of her students, when what they really wanted was to hear the sordid details of the case: How and how much did they torture her? Was she afraid she would die? Was she in a lot of pain . . . ?

It was Amparo Gutiérrez, the PE teacher, who asked her about it the second week, right at the end of a meeting about discipline and protocol.

"That must have been awful, you poor thing," she said, and noting that Clara didn't respond, she went on, "but you won't need to worry about that here. Our girls can be a little difficult, depending on the group, but they come from good families. They aren't a bunch of wild fillies, no, and they aren't criminals either. It's important to maintain order and discipline with girls this young, that's what we do here: we teach them how to behave themselves. Or at least, we try." She sat thinking for a few minutes, then blinked very rapidly. "But are you o.k.?"

Fortunately, Ángela Caicedo came to her rescue. She interrupted them in such a way that her entrance felt neither abrupt nor rude—there are people, her mother had said, who can do anything without others taking it personally—and asked Clara a question about historical novels and their filmic adaptations. A few minutes later, Amparo Gutiérrez gave up and left, chatting with Carmen Mendoza, the natural science teacher.

"Do you want a coffee? I could use a strong one," Ángela said, standing up. It was then that Clara realized she was tall because she wore heels that almost resembled stilts. That day she was dressed in light blue: a knee-length skirt and a cotton blouse with a zipper down the back. There was something in the tone of her voice, a genuine whatdoicareism that assured her she wouldn't ask any personal questions.

That was the first and only time she went for coffee with one of her colleagues.

Most of the teachers at Delta had been there for more than five years: Ángela had been there for seven; Alan, twenty; Carmen, eleven; Amparo, nine; Patricia, twenty-five. She knew that the person who had previously held her position had just retired, and that's why she had been able to join the staff. Everyone spoke highly of Marta Álvarez—the former language and literature teacher—but Clara thought they seemed insincere: they used clichés to describe her work at the school, stock phrases that could have been applied to any other professional who'd devoted their life to any other job. Furthermore, her impressions of her new coworkers told her that they were similar to her ex-colleagues: the faces and the surroundings had changed, but not the personalities of those who chose to teach. Amparo Gutiérrez, for example, was a muscular woman with pronounced crow's feet who thought they should increase the mandatory hours of physical education each week and who seized every opportunity to rattle off her speech, "Mens sana in corpore sano," in the teachers' lounge. She was the kind of person who—in the opinion of the dead mother who inhabited her mind—liked to hear her own voice, and that's why she talked regardless of whether anyone else was interested. Unlike Alan Cabrera, who went out of his way to please the others—several times a week he brought in chocolates or sweets and left them in the middle of the teachers' lounge, he made his racist jokes, talked a bit about the Work, and offered to assist in any matter (even those beyond his abilities)— Amparo said whatever came into her mind without worrying how it might be received. The teachers listened without contradicting her, not because they agreed but in an attempt to escape her intensity. Only Carmen Mendoza—the natural science teacher who crossed herself every time she turned on her computer—dared to engage in debates with her.

Clara understood later that she did it because they were friends.

The third week, still without any hint of an oncoming panic attack, Clara concluded that she had made the right decision in interviewing for the language and literature opening. The Delta Bilingual Academy, *High-School-for-Girls*, seemed to have everything under control, and so did she. Her anxiety didn't disappear in those weeks, but became manageable again. And even though the nightmares and visions of the *M&M's* breaking into her house didn't stop, at least while she worked, she was able to forget about them, along with the fear that floated under her ribs like a balloon. Around that time, she realized the only colleague whose company she could tolerate was Ángela Caicedo. Clara felt she could count on her to slip her out of situations in which her anxiety gave her away as a nervous and obsessive person. The two of them had an unspoken agreement: when they needed information or special

assistance with something, each one only turned to the other—
maybe because they both knew that neither would try to start
a conversation or ask for something in return. She had noticed
with admiration that the other teachers didn't judge her com-
panion's distant attitude to be strange or aggressive; instead, they
accepted it, because she was friendly in her distance, in her way of
not connecting with the rest. Patricia-the-dean was also sparing
and distant, but she was surly and lacked even a shred of Ángela's
elegance. That's why Clara began to imitate her mode of integra-
tion: she politely greeted everyone upon arriving in the teachers'
lounge, answered their questions, helped others when they asked,
and always said good-bye with a smile. It was that behavior that
allowed her to abandon her own technique. She no longer had to
make comments or initiate trivial conversation three times a day
to be cordial, because no one expected or missed it. She soon realized the teachers at Delta—unlike the ones at the school where
she used to work—weren't trying to get to know her, but to work
with her.

Despite that almost perfect atmosphere, she sometimes heard
allusions to past conflicts, situations that, in the majority's opinion, had been generated by students. Once, she learned, a student
who had gotten pregnant and was about to drop out of school—
her parents wanted to take her to another country and force her
to have the child there—jumped from the second floor of the high
school. Both the girl and the fetus survived, but a teacher who
no longer worked there reported in the rector's office that Alan
Cabrera had set aside time to discuss the sin of abortion with
the student and her friends. The pregnant girl had left one theology class so distressed that soon after, she jumped from the second floor. The teacher who reported the fact also complained on
social media about Delta's institutional policies and accused them
of perpetuating violence against women. That teacher, of course,
was fired, but others still there resented the belligerent speeches
Alan Cabrera made in his classes, though they never dared to discuss it beyond the school's hallways. In such cases, Clara thought,

nothing could be done: the students' parents were in favor of the kind of education they provided, and because of that, year after year, they paid enormous sums of money so Opus Dei could hold various ceremonies and events. "This is an ideal place to work," Ángela told her the day they got coffee together. "As long as you're able to go deaf, blind, and mute from time to time."

On another occasion, Clara learned, Carmen Mendoza got into an argument with Lidia Fuentes, who taught art appreciation, because a student had told Carmen that Lidia denied the credibility of Darwin's theory of evolution in class. Because it was a religious matter, Alan Cabrera intervened and was able to quell the animosity, even though Clara thought she noticed Carmen Mendoza avoiding both Lidia Fuentes and Alan Cabrera in the teachers' lounge.

"Conflicts between teachers don't last very long here," Ángela told her once while they were waiting in line for lunch. "And the girls are almost always involved. That's why they never last. They're ridiculous."

But as the start of classes approached, Clara again began to unexpectedly tremble, become agitated, pick at the delicate skin between the fingers of her left hand, scratch her thighs at night, and, above all, see *them*: Malena Goya and Michelle Gomezcoello, two short shadows walking around in her house in the early hours, clawing at the walls, chewing all the table legs. The insomnia—the only thing she would have preferred not to have inherited from her mother—forced her to lock the door to her room and ignore the footsteps and laughter she heard even though she knew they were coming from her own head. Clara was terrified of her mother's nights. When she was alive, Elena Valverde would walk around the house in the dark, locking the doors and windows so no one could come in. Once, Clara had a friend, but her mother never let her invite her over for a slumber party. "Do you really think it's safe to let a stranger come in and sleep alongside us?" she asked, offended, and since Clara wanted to be like her in every way, she began to detest the idea of having visitors in her home. When someone rang the doorbell, Elena always opened the door but never let anyone in. "I don't like people seeing my things, Becerra." "Be careful letting your friends in, because I'll rip you to pieces." On nights when she had insomnia, her mother would drag her feet from room to room, and Clara would try not to fall asleep, but she would, and it was terrible because on the weekends, she would wake up just as her mother was falling asleep, and sometimes the doorbell would ring, and there'd be no one to open the door.

"You look awful," Amparo told her at a meeting the rector called two days before classes started, at which she reminded the teachers of the necessity of complying with the list of books approved by the institution and emphasized that if they wanted to work with something new, they should tell their respective coordinators, who would submit it for board review. She also talked about the importance of incentivizing the "gifted" students to register for classes in which they could develop their abilities to competitive levels—the Delta Bilingual Academy, *High-School-for-Girls*, was interested in winning as many championships and contests as possible because (in the rector's words) their students needed to be in the showcase. Furthermore, she asked teachers to try to handle discipline in the classroom rather than making students leave class. "That has to be the last resort. Ideally, we should be able to modify our girls' behavior in other, less exclusive ways," she said. "When we ask them to leave class, we're telling them we can't handle them, and that is a sign of weakness."

Some parents had complained the year before about their daughters' repeated expulsions, Ángela told Clara under her breath, and the rector, always accommodating with clients, was unwilling to upset them.

"With all due respect," said Rodrigo Zúñiga, the math teacher, "I don't believe any of us take it lightly when we ask our students to leave class. These girls . . . well, some groups are out of control. They treat us like their employees, they have no respect for us. The humiliation, in certain cases, has reached an intolerable level, such that even more drastic measures—a special sanction, a permanent expulsion—would be warranted. We all know what happened with Marta. Situations like that cannot be permitted!"

That's when Clara learned that Marta Álvarez, her predecessor, had suffered a pre–heart attack when a group Ángela defined as "especially challenging" played a prank. The girls had decided to create their own version of the Clutter family murder from Truman Capote's *In Cold Blood*—required reading that semester—the same day Marta had planned to teach a lesson on the book. When Marta Álvarez, sixty years old, entered the classroom that afternoon, she found the bodies of her students languid on the benches, bloody pillows under their heads. Two students were still standing in the middle of the room, one of them holding a revolver, and that's when it happened.

"The poor thing couldn't even scream, she collapsed in the doorway," Ángela told her. "She was o.k. in the end, but we all know that's why she retired."

One of the two students who pretended to murder her classmates had taken, without permission, a revolver from her father's collection so the prank would be more realistic. Ángela explained that they even bought fake blood from a costume shop.

"But . . . they were punished, right?" Clara asked, picking at the delicate skin between the fingers of her left hand.

"Of course. The girls were suspended for a week."

"One week?"

Ángela, who noticed Clara's incredulity at the lightness of the punishment, fluttered her hand in the air to diminish its importance. "You have to remember that, yes, this is a school, but it's also a business. These girls come from important families."

"The revolver wasn't loaded," Ángela said.

"It was a joke made in very poor taste, by two girls who didn't know how to measure the consequences of their actions," she said.

As they were leaving the meeting, Clara dared to ask one final question.

"Will those two students be in any of my classes?"

And Ángela nodded.

VIII

A: Miss Clara, why do you think girls always go to the bathroom in pairs?

C: I don't know.

A: Think about it. Why would a girl do something private accompanied not by three or four or five, but by one, her equal?

C: That's a different question.

A: No, Miss Clara. It's the same one.

C: This has nothing to do with the topic for today's session, Annelise.

A: But answer me, please. Why do girls always go to bed two by two at sleepovers?

C: I want you to open your book to page 148.

A: Why do girls shower with their best friends?

C: Annelise!

A: Why do they greedily watch over them?

C: Señorita Van Isschot!

A: Why do they love them so much that they would rather see them dead?

IX

Dr. Aguilar:

Fernanda: I didn't kill my dead brother, Martín. I didn't kill my dead brother, Martín. I didn't kill my dead brother, Martín. I didn't kill my dead brother, Martín. There you go. See? I wrote it a million times. I really believe it. I know perfectly well it was an accident, even though I don't remember, because I was reeeally little, *you know?* Also, it doesn't matter if I did it or not, because if I did and I don't remember, it's as if I didn't do it. And I was reeeally young, so if I did let him drown, it wasn't because I was bad but because I was stupid and ignorant. I mean, at what age do children learn that killing is wrong? Do you know anything about that, or . . . ?

Dr. Aguilar:

Fernanda: No, I'm not mad, it's just that . . . Ufff! I'm bored of talking about Martín. I have tooons of other problems that are muuuch more interesting, *you know?* Because I'm at the age when things happen to me. There's sooo much we could talk about! I have problems, trauma and whatnot, that would shock you. But why do they call adolescence the donkey phase here? Why not the parrot phase or the tapir phase?

Dr. Aguilar:

Fernanda: *Wrooong.* What I said that day was that I felt guilty about my mom not loving me, not about Martín's death.

Dr. Aguilar:

Fernanda: *Of course.* Guilt is boring, that's why I avoid it, but . . . I know my mom doesn't love me. In fact, I know she's afraid of me.

Dr. Aguilar:

Fernanda: It's difficult to talk about, *I guess.* I think about my
mother a lot. I never see her, because she's reeeally busy, but
I think about her a ton. For example, I realized not long ago
that she doesn't love me. She never loved me. And don't think
I'm saying this out of resentment, because I'm not. The truth
is, I don't care, because I'm grown up now, or almost grown
up, *you know? Anyway,* I think it's because of Martín. Because
she knows it's possible that I saw him drowning and did
nothing to save him, or that I pushed him, I don't know. It's
possible, and don't say it isn't, because I'm smart, and I've considered all the possibilities, and that's a possibility. Anything
could've happened. That's why every time they talk about
Cain and Abel in church, she cries. I notice, *you know?* We've
never had a normal relationship. *I mean,* like other mothers
and daughters. It's the same with my father, but still, you would
think with my mom it would have to be . . . I don't know, different, because there's nothing greater than a mother's love,
blah, blah, blah, right? Every time I come here, I think: *What
am I going to tell Doc today?* But this time I didn't think about
it much. *Anyway,* I think she has tried to love me, and that's
the problem. It shouldn't be something you have to force, *you
know?* Loving your own daughter. And it's strange, because
she's always telling her friends how important it is to be a
good mother, how we—women, *I mean*—come into the world
for that purpose, how precious it is to care for someone, blah,
blah, blah. But she does it because she's the president of the
National Association for the Defense of the Family, and, as
you know, she organizes a looot of marches against abortion
and gay marriage and things like that. *Anyway,* ever since I was
reeeally young, I've been seeing posters and leaflets about that
stuff in my house. Sometimes Mom invites her friends from
the association over for dinner, and I don't like it, because they
come wearing fetus shirts and eat dinner and smile and make

jokes while I'm forced to look at the bloody fetuses on their shirts, and *of course*, it grosses me out. Do you think people in favor of abortion are pro-death?

Dr. Aguilar:

Fernanda: o.k. Once I asked my mom that, and she laughed at me, but I know that's what she thinks, that they're pro-death. That's why she calls herself pro-life, *you know?* I know a lot more about my mother than her friends from the association do. Things they couldn't even imagine.

Dr. Aguilar:

Fernanda: I don't know, like that she's a little, let's say hypocritical. *Just a little bit. I mean,* I find it weird that she defends babies that way when it's clear she doesn't want to be a mother, or at least not mine. For a looong time I played dumb, because facing something like that is hard, *you know?* But I think I always knew it: for her, I'm, I don't know, a chore. An obligation. *Something like that.* We can all tell when we've been rejected or when someone doesn't want to be with us, and I sense that with my mother aaall the time.

Dr. Aguilar:

Fernanda: Because she never wants to be alone with me, and when she can't avoid it, she looks at me in this reeeally ugly way, as if she were looking at a rat or something scary. She tries to hide it, *of course*, and anyone watching would say I'm making it up, that she doesn't look at me like that or that I'm exaggerating, but nobody knows her like I do. In front of her friends, she's reeeally affectionate toward me, but at home she's never like that. It's not that she treats me badly, it's just that I've spent more time with Charo than I have with her over the course of my life. And that's not normal, is it?

Dr. Aguilar:

Fernanda: Before, when the three of us would go out, *I mean* Dad, Mom, and me, she was aaalways somewhere else. *Like, I mean,*

I don't know. It felt like she'd get bored with us. Like she didn't want to be there. *Of course*, at times, she's been good to me, mostly when I was little, but she would always go back to acting . . . weird. Like she didn't want me getting too close to her. For example, if I insist that we do something together, she runs away. Literally: my mom runs away from me. She locks herself in her room or leaves the house every time I try to get close to her or talk to her. Sometimes I get to thinking about how horrible it is to be rejected by your own mother. *I mean*, if from the beginning not even *she* loves you, who possibly will in the future?

Dr. Aguilar:

Fernanda: *I know, I know.* I know there are people who love me, I'm not that much of a *drama queen*. Anne loves me, for example. A lot. My friends also love me. Dad, too, even though he barely has any time for me because he's always working. But Mom . . . Sometimes I think she doesn't like it when I'm with Dad. *I mean*, sometimes Dad has the day off and wants to take me fishing or something, and Mom says he'd better not. And she always finds an excuse, like that I have to do chores, or study, or go to church, I don't know. She always finds a way to keep the three of us apart.

Dr. Aguilar:

Fernanda: I'm not saying she hates me, just that she's afraid of me.

Dr. Aguilar:

Fernanda: Because she thinks I'm bad. That I killed Martín. Or that I could have killed him, *you know?* That it could have happened. And I feel guilty because maybe I'm not good, and I don't realize it. *Maybe*, I'm bad. I don't know. Or at least *not good enough*. Look at me, do I look bad to you?

Dr. Aguilar:

Fernanda: Well, looks can be deceiving, Doc.

Dr. Aguilar:

Fernanda: It's not just that she sees me as a possible murderer, she also thinks I'm a pervert . . . You know, the thing about me touching myself down there when I was little . . . *I mean*, the masturbation thing. We've never talked about that, she and I. It's not something she would talk about with anyone. It disgusts her. She did come and tell you about it, but she didn't talk about it with me. It's not the kind of thing we'd discuss at home. And she sees it as a sin, as something reeeally bad. *Maybe* she thinks I've been bad since I was born. Like Anne's mother, who's always criticizing her. At least mine doesn't criticize me. She doesn't say anything about me, *true*, but she doesn't criticize me. That's why Anne says she would rather her mother be afraid of her than be afraid of her mother. That woman really is scary.

Dr. Aguilar:

Fernanda: For a while, my mom and her mom were friends, from badminton club. They weren't good friends or anything like that. They just played together. And a few years ago, they got together and came to our school to complain about that girl getting pregnant. They demanded she be expelled because she made the school look bad, *you know?* Something like that.

Dr. Aguilar:

Fernanda: No, *I mean*, I do love my mom. I reeeally love her. And I guess there are times—hardly ever, but still—when she loves me. But if my mom were Annelise's mom, for example, I wouldn't love her. *I mean*, that woman is home all the time, but she's always ignoring Anne. And if she does pay attention to her, it's only to criticize her for things that don't even make sense. She tells her she's stupid, but Anne isn't stupid: she's reeeally smart. And sometimes she hits her. My mom doesn't hit me. If I compare them, I have the better mother, *I guess*.

Dr. Aguilar:

Fernanda: No, and I'll never tell her, because I can't talk about the things I think about with my mom. I can't get it out. *I mean*, it's a little sad, but she doesn't know anything about me. And sometimes I realize something else: I don't know anything about her either. And that, I don't know, scares me. Not her, *of course*, but how the people closest to you can be complete strangers. *Like*, I don't even know what she likes or if she has a favorite color. Or if there's anything in the world that she wants, besides keeping people from getting abortions and gays from marrying. What do you think Mom would do to me if I were a lesbian?

Dr. Aguilar:

Fernanda: *Maybe*, but Anne told me something once that really scares me because I think it's true: one day, we'll be like our mothers. And I don't want to be like that. I want to be the way I am now forever.

Dr. Aguilar:

Fernanda: If I were a lesbian, what do you think would happen?

X

"There's a crocodile! A crocodile at the edge of the mangrove!" Fiorella shouted several times, drenched in sweat and running inside the building, where her voice expanded into a bone alarm.

The first to appear were Analía, Ximena, and Natalia, but Fernanda and Annelise pushed their way through, their bodies reeking of onions and boiled vegetables. "I don't see anything." "Ouch!" "Get out of the way!" Fiorella's rubber shoes made a smacking sound on the stairs, like Ximena and Analía's hands when the dare was to slap each other without screaming. "There!" they exclaimed in unison, but they could only make out a saurian tail sinking into the water as if it were the oldest extremity on Earth. "It was enormous, and it was dragging its belly," Fiore described, gasping all the humidity out of the afternoon. "It had teeth like a saw and pasty scales." "It was like a squashed horse." "It was like if all the moss caught fire." As she was talking, Annelise gnawed her lips pink the way she did when the dare was to cut her belly and then have Fernanda lick it. "It had the eyes of a cat on the prowl." "Its tongue was so long it fell out of its mouth and flattened all the flowers." With the beginning of the rains and the rising tide, the building had become the stopover for big, colorful snakes, bats, crickets, and more frogs and lizards than ever. "You have to be careful with snakes," said Ximena, but Annelise liked reptiles. "I like reptiles," she said when the dare was for Fernanda to lie on the ground where a yellow-striped snake was slithering. Sometimes the rain formed little waterfalls on the stairs that Natalia rolled down when the dare was to fall dramatically from the second floor to the first. But they knew how to deal with the wild water and talk over the humming of insects. "Vampires!" Analía screamed, running from the clouds of mosquitoes that covered their legs in hot, red ridges. "Don't scratch: dig your nail in like this," Ximena recommended, making an *x* with her thumbnail over the welts wet with saliva. "My spit smells like pork." "My spit smells like licorice." The climate of lightning bolts and vermin nourished them during the afternoons when they told increasingly sensationalist horror stories. The appearance of the crocodile, however, was special, because it launched a new obsession for Annelise, who soon wanted to see it up close and with that, surpass any dare her friends had ever completed. "Did you know a crocodile's bite is more powerful than a lion's?" she mentioned to Fernanda-princess-of-the-tightrope-walker-exercises as they got into the pool at her house. "Did you know crocodiles are the biggest reptiles on Earth?" The possibility of seeing it again, or of it entering the building like the snakes, bats, and geckos, scared Fiorella. "That's what all this is about: overcoming fear," Anne told her as they walked along the edge of the third floor, the dare being simply to not die. "I think Anne is going a little too far," Ximena dared to say, and Fernanda heard her. "If you're going to be a *baby*, then get out of here," she shot back, her voice full of spurs, her eyes narrowed. Sometimes the dares were painful, like when they had to take a punch to the mouth or stomach without falling, but more often, they were just humiliating, like when Analía had to be Annelise's bitch for four hours straight and say *woof woof* and lick her knuckles and pee on the roots of a tree; or when Fiorella had to pretend she was laying a lizard egg only to fling it against the wall; or when Ximena was Fernanda's slave and had to kneel before her and kiss the tips of her shoes and let her step on her hair. "We shouldn't do things this dangerous," Natalia said when she saw Fernanda sitting on the windowsill with her feet dangling in the air, softly singing megustanlosavionesmegustastú, her skirt opening like a petal on the verge of drying out. "Don't become one of those people who don't know they like this stuff," Annelise said one afternoon when Analía got really scared because Fernanda had fainted during the strangling game. "It only makes sense if it's dangerous," she told them. "It's only fun if it's dangerous." Having to watch while Fernanda and Annelise played at strangling each other made Fiorella uncomfortable, but it didn't make her uncomfortable watching her sister roll down the stairs like Scarlett Johansson's double in a high-risk scene or watching Ximena slap Annelise. At home, they all sat up straight and went to church and ate with four utensils and two different kinds of glasses and used cloth napkins and never said bad words and smiled demurely and kept themselves dry and clean and prayed before going to bed and before eating and silently thought about truly frightening horror stories, because getting scared was exciting, up to a certain point, but never to the extreme like Annelise, who wanted to look the mangrove crocodile in the eye even after Fiorella had told her it had a tongue like a condor's corpse in the crags. "What do you think a crocodile's breath smells like?" Annelise asked Fernanda in math class. "Like crabs, monkeys, and turtles." "Like egrets, anemones, and snails." At school, the six of them behaved the way they had before the discovery of the building, even if they were alone and no one could see or hear them, because outside, everything was still the same, although among them nothing was, and the *croak croak* of the toads and frogs was already a symphony that entered their bodies each time they played at what they couldn't understand but what felt better than anything else. "Anne, don't do that!" Ximena screamed whenever she saw her walking along the brink of any precipice. "Nothing is going to happen to me. Today I'm possessed by God," Annelise would respond from the edge of the third floor, her arms open like the wings of a small plane. They never discussed the fact that the tightrope-walker exercises had made them an even more perfect group, rounded and impenetrable. "So you think if you face the crocodile, your drag-queen God will protect you?" Fiorella asked with her brows knit tightly together. "Maybe yes, maybe no," she said. "The White God doesn't care." Ximena, the spaciest of the girls, believed for several weeks that the drag-queen God and the White God were the same, but Fernanda set her straight: "The White God is new." "The White God is what we are when we're here," Annelise explained to the group on an afternoon she spent watching the shore. "Did you know crocodiles can't chew?" "Did you know crocodiles have more than seventy teeth?" The others didn't like when Fernanda and Annelise strangled each other or walked along the edges of the building, because those things seemed more serious than hitting or cutting each other or throwing themselves down the stairs. They didn't like the colorful snakes that entered the building either, but occasionally they pretended to hunt and domesticate them on the floors they slithered across. "It's too risky to get close to a crocodile," Fiorella remarked while Annelise waited for the saurian tail to emerge from the water. "Your eyes are going to get tired," she said later, watching the sun fall in a stripe across Annelise's forehead. "Your lips are going to burn." "Your eyelids are going to burn." Baby iguanas and mother iguanas also entered the building, whipping their tails when Ximena approached to step on them because she didn't like reptiles. "I don't like reptiles," she said the week she told a horror story about witchery and chameleons. They began to perfect the Wednesday stories with the sudden inclusion of the White God as a joint anxiety, as if the atmosphere of the unutterable in Annelise's head were producing in them a lunatic vertigo. "What happens when we see something white?" Annelise asked Fernanda without waiting for a response. "We know that it will be stained," she told her, smiling milkily. When they slept together, they intertwined their legs and brought their noses close, and, in the midst of the darkness, Annelise tenderly asked her to strangle her. "Did you know a crocodile can grow up to three thousand teeth?" "Did you know a crocodile's mouth hurts when it bites?" Then Fernanda embraced her neck with her soft-as-silk, soft-as-cotton hands and squeezed a little, and a little more, and then she let go and massaged with her smooth thumbs, her silky-smooth thumbs, the cartilage that surfaced like an Eve's apple under her fingers as Anne parted her lips. It didn't upset Fernanda to satisfy the desires of her *best-friend-4ever*-never-change-baby, but she also didn't feel what she saw settling into Annelise's face when she squirmed in bed and asked her to press harder. "You have the neck of a jellyfish," she told her, caressing the liquid geography of veins and arteries across her Snow-White skin, her Bette-Davis skin. Every now and then, small bruises remained, which the two of them photographed and uploaded to their private Instagram accounts. "This is green. This is purple. This is blue." 288 likes. 375 likes. 431 likes. Then they covered them with mom makeup, thanks to the foolproof steps in the YouTube tutorials that also taught them how to line their upper lids just like Lana Del Rey. "Did you know crocodiles mate underwater?" "Did you know crocodiles hold their babies inside their jaws?" Ximena, Analía, Fiorella, and Natalia were jealous of Fernanda and Annelise's friendship, but they also knew that all the girls in class were jealous of them for being part of such a perfect group, which is why they pretended not to be bothered when the two whispered things to each other or laughed while looking at each other's lips or caressed each other's earlobes during break. "How I wish you could hold me in your jaws," Annelise whispered to Fernanda one early Saturday morning in bed, and she confessed to her, just like that, what she really wanted her to do. "It'll be like everything else, just different," she told her. Her eyes shone like Christmas lights. "It came to me in a dream." "It came to me in the blink of an eye." Once, Fernanda dreamed that Annelise lay down on the ground on the first floor and that, leaning back on her elbows, she looked a giant crocodile in the eye as it advanced toward her from the other side of the room. Then Annelise opened her legs and threw her head back while the crocodile, like a son that returns to the puddle of his origin, penetrated her until it disappeared. "Why is the White God white?" Natalia asked right before telling her own horror story. "Because white is the perfect silence," Annelise responded with apparent solemnity. "And God is the horrible silence of everything." That afternoon Fernanda thought of her next story: a mother with postpartum depression and a baby making her nipples bleed. Spoiled milk. Bloody milk. "Love begins with a bite and letting yourself be bitten," Annelise said. In the end, the baby would eat the mother, because that's how love is. "My little gator," she would say to her tiny son. "My little smitten shark." "I've read that some mothers get turned on when they breastfeed their children," Analía said, disgusted, looking at her squirrel-colored, kiwi-colored nipples under her wrinkled school blouse. Fernanda and Annelise told stories about maternity and cannibalism that terrified Analía and Ximena and made it difficult for them to drink milk at breakfast. "Did you know Miss Clara dresses exactly like her dead mother?" Annelise said after she began taking extra language and literature classes on Friday afternoons. "I think Miss Clara is afraid of us." "I think Miss Clara wants us to stay far away from her." The crocodile did not appear on the shore again, but Annelise drew it in her notebooks and on the walls of the building. *How I wish you could hold me in your jaws,* Fernanda repeated in her mind before giving in to her *best-friend-4ever*-never-change-baby's proposal. "But if I do that to you, the others can't find out," she told Annelise even though she'd already said if she did it, the others couldn't find out. Fernanda believed that Miss Clara was easily scared because she barely blinked and folded her arms during break. "We've all bitten our mothers." Annelise thought it would be fun to scare her. "We've all fed off our mothers."

XI

Clara couldn't sleep that night. Nevertheless, she lay immobile on the old cot, determined not to make it creak with even the slightest blink. She wanted to hear the early morning of the forest: the song of lunar beings crawling under the gaze of a white eye. She believed the sound of what cannot be seen would calm her. She believed that if she didn't move, Fernanda would stop screaming. Those screams silenced the forest, but Clara didn't blink. The cot didn't creak. Outside, the animals hunted. *Animals never stop hunting,* she later thought, when the screams did stop. The noise of the night creatures was vast and distant like death's feet. It wasn't the first time she set herself the challenge of ceasing to exist so that everything else could exist. Her mind worked better in those conditions: when she didn't move a muscle. During her adolescence, the doctors told her that her physical exercises were really a catatonic state triggered by psychological factors. No one understood that it was a voluntary condition, a decision that required extreme discipline. The living body demanded action, and putting it on hold was the nearest thing to fighting against that life; in order to think, however, some things had to be very still, like a cadaver or sleeping volcano.

"Anxiety disorder," they had diagnosed when she turned sixteen. "Panic disorder," they later added to her sentence.

"Excuse me, Doctor, but what is that supposed to mean?" her mother had asked, and even though they explained it, she couldn't understand. A lot had changed since then. Now, for example, she could think without words. Her body incarnated a sacrificial logos: a language in which the verb could not stand up straight. It had been hard to accept, after so much time spent trying to express herself, that nothing she said resembled what went on in her head.

The symptomatology of her fear was mute but gasping. "Get those cockroaches out of your mind, Becerra. All right, just tell me, what is it that makes you so panicky?" her mother asked before her vertebrae turned against her and she understood. Panic is panic, Clara would have liked to explain: words are a finicky, miserly fiction, a trap that hides organic chaos behind a false dramaturgy of order. Perhaps that's why she liked correcting her students' texts, working with neat and normalized writing: because it was better to set your feet on the cement of verbal logic than lie naked in the ocean of your own mind.

But fear—she would have liked to tell her mother
before she died—was biological and had an
inhuman language.
Now Clara knew thought did not require words.
Now Clara knew there were things that could
only be thought without words.

Before the sun came up, she rose from the cot and went downstairs. Fernanda was sleeping on the table, her eyes bulging from her eyelashes like two quail eggs. She wanted to lick them, but the desire horrified her. In silence, with her pulse gnawing at her jaw, she expelled herself from the cabin, and the absolute darkness floated into her ears like a lullaby. Thinking with the body was a disconcerting sensation: assuming the marks, the folds, the history of the bones that unfurled the beasts in her throat. "Within every woman and every man, there's a new round of the mythic fight between the logic of the mind and the logic of the senses," she once told her students, but back then, she didn't yet understand the true extent of the material experience. To understand it, she had to see herself reduced to her flesh, like the tortured; those beings made of arteries, bones, saliva, blood . . . So filled with their own being, and nevertheless, so incomplete in everyone else's eyes. She, despite having known torture, did not feel her conscience was mutilated or dismembered, but rather that it was swollen in every one of her organs. That's how she walked among the trees, like a blind woman, overflowing with physical thought that neither could nor should be articulated and that had to do with the horror she experienced when she closed her eyes and saw braids and birthmarks. Images and not words. Sensations and not meanings. "Poetry is an attempt to create the experience of the unsayable," she'd told her students many times. The affirmation of all that is human in the haze, while on the other side, animals hunt.

"What's the only animal that's born from its daughter and gives birth to its mother?" asked her sphinx-of-the-mangroves-mother, staring into space and beating the ground with a stick to extinguish Clara's deep silence.

A forest is bigger from within than from without, she thought so as to avoid clinging to the maternal riddle.

She walked along, clawing at trunks and tripping over thick roots that scraped at her bare feet. For a moment she felt as if she were fleeing from what she had done and, repulsed by the idea of that weakness, let herself fall onto a rock that resembled a curled-up man. It was so cold that her teeth began to hurt, like tiny hearts beating in her gums. Her breathing was erratic, and a familiar crawling sensation began to spread from her open palm to her neck. She knew she could control the fear of death that swung just like a pendulum over her tongue when her anxiety symptoms intensified. She had experience thinking with her muscles, and, moreover, this time was different: this time she wouldn't have to worry about something as simple as dying. What really kept her from sleeping, what suffocated her and provoked daily dizzy spells, wasn't death but the possibility of once more being afraid of dying; that sensation of extreme anxiety, that feeling of each of her cells shooting off in a different direction—just like when the *M&M's* stuck a sock in her mouth so she wouldn't scream—was unbearable. She could never fully explain what she felt when the palpitations, the sweating, the tingling arms, the trembling started. She could never have told her mother, dying on a hospital bed, her spine turning into a boa constrictor, that being afraid of dying was worse than dying.

"A panic attack is like drowning in air," she tried to explain to her once, and perhaps because it seemed incomprehensible, it was the best description of her illness she had managed so far.

A panic attack is like burning up in water, falling upward, freezing in a fire, walking against yourself, your flesh solid and your bones liquid, she thought. No word, however, could describe the tachycardia that, in that instant, was transforming her chest into porous rock. Her skull was heavy, full of thorns and backpacks, but beyond her head loomed the volcano. *Volcanoes are also bigger from within than from without,* she told herself, watching the spectacle of the purple sky getting light while the lines of one of her favorite poets returned to her lips like water: "For beauty is nothing but the beginning of terror." Perhaps because what's beautiful precedes horror, she left her book about volcanoes unfinished: in order to finish there, on the other side of the mist that sometimes covers the view of a snowy peak, hunting alongside the hunters.

"We live in a caldera: there are almost a hundred volcanoes in this country, and more than twenty are active," her mother once told her. She had always been drawn to landscapes that insinuated their own destruction. "There is nothing more sublime than a mountain that burns," she said as she looked through her collection of photographs of Cotopaxi, Antisana, Tungurahua, Chimborazo, Pichincha, Sangay, and Reventador. "It seems impossible, Becerra, that hell lies beyond these glaciers." Sometimes, the beauty of the icy craters, combined with their potential to annihilate, provoked in Clara an immense urge to cry, but they also made her feel less alone, as if her illness were part of the magma boiling under the frozen sky of the cordillera.

The fear—she would have liked to tell her mother—was telluric: that's why, as the forest consumed the first rays of sunlight, Clara's shivering grew in intensity like an earthquake of the flesh.

The cabin and the forest, a few kilometers from the volcano, were the perfect backdrop against which to be brave for the first time. After all, walking toward life required the same strength as walking toward death: the same courage, the same broken nails. She had to be able to cleanse herself of the confusion of cold and heat that converged in the vertical river of her torso. She had to understand that a perpetual horror repeatedly distancing its victim from the order of the world could make anyone lose the will to speak. A horror like the one she was experiencing now, sweating trees of water down her back, was inexplicable and expanded within her body like a millenary explosion in the throat of God. She had wanted to convert her book of volcanoes into a poem about that feeling she knew so well; write some verses from her interior full of hair and pubescent voices and other people's verses, but not even she, in the deepest part of herself, knew why she had begun such a useless task. It was clear to her, though, why she had taken Fernanda to that elevated forest, suspended in the sky before a dormant volcano, and what she needed from her before everything was over. Because even though she was dragging the thing out, she knew that time had not stopped, that they could be found at any moment, and that wasn't part of her plan. Her plan was for the police not to find them too soon.

She had consciously crossed a mysterious border, on the other side of which she believed she would come face-to-face with her own limits. But beyond the squall, there was only the squall and a fresh bite awaiting her.

Sitting in the midst of the sunrise, her lungs folding up like shy bats at the bottom of her thorax, she again remembered the riddle: "What's the only animal that's born from its daughter and gives birth to its mother?" *Poetry, the universe, death, God.* "Would you have loved me if I had solved it?" she had asked Elena as she approached death. Her aunts and uncles told her, when she was ten, that she couldn't dress like her mother or desire her so absolutely. "Poetry gives birth to the poetry that engenders it," she attempted at twenty-four, but that wasn't the answer or the truth. "Death breastfeeds the death that births it." Shortly before, her grandparents had explained to her that an umbilical-cord love was pathological. "Mom, would you have hated me less if I'd told you that unique animal was us?" she whispered to her mother's inert body, covered by a sheet in her imagination. Everyone else's words were soft mandibles combing her during her early-morning insomnia, but there was a time when she'd searched within them for an untouched place to graze, a narrative construct that would make sense of her world drowning in nouns.

"What's the only animal that's born from its daughter and gives birth to its mother?" she had asked Annelise a month ago. "God," Annelise responded immediately. "Because my God is a hysterical wandering womb."

Clara believed in Annelise's concept of God: a presence like a dream in which the sun rose from the crater of a volcano, just as it was doing in that moment. A white mist became visible, and she saw a gray rabbit very close by, prowling around the coarse roots of a tree. She hadn't brought food, but now she was hungry. She had left the empty car a kilometer from the cabin: an old piece of junk that had belonged to her mother and had, against all odds, managed to carry them here, to her dead grandmother's old cabin. What would Elena say if she could see her in that moment. *Nothing,* she thought: she would pound on the floor with her improvised cane, like Tiresias's in Martha Graham's ballet, and cry like a mourner, or like Oedipus before he gouged out his eyes. "I knew you would make me regret giving birth to you," she'd say. "You're a sick little girl." She still had an acrid memory of the first thought that came into her head when she saw her mother die. She was twenty-five years old, and as she observed the scaly skin of her mother's face, already decomposing, already dying, she thought about her car. *Now it will be mine,* she thought. *I'll reupholster it, I'll service it, I'll paint it a color I like, a flashy pink, I'll renew the registration, I'll pay the insurance . . . Now that the car is going to be mine,* she concluded, *life will be mine. I'll travel, I'll move, I'll change.* But after the funeral came the debts, her studies, her work. And the car wasn't reupholstered, and it wasn't painted a flashy pink, but it was serviced, the registration was renewed, the insurance was paid. Clara did what she had to do, but now she was doing what she wanted. And what she wanted was to teach something important to Fernanda, to teach her a real lesson. To be a good teacher and give her not the floor but the wound: the greater knowledge that can arise only in the flesh.

A vegetal silence of meanings.

A new state of consciousness.

Clara knew she had tied up her mother's neck with her umbilical love.

Now she tied up Fernanda, because a good teacher is a mother, and a student is a daughter.

"Sometimes I like to imagine that the universe is God's corpse decomposing," Annelise told her one afternoon when she had extra classes. "Imagine, Miss Clara, if we were just that: God's enormous floating carrion."

She had thought it would all be over before she got hungry, but she was wrong. She needed more time to be a good teacher. Even though she was cold and the shivering was unceasing, she stayed in place with her eyes on the rabbit that nonchalantly approached, rummaging among the dry leaves and earth, as if Clara were part of the landscape and not a potential predator. *But the landscape is always a potential predator,* she thought as she listened to the sound of her breath, increasingly like a washing machine. In her life, the problem had been that absurd and exhausting struggle, maintained for years, against what she was and what she assumed she should not be. *Women do not make themselves,* she thought. *Women are made by their daughters and their mothers. To fight against your skeleton is to fight a war impossible to win.* Nature could only be transformed to a certain extent, and its center was untamable, but in that moment, Clara accepted the untamable in herself, because when she didn't try to control the symptoms of her fear—as in that moment, when the tachycardia began to cede and her heart swam and slackened—the panic attacks weren't as terrible. Her corporeal thoughts were small flowers growing on the cactus of her mind: the most delicate, the softest, and most alive on Earth, just like the rabbit brushing against her toes and breathing in the smell of her blood.

"Fernanda and I aren't friends anymore," Annelise told her after she pulled Fernanda's hair and Fernanda split her upper lip with a punch. "I hate her, and I think I'm gonna throw up."

She had kidnapped one of her students to educate her on the only thing that mattered, but she had no idea how to do it. Part of the job was in motion, but with no path or promise. And while the symptoms diminished to a distressing rhythm, she submitted herself to the horror of her cells dismantling her extremities, to the vertigo of her pelvis.

"Do you want me to tell you what my best friend did to me?" Annelise asked her.

The body was the only reality for a mind that fed on deserts, but hers couldn't offer anything more than that world of unbearable sensations and the vengefulness that concealed her ultimate desire.

"If I tell you, do you promise you won't get mad?"

XII

A: What's the only animal that's born from its daughter and gives birth to its mother?

F: What?

A: It's a riddle.

F: Where did you hear it?

A: I heard it from Miss Clara-fied-butter.

F: Miss Clara-clear-as-water, Miss Clara-crystal-clear.

A: I listened and said God. But that wasn't the right answer.

F: *It's so creepy.*

A: Miss Clara says there is a right answer.

F: *It's so fucking creepy.*

XIII

"Shhh!" Annelise motioned, bringing one finger to her painted lips when Ximena tripped over Fernanda's father's bearskin rug. "She'll hear us." "She'll catch us." All the lights were off, and they were tiptoeing, barefoot, their high heels in hand, through a room full of traps in the form of furniture, vases, and expensive sculptures. "Ay, I'm dying!" Analía let out. "Shhh!" Fiorella and Natalia motioned in unison. It was one in the morning, and Charo was sleeping. The chauffeur was on vacation. Fernanda's parents were traveling. *Ticktock* went the old pendulum clock that stood against the wall with the piano no one knew how to play. "We can have the sleepover at my house," Fernanda had suggested last weekend. "No one will be keeping an eye on us. No one will notice." The college guy with green eyes and a tattoo on his wrist was waiting for them in his black-Batman-convertible next to the park in the center of the gated community. They were running ten minutes late because Fiorella and Natalia had called their mother to tell her good-night. "Have fun with your friends, girls, and don't go to bed too late." "It's Friday, Mom." "We're painting our nails." "We're gonna play PlayStation." "We're gonna do our hair like Lady Gaga." "We're gonna do Amy Winehouse makeup." "We're gonna model like Kate Moss." "We're gonna sing like Lorde." None of their parents knew that for years they'd been using sleepovers as an excuse to drink Ximena's mother's wine, touch Annelise's father's revolver collection, smoke Charo's cigarettes, and watch hentai on XVideos and PornTube. "Why does he cum on her face?" "Nasty!" "That's not what my vagina looks like." "So many veins!" "That's a nipple?" Sometimes the sleepovers were also an excuse to escape to parties with college boys who had driver's licenses and facial features like those of Hollywood actors, but they never told the boys anything about the building or what they did there. "Do you think our tightrope-walker exercises are like the mortifications Mister Alan talks about?" Analía asked when her dare was to withstand Fiorella stepping on her hands. "Are you crazy?" Annelise responded. "Unless they're mortifications for the White God, in which case, yes." "Then this is what we're doing for the rapture." The night of the sleepover, they dressed up the way they thought older girls did, the ones who went to parties and drank and danced and did everything Mister Alan said was typical of women who were then raped or killed on the street. "How do you put this on?" They covered their bruises with makeup. "Oh, like that." They put perfume on their collarbones. Ximena messed up her eyeliner and stained her face black. She was the least pretty of the group: the least funny, the least intelligent, the one who stuffed her bra with wads of toilet paper and wore her hair like Annelise and Fernanda did even though it didn't look good on her. "Do I look o.k.?" she had asked earlier, in the bedroom. "Oh yeah. You look gorgeous," the twins told her. "You look like you're nineteen." "I think you could pull off twenty." As they were sneaking out, Analía, Fiorella, and Natalia tried to contain their laughter at the glittery bow clipped above Ximena's bangs. There were some ridiculous things that only ceased to be so on certain skulls, they thought. Fernanda, for example, wore a sequined ribbon on hers, but she was elegant, and even short boyish hair, à la Emma Watson or Kristen Stewart, flattered her diamond-shaped face, her flamingo-like neck. "Put some red lipstick on," she had told Annelise an hour before. "Do you like it?" "I love it." Fernanda liked Annelise's lips, Annelise's freckles, Annelise's black hair. "Wow, that dress looks amazing on you." They all knew that someone like Anne required nothing more than that shade of lipstick. "Shhh!" "Chucha, shut up!" At the building, Annelise was always first to complete the truly dangerous dares. "Fer, how do you open the door?" The first to kill a snake. "It's open." The first to walk along the edges of the third floor. "We did it!" The first to swim in the mangrove, even knowing a crocodile was there. "Hurry up, or we'll never get to the park."

Fernanda was also the first, but only sometimes. "What's his name again?" Natalia, the flirtatious twin, asked. "Hugo," Fiorella, the shy twin, answered. Ximena couldn't walk in heels and wobbled as she tried to keep up with the group on the silent street of the gated community with a pool, a sports club, a mall, a church, and twenty-four-hour armed security. "They're shoes, not stilts," Analía told her, laughing and taking a video with her phone. Analía was the funniest one in the group, and she often made fun of Ximena, because she thought that if she did, no one would make jokes about her being slightly overweight. "Wear my shirt, it's prettier," Fernanda had told her half an hour earlier, not realizing that Analía wore an M and she wore an XS. "No thanks, I like this one," she said, pulling hers out of her Sailor Moon suitcase. At school, they said that Analía was otaku, but her friends knew that she was only a fan of four anime and had never read a manga. "Stop recording me," Ximena screamed. "Shhh!" "But we're not even inside anymore!" "Oh, come on! What, you think people here don't sleep?" "It's Friday!" The college guy named Hugo was waiting for them outside the black-Batman-convertible, smoking. "Ufff, so handsome," Ximena blurted before biting her bottom lip. "Don't even think about it," Natalia said, tossing her hair. The Barcos sisters were indistinguishable except for a birthmark on Fiorella's shoulder. They started training in classical ballet at age six, but at the building, they told horror stories about strange objects and sick bodies hidden in the corners of rental homes. "Hey, girls, how's it going?" he said, crushing what was left of his cigarette into the sidewalk. "*Sorry* we're late, it's just that my friends are idiots," Annelise said, looking at Fiorella and Natalia, who both made a face. "*Nice!*" They got in the car, praising the color of the leather seats. "Thank you, thank you." Fernanda didn't like having to sit in the back, far from Annelise. "Should I put some music on for you?" It was their first time going to a college party with the college guy with green eyes and a tattoo on his wrist, named Hugo. "*Obviously!*" They usually went with boys who were studying law at the Universidad Espíritu Santo, but Hugo was studying medicine at the Universidad Católica and was one of Annelise's most recent Instagram followers. "Are you sure he isn't a psychopath?" Fernanda had asked her two days earlier. "Chill out, he's the cousin of one of my brother's best friends," she answered. "I know him. I know he isn't crazy." At the first stoplight outside the gated community, a man with an amputated arm approached, asking for coins, and Hugo chose to smash the button that controlled the canvas top. "Even better: this way, our hair won't get messed up," Fiorella said, running her fingers through her blond locks. Her sister had her eyes fixed to the rearview mirror, and when they met the gaze of the college guy with green eyes, a tattoo on his wrist, and a cleft chin, she smiled. "Did anyone bring a comb?" Neither Fiorella nor Natalia had ever had a boyfriend. "No one?" Nor had they kissed a boy, though they came close at the last party. "If you hadn't said that to him, he definitely would have kissed me!" Natalia had screamed at her sister afterward. "He didn't like you, he liked us both!" Fiorella corrected her. "He wanted to kiss us because we're twins! He wanted to kiss us because we're identical!" No teacher could tell them apart, but Fiorella felt uglier than Natalia, even though the only difference was a birthmark. "No one?" That's why the college parties undermined her self-esteem, unlike the afternoons at the building, when it was her turn to dance barefoot where colorful serpents gathered. "Ouch!" Natalia blurted out when Fiorella elbowed her in the ribs so she'd stop winking at the rearview mirror. "Do you like reggaeton? Hip-hop?" Fernanda didn't find it amusing that Annelise was up front alone, nor that Hugo—the college guy with green eyes, a tattoo on his wrist, a cleft chin, and wavy hair—stared so much at her lips. The last time they went to a party, a redhead with dreads kissed Annelise. "Well? How was it? What did it feel like?" they asked her back at home. "Gross," she said. "He had bad breath," she said. At the building, when the two of them walked along the edges of the third floor with their arms open, they never looked down. "It feels incredible, right?" Annelise said. "To feel like you could die and then not die." They were the only ones who did acrobatics like that because the others were afraid of falling. "Cowards," Fernanda would say, and then she'd look at the sky and carefully put one foot in front of the other. "Will there be a lot of people?" she asked the college guy with the black jacket, named Hugo. "A lot, yeah." Their perfumes mingled. "He's just like the guy from *Twilight*," Ximena whispered to Analía, and the twins heard her. "Back here, they're saying you look like Robert Pattinson." "Do you think you look like Robert Pattinson?" The red brought out Annelise's freckles, which Fernanda was monitoring from the right side-view mirror. "I get that a lot." Ximena and Analía were fans of the *Twilight* saga, even though they had only watched the movies because reading the books sounded totally boring to them. "*Harry Potter* is a hundred times better," opined Fernanda. "Avada Kedavra," Annelise would say, pointing her pencil in Mister Alan's direction as if it were a wand. "What a shitty job," said Analía when two security guards with rifles took down their names and the license plate number of the black-Batman-convertible before allowing them inside another gated community with a pool, a sports club, a mall, a church, and twenty-four-hour armed security. "Will there be beer?" Ximena asked, even though she didn't like beer. The college guy with green eyes, a tattoo on his wrist, a cleft chin, wavy hair, a black jacket, and blue Chuck Taylors laughed. "Of course," he said as he opened the car door for Annelise. "Idiot," murmured Natalia, cringing. Fernanda ignored the hand Hugo extended and stepped down without his help, straightening the skirt that had inched up her thighs. "You look like the girl from *Stranger Things*," he told her, gesturing to her short hair and the sequined ribbon. "Oh? Who's that?" Ximena asked. "Millie Bobby Brown," Analía explained, exasperated. "Google her." The red of Annelise's lips smiled. "Yeah, you really do look like her." At the building, they had all made cuts below their left butt cheeks in acceptance of the White God in Annelise's stories. "This is your initiation, Fiorella Barcos Gilbert," Annelise said aloud before cutting her skin. "Because in the white age you are, and white are your thoughts." "Because you saw the white animal emerging from the water, because you open yourself to the

mother-God-of-the-wandering-womb." Not even Fernanda fully
understood what they were being initiated into with those scars,
but the game was interesting because it was an enigma, and
because it made them feel that they belonged to something special.
"Today's story is like no other: I'm going to tell you about the first
and most abhorrent apparition of the White God, witnessed by a
young girl in her white age," Annelise recounted one Wednesday
afternoon while the others, scared from the start, sat in a perfect
circle and listened. "No one ever found out what happened to her,
and her name remained unutterable until two terrible murders
shook two tiny towns in Eastern Europe." When they listened to
the stories about Annelise's White God, they all got scared and
went home with the sensation that someone or something was
stalking them, that a divine and monstrous power might reveal
itself to them at night, in the early hours, and that none of them
would be able to close their eyes to protect themselves. "Those stories aren't true, are they?" Ximena once asked. "Of course they're
true," Annelise said, standing next to one of the building's windows. "You aren't questioning the White God inside their temple,
are you?" Ximena didn't think it was safe to question a god from
within their territory. "Let's go in," Hugo said, pulling a new cigarette from his jacket. "All the earthquakes are Them," Annelise
claimed when the earth shook and the building rocked like the sea.
Magnitude 4.2. Magnitude 6.5. "Is my hair messed up?" Fiorella
asked, but her sister ignored her. The party was in a big house from
which emerged colored lights, shouting, and reggaeton. "*Cool*,"
Ximena said, starting to dance too early. The volume was so high
that Fernanda felt it resounding unpleasantly in her organs. "In
horror movies, things always start to go bad at a party," she whispered into Annelise's ear, and Annelise sweetly took her hand. "I
guess we'll find out." People were dancing in the backyard, but
inside they were drinking and exchanging shrieks, smoke, and beer
cans. "You can barely see in here," Analía said, waving away the
smoke. "You just have to get used to it," said Fiorella. "Just wait,
our hair's gonna smell like weed." "Just wait, they're gonna try to

get us drunk." Ximena scrunched up her nose: "I'm not trying any of that stuff, it tastes bad." But at the building, she had been the first to lick a drop of Annelise's menstrual blood. "What's it taste like?" Analía asked her then. "It tastes like a rusty snail. It tastes like algae and liver." Hugo led them to a round table where three friends from his program were waiting. "Gabriel, José, and Gustavo," he introduced them. Natalia was annoyed that they looked at Annelise first, so she showed off her cleavage by throwing her shoulders back. "How old are you all?" asked the one named José, whose nose was too small. "How old are you?" Anne shot back. "Older than all of you," and he laughed as if he were whinnying. "Well, we're younger," she said, thinking that there were horses less horselike than José. Fernanda sat down on Annelise's left. "Are you from Delta?" Hugo, on her right. "That's a good school, my cousin went there." They offered them beer. They offered them peanuts. "I hope none of you have boyfriends." Analía didn't understand how they could talk with all the noise, although Mister Alan said that at parties, no one wants to talk. "Girls like you should beware of parties," he told them. "Girls like you need to learn to pace yourselves." At the building, they explored their bodies in silence and listened to the wind, which sounded just like the cry of a woman. "How awful!" Fiorella would say. "It sounds like La Llorona." La Llorona was one of Annelise's favorite legends. "Once, many centuries ago, a woman went mad and drowned her baby in a mangrove full of crocodiles, but afterward she regretted it, and she was able to pull the almost-intact cadaver from the green water. It was only missing one thing: its pinky," she intoned in the white room, which is where they could most strongly hear the wind wail. "Ever since then, La Llorona has been searching for her son's lost pinky among other people's fingers. She rips them off with her teeth to try them out on the tiny cadaver. On the miniature cadaver." Fiorella and Natalia gripped each other. "But finding that they don't fit, she feeds them to the turkey buzzards." It surprised Fiorella that a mother could be so scary. "Guard your pinkies if you hear La Llorona's interminable wail!" Annelise would say, her voice

deep, as if from beyond the grave. "Close the doors and windows!"
"Close your eyes and protect yourselves from her jaws!" José ran his
tongue over his teeth. "Do you wanna dance?" Out in the countryside, people believed that La Llorona stole children and drowned
them to try and get the crocodiles to return her baby's pinky. "A
mother that drowns her son must be a man!" Ximena said, covering her ears. *But a mother could take a life as furiously as she'd made
it,* thought Annelise. "La Llorona doesn't take babies, Nandita,
dear," Charo told Fernanda one night. "Living people do. The living are worse than the dead." Fiorella, disinterested, looked out at
the yard. "We don't wanna dance yet," she said, and Natalia stuck
out her tongue. Although Charo was from the countryside, she did
not believe in La Llorona, nor in the Ecuadorian Dama Tapada, nor
in Tin-Tín. "Sometimes it's just the mamas themselves, they kill
their babies and throw them in the river," she said. "Why are you
speaking for everyone?" Annelise was sure that the crocodile they
had seen from the building was white and that in its belly was La
Llorona's baby's pinky. "A mother would never kill her children,"
Natalia said after hearing one of Fernanda's stories about mothers
and daughters who lose their minds. *"For real?* What world are you
living in?" Fernanda responded. "Mothers kill their kids aaall the
time." Fernanda and Annelise read creepypastas for inspiration
when it came time to create their own horror stories. "And kids
also kill their mothers." Their favorites, aside from the classic "Jeff
the Killer," "1999," "Ben Drowned," "Sonic.exe," and "Slender
Man," were the ones featuring mothers and daughters in strange
situations. "The Mr. Dupin one is awesome!" Annelise said after
sending the creepypasta.org link to their WhatsApp group. "It
won't scare me if I read it," Analía wrote. *Tap.* Send. *Xime is typing.*
"Lazy shit." Gustavo, the college guy with muscular arms, plunged
his eyes into Natalia's cleavage while Fiorella pretended not to
notice. "Wanna play Never Have I Ever?" The Mr. Dupin story
was called "Mother's Love," and it was about a daughter who woke
up to the sound of her cat lapping up water in the hallway. "Of
course, then she realizes the cat is with her, sleeping in her bed, so

she gets up, goes over to the hallway, turns on the light, and . . . guess what she sees," Annelise was talking to Analía, because she was the only one who hadn't read the story. "Her mother?" she asked in a soft, brittle voice. "Yes, her mother!" Anne screamed, making her tremble. "On all fours, drinking like a beast from the cat's bowl." Ximena sighed, resting her elbows on the table, sad because the college boys had barely noticed her makeup or how good her jeans looked on her hips. "Sure, let's play," she said. Analía was sad for the same reason, but she didn't want to show it, and she was annoyed that Ximena was being so obvious. "Then what happened?" she had asked, intrigued by the Mr. Dupin creepypasta. "The daughter looked at her mother, and the mother looked at her daughter," Annelise went on. "She bared her teeth and stuck out her exceptionally long tongue before running at her like an animal, but the daughter was quicker and shut the bedroom door, which the mother clawed at and pounded on, bellowing." At the college parties, Annelise never told horror stories. "And?" Analía insisted. "Then what happened?" The boy with blue hair, named Gabriel pulled a bottle of tequila from under the table. "If after that, you heard the voice of your mother, the one who takes care of you, who loves you more than anyone else, and she asked you, concerned, if you were all right, asked you to open the door, what would you do?" Ximena, Analía, and Fiorella looked at Annelise as if asking for her permission to play with a kind of alcohol whose proof exceeded 30 percent. "You aren't gonna chicken out, are you?" Fernanda smiled, irritated by the question. "Us?" She took her glass and slid it toward Gabriel. "That's how I like it!" At the building, they were very brave: the girls who leapt over their fears. "You're really pretty," Hugo told Annelise, running his finger over her shoulder as she stiffened. "Cradle-robber!" some sweaty college girls in skimpy clothes yelled from the backyard. "I can't help it if I like 'em tight," said Gustavo, smiling at Natalia and Fiorella. Fernanda really liked the creepypastas about twins: her favorite was the one that described the ritual of the mirror, candle, and armoire. "We all have a double," she told her friends once, during break. "To find yours, you just have to shut yourself up in an armoire with a mirror and a candle." Ever since they discovered how special the white room was, they didn't tell the horror stories anywhere else. "Inside, you have to knock on the mirror twice and look at yourself without breathing, and that's when it appears." The college guy with the tiny nose and the birthmark on his forehead, named José poured a little tequila in her glass. "Never have I ever fucked in the shower," he said, but only Hugo drank. "I knew it, jueputa!" "You crazy mothafucka!" *It's no big deal*, thought Ximena, that she had marks from when her dare was to let Annelise, Fernanda, Analía, Fiorella, and Natalia write their names on her back with the sharpened tip of a pencil. "My turn," said the college guy with blue hair and thin lips, named Gabriel. "The ritual works, and that's why you have to be really careful, because our doubles take the true shape of our souls. If you're a bad person, what you see will be evil." Ximena gulped. "What if I'm bad but I don't know it?" Annelise spoke in her catacomb voice: "Then you better not try it." Gabriel raised his glass: "Never have I ever kissed a man." *What a stupid game*, Natalia thought, watching Annelise and Fernanda scrunch up their faces as they drank. "It tastes like acetone." "It tastes like menthol." Hugo and his friends fist-bumped. "I told you, locooo!" And he looked at them: "How many times?" "With boys your age or ours?" Analía squinted. She could handle the creepypastas, but Annelise's stories gave her nightmares. "You girls haven't ever kissed anyone?" the college guy with the muscles named Gustavo asked the twins. "If you want, I'll teach you." The music made the glasses shake, and in the backyard, someone began to spray people with a hose. "Bacán! Tits are gonna be out soon, boys." One of Annelise's favorite creepypastas was the one about a mother who cooked tender pieces of her breasts for her child. "Legend says it all starts with reading an unpublished poem by an unknown author that circulates on the internet." "They say every mother who reads it ends up doing the same thing: amputating her breasts and feeding them to her children." Analía took a boomerang of the party and uploaded it to her Instagram story. "I wanna do one too!" Ximena said, and she also took a selfie. José stroked his chin. "If you want, we can get up and take the pictures for you." Ximena made a duck face. "If you want, we can take a picture of all of us." There was lots of traffic on the stairs and a line for the bathroom. "Ha ha, very funny," Fiorella said, and her sister touched her tongue to her nose. The creepypasta forums were riddled with photoshopped pictures, but Annelise only liked the ones that looked real. "Never have I ever taken naked pictures of myself," Gustavo said, picking the game back up. Fernanda hated that the older boys thought they were smarter than them. "Things are heating up!" Gabriel blurted, excited by the possibility of a confession. *Don't do it,* Fernanda pleaded in her head. *Don't do it. Don't do it.* But Annelise took a big gulp, and the boys opened their eyes wide like hunting owls. "Wooo!" The floor was littered with alcohol, plastic cups, and candy wrappers. "Now it's a party, boys!" Fernanda wanted to punch the college guy with green eyes, a tattoo on his wrist, a cleft chin, wavy hair, a black jacket, and blue Chuck Taylors, named Hugo when he looked at her best friend's legs. "You really have *nudes?*" Fiorella asked, shocked, even though at the building she had taken off her underwear and launched them into the mangrove on a dare. "Did you take them for a *crush?*" "Or did you do it *just for fun?*" Anne didn't even blink: "I did it for me, because I like looking at myself." Next to her, Hugo's mouth hung open, and Fernanda knew that he and all his friends were picturing Annelise naked. "This is boring," she suddenly said, letting go of Anne's hand. "Where are you going?" Anne asked, but Fernanda didn't answer. Something strange and hot squeezed her throat, and her feet carried her to the yard, where almost everyone was dancing, soaking wet, and you could see the girls' nipples. *Now she'll come,* she thought, convinced. *Now she'll come for me.* She had stopped having fun at the college parties a while ago. *Douchebags. Idiots. Assholes.* A while ago, she had figured out what they wanted, those boys who had never done anything like strangling or being strangled or lying down on a floor full of snakes. "What did it feel like?" Annelise asked her after the last party, when a college guy who looked like Johnny Depp from *A Nightmare on Elm Street* touched her under her panties. "*Weird*," she answered. "It hurt, and I liked it." Very handsome boys took her breath away, and sometimes, if they kissed her well, her underwear got wet. "I want to kiss!" Natalia yelled into the room of desires. "I want to kiss! I want to kiss! I want to kiss!" Analía had given her the solution: "Kiss me." But Natalia looked at her with disgust. "I'm not a lesbian! That's a sin! I like men!" Fernanda was happy to see Annelise coming out to the yard, dodging the dancers and walking in her direction. "It was a joke, dummy. I also like men." In the building, Fernanda had painted the only room without windows white, not knowing that it would become the center of the group's ceremonies. "Why'd you leave?" Not knowing that one afternoon, she would hear a scream and run up the stairs, terrified, to see Annelise half-naked, emerging from the room, trembling, bathed in sweat, looking shaken. "I hate them," Fernanda explained. "I can't stand them." "I don't like them." That afternoon, she said she had seen something in the whiteness of the wall. Something that was moving and that she then felt on her skin, like a live rat, and that's why she had to take off her uniform. "I get it," Annelise said, her lipstick a little smeared and her freckles like cocoa powder. "Should we teach them a lesson?" And then, the White God. And the fear the room inspired at all hours. "Should we take them down a notch?" Fernanda loved that Annelise always knew how to lift her spirits. "Let's," she said, and hand in hand again, they walked back. When they were eleven, they watched *The Exorcist* on an iPad, hidden under the sheets with the red ponies, together in the darkness with dozens of stuffed animals and collectible dolls watching over them, and they were so scared that they held each other all night. "It must be awful to have to take care of a daughter possessed by the devil!" Two years later, Annelise wrote an essay about the movie for the creative writing teacher. "I would lock her up." And the teacher said that Annelise had an "exceptional talent" for telling stories. "I would kill her." Fernanda got good grades on her papers for language and literature, but only Annelise was forced to participate in interschool fiction and poetry contests, even though she never won. "I do a bad job on purpose," she said proudly. "I lose so they'll leave me alone." At school, the teachers thought Fernanda lacked special talents, but at the building, she was the only one who had dared to shoot Annelise's father's revolver into the walls. "Seriously, if you do that again, I'm out," Fiorella told her. "It was so loud." "It sounded like death." The college guy with green eyes, a tattoo on his wrist, a cleft chin, wavy hair, a black jacket, and blue Chuck Taylors, named Hugo applauded when they returned. "I missed you, girls!" His wavy hair was identical to what they drew on Jeff the Killer fan art on creepypasta.org. "Finally," said Ximena, looking sulky because Gustavo, Gabriel, and José had sat back down next to Fiorella and Natalia. In Annelise's stories, the White God only revealed Themself to girls their age, and the vision was so disturbing that it transformed them forever. "Are we going to keep playing?" Analía asked as she stopped taking selfies. "Yeah, but we're going to play something else." And Fernanda perched on the table. "Do you wanna do something really fun?" Hugo and the others looked at them with curiosity and lust. "This house has a rooftop terrace, right?" The stairway that led there was near the garage. It was metallic, and there was vomit on the first step. "Gross, gross, gross, gross, gross!" Analía repeated when it was her turn to navigate the yellow puddle containing tiny pieces of carrot. Fiorella knew that Natalia wasn't attracted to Gustavo but that she wanted him to like her because she loved to feel like the center of attention. *Tac, tac, tac, tac,* went their heels on the trembling stairs. "Xime, would it kill you to smile," Analía pleaded, even though deep down she wanted to hit her for making her sadness so evident. *Ay, pay attention to me!* Analía thought. *Ay, nobody wants me!* "Do you think someday a boy will like one of us?" Ximena quietly asked her. "Wouldn't you like to be more like the twins, or Fernanda, or Annelise?" Analía hated that Ximena grouped the two of them together. *I'm not like you,* she thought about saying. *I just need to lose a little weight.* On the rooftop terrace, there was a couple making out and groping each other under their clothes, but Fernanda chased them away by shouting: "Get a room!" Grotesque laughter. Analía recorded them running away and posted the video to her Instagram story. 54 views. 123 views. 234 views. "All right, we're here," Hugo said, looking even more like Robert Pattinson in the moonlight. "So, now what?" Fernanda and Annelise exchanged a glance. They had practiced it so many times at the building that doing it there felt like a joke. "Now we're really going to play." They took a deep breath. "Here I go." Fernanda ran toward the edge of the terrace and hopped up on the wall that protected people from falling. "Careful!" The college boys held their breath. "Are you crazy? Get down!" Hugo yelled. "She's going to kill herself, locooo!" Gabriel yelled, pallid. "Someone grab her!" Before they could stop her, Annelise did the same thing, jumping onto the opposite wall and teetering but achieving stability by opening her arms like a little toy airplane. Gustavo closed his eyes. "Fucking hell!" Fiorella, Natalia, Analía, and Ximena excitedly applauded their friends' feat. It wasn't every day that they could show off the abilities of their group, such a perfect and interesting group that it was. "We're going to play a game where whoever falls loses," said Fernanda, walking like a cat along the wall. "If you don't fall, you can ask any one of us for anything," Annelise said, moving quicker than Fernanda. "What?" "Get down, chucha!" When they got to the corner, both wobbled, and Hugo clasped his head. "They haven't even taken off their heels!" But they managed to recover from that setback. "We do this aaall the time," Fernanda said pedantically. "Let's see who's the bravest." Annelise hopped down, and the boys let out their breath. "Verga!" Fernanda copied her, letting out a groan when she landed wrong because of her heels. "That's dangerous!" said the college guy with blue hair, thin lips, and bushy eyebrows, named Gabriel. "That's why doing it is so awesome," Fernanda said. "No one wants to try?" They crossed their arms. They put their hands in their pockets. "It's not that hard," Annelise said. "Even two girls in heels can do it." Hugo looked at his friends and laughed. No boy likes it when a girl suggests she can do something better than he can. "All right." His laugh was filthy. "But if we play your game, we can ask for anything?" Fernanda nodded. There were no limits on the content of the dares at the building. "Anything." And she fluttered her eyelashes. "As long as you don't fall." The college boys studying medicine at the Universidad Católica circled up and discussed for a few seconds. "I didn't think they'd have the balls," Natalia said, imitating Gustavo's way of speaking. Fiorella looked at her with horror. "Don't be crass!" The creepypastas that scared them the most were the ones in which something macabre was unleashed after a phrase, prayer, or spell was uttered in front of a mirror. The college guy named José with the tiny nose and the birthmark on his forehead sat on the wall and, little by little, stood up. "I bet even your pancreas is shaking, cocksucker!" shouted Gabriel, the one with blue hair. "Can we ask them to take off their clothes?" José took unsteady steps and stayed crouched down like a goblin. "Yes," Annelise said, smiling. "You can ask one of us to take off our shirt, for example." Analía didn't like the idea of having to take off her shirt, because she wore an M and not an XS. "And then it'll be our turn." Neither Fiorella nor Natalia nor Ximena nor Analía had walked along the edge of the third floor of the building. "Are we going to have to get up there?" Ximena quietly asked Annelise. "Shhh! Of course not." Of the group, only Annelise and Fernanda took risks; that's why they were the best and made all the important decisions. "Can we ask for a kiss?" On the wall, José was sweating and looked like he was about to piss himself. "You can, if you don't fall." At the building, Natalia worried her friends would slip and crash to the ground. "Then I know what I'm asking for." But in that moment, she was thrilled to see that the college guy with the tiny nose and the birthmark on his forehead was so afraid of falling. "I did it, locooos! I did it!" shouted José, pounding his chest like a gorilla after returning to the ground. *He looks like a boy, not a man*, Natalia thought, and she wanted Gustavo to get on the wall so she could see how much of a boy or a man he was. "Did you see that?" She preferred the short films based on creepypastas and circulated on YouTube, like "The Smiling Man," the story of a boy who had the misfortune of meeting a smiling man in the middle of an empty street. "Reading it scared me more," Annelise said, but it had disturbed Natalia to see that man embodied in an actor with a demented smile, walking the same way José had on the wall. "I'm asking for a kiss, guapa," he said to Fernanda, pointing at her with his index finger. "Kiiiss, kiiiss, kiiiss!" the rest chanted, even though Annelise got very serious. In reality, neither Natalia nor Fiorella nor Analía nor Ximena preferred horror to romantic comedies, or dramas, or fan fiction about Selena Gomez and Justin Bieber. "*Fine*," Fernanda said, and she walked toward José without concealing her boredom. But those were hobbies that had nothing to do with the building or with what Fernanda and Annelise got up to on their own. "Go on, dude, go on!" Gabriel shouted. "Wooo!" Ximena was sure that the college guy with the tiny nose and the birthmark on his forehead, named José wasn't a good kisser, because his tongue moved as if he had epilepsy. "Poor Fer," she remarked aloud, and the twins laughed. "She's getting kissed by a horse." Meanwhile, Annelise returned to the wall and this time moved cautiously backward. "Look at her, chucha!" "That chick's crazy!" Everyone knew Anne loved it when they called her crazy, and that's why there were insane asylums and hospitals in her stories. "Loooca!" they crooned at their friend. "Loooca!" "Loooca!" When José let go of Fernanda, she wiped her lips with her forearm. "*We all go a little mad sometimes*," Annelise said from the sky. And Fernanda repeated it: "*We all go a little mad sometimes*." Hugo applauded the remark, not understanding that they were quoting Norman Bates. "A black-and-white movie? What a drag!" Natalia had said the day Fernanda told them about *Psycho*. "If I watch it, I swear I'll be yawning the whole time." "If you make me watch it, I swear I'll fall asleep." Ximena, Analía, Fiorella, and Natalia admired Annelise's beauty when, unscathed, she came down from the wall. "What should we ask them for?" they wondered, anxious. "Let's ask them to take off their shirts." "No, their pants." "Let's ask them for kisses." "No, let's ask them to let us spit on them." "What if we pee on them, like at the building?" "They'll flip out if we ask them to let us do that!" Annelise winked at Fernanda the way she did when she was planning something and didn't want to say it. "I know." And she turned toward the college boys who studied medicine and were members of the Student Association of the Universidad Católica: "One of you is going to have to lick my heels." Analía's jaw dropped. The twins wrung their hands. Annelise's heels were medium-height Jimmy Choos that showed off her beautiful toes. "Or we end the game here, and we win." The boys were so surprised by the proposal that they were mute for a few seconds. "Fuck off!" "Be serious." José scratched the crown of his head: "Hang on, you can ask for that kind of thing?" Gustavo snorted just like a bull. "No fucking way am I going to lick a girl's shoes." Analía pointed at them mockingly. "What, you don't have the balls? Boooo." Tense lips and furrowed brows. Fiorella didn't like that her friends used the slang of the college boys they went out with; it made her feel like they'd lost their class. "The other game was just alcohol and confessions, big deal!" Fernanda said. "This is real, only fit for the strong." Their smiles began to fade, and the air tensed, just as Annelise loved for it to get when she wanted to intimidate others. "Why do you like scaring people so much?" Fernanda had asked her before they started high school. "Because it makes me feel big, like my mother." "Because I have to work my imagination to do it." Hugo shooed a fly from his cheek, and Fiorella noticed he had the cheekbones of Ezra Miller. The cheekbones of Ed Westwick. "Supposedly everyone here wants to have a good time." Annelise's responses always satisfied Fernanda, even when they were unclear. "I'm having a good time," she said, allowing the wind to lightly lift her skirt. "And I didn't chicken out when I had to kiss your friend." From the rooftop terrace, Ximena counted three stars, her head leaning back, until suddenly one went out. "o.k., o.k.," Gabriel said, walking toward Annelise and surprising the group. "We aren't going to give up, but you can't either, princesses, and just wait till it's our turn." Fiorella doubted that Annelise and Fernanda had considered what might come to pass if things didn't turn out as they wanted them to.

"Let's see who gets the last laugh . . ." If the boys asked them to do something worse: something that would get them in trouble. "Go on, lift up your foot." At school, they were warned many times to protect themselves from boys. "Duuude! Are you really gonna do it?" Told to demonstrate that they were respectable young women so they would be treated with respect. "Don't worry, dude: it'll be quick." And they, in Fiorella's opinion, were not coming off as respectable. "We'll get our revenge later." Fernanda smiled, watching the college guy with the blue hair and thin lips named Gabriel draw his pink tongue over Annelise's right heel, barely containing his retching. "Hopefully Anne didn't step in the puke on the stairs," Ximena whispered to Analía. His pink tongue cleaned the left heel, leaving it slobbery. "My turn," said Hugo, climbing up on the wall while Gabriel spit and murmured words that Fiorella would never dare say. "You have to do it like Anne," Fernanda reminded him, smiling for the second time all night. "You have to walk backward, verrry slowly." Gustavo rubbed his neck, unaware that his knee was trembling and that Natalia was watching with pity, as if he were a castrated dog. "Maybe you better get down, dude." Hugo started strong, but he was having a hard time keeping his balance. "Let's go, dude, you can do it!" He looked like he was on the verge of falling with each step he took, and watching him, Fernanda remembered those times when she had walked along the edge of the third floor of the building, murmuring to herself: "If I die, it'll be quick." "If I die, I won't realize it." Fiorella glued herself to her sister's shoulder. "Now they're gonna ask us to do something horrible." "Calm down," Natalia ordered. "They're gonna ask Anne, not us." In the midst of the noise and Hugo's acrobatics, Fernanda thought about how incredible it was that there were periods of time in which death meant nothing for her. "How do you know?" Periods of time in which she felt that living and dying were the same thing happening at the same time, every second. "Anne was the one who got us into this!" Or in which her most extreme happiness converged with moments when everything could also violently stop. "She's the one who'll get us out of it!" And there, thinking about that, she noticed that Annelise was getting nervous because Hugo was not falling. "Are you o.k.?" she asked. "We can always run *if this gets ugly.*" Annelise forced a smile. "*If this gets weird, we can always call a taxi.*" Her hands sweat when Hugo gracelessly overcame the challenge, shaking until the last step, the adrenaline painting his face with an incomparable emotion. "*Fuck.*" His friends applauded and shouted his name when he returned to the safety of the ground and the dry leaves. "Huuugo!" "Huuugo!" It was the excitement of having grazed death with his sex that made them jump up and down. "Huuugo!" The college boys who studied medicine and belonged to the Student Association of the Universidad Católica gathered around him. "Huuugo!" They smacked his back. "Huuugo!" They smacked his shoulder. "Huuugo!" Neither Fernanda nor Annelise liked that they'd brushed against what was theirs. "We're fucked," Ximena said, raising her eyebrows. The sex within death. "It was fun while it lasted," Analía added. Farther off, the college boys brought their heads together for an improvised secret meeting. "Well, what were you expecting? This was stupid from the beginning," Fiorella said. "What if he fell?" Fernanda took off her shoes and clambered up on the wall again. "Then what would we have done?" *The problem is that he didn't fall,* Fernanda thought without remorse. *It would have been better if he had fallen.* The boys watched her increasing the difficulty of the challenge, running from one corner to the other before landing on her feet next to Annelise, her double. Her twin of ideas. "Whoever's next will have to do the same thing!" she told them, intending to teach them a lesson. "Wait, wait, wait! First Anne has to do whatever I ask," Hugo said, with Gabriel on his left. Months ago she had read a creepypasta about a girl who killed her friend by shooting her with her finger. "And because I'm a *gentleman,* I won't make you lick my boy's shoes or anything like that," he told Annelise. In that moment, Fernanda would have given anything for her finger to be capable of the same. "I'll go easy, a true caballero." *Jerks,* thought Fernanda: they were enjoying their moment of glory. "In fact, what I'm gonna ask you for is minor." They savored it with the tips of their tongues. "Almost nothing compared to what you did to Gabo." They consumed it little by little, just like a candy. "You just have to show us one of those pictures you said you took of yourself." Fernanda scratched at the floor with her toes. "One of the ones you're naked in." *Bang!* Natalia thought. *So that's what they wanted.* In her head, the punishment had been much harsher and crueler. "Well, it could be worse, right?" Everyone realized that Annelise felt relieved, even though she tried to hide it so the boys wouldn't change their minds. "He likes Anne," Fernanda quietly said. "That's why he's been so *nice.*" It made Ximena uncomfortable that the college guys who studied medicine and belonged to the Student Association of the Universidad Católica wanted to see a minor naked. "These guys have no imagination," Analía remarked. "Or they just wanna get off," Natalia added, and Fiorella jabbed her with her elbow again. "Ouch! Stop hitting me!" The moon showed its perfect roundness, just like in the werewolf movies. "How stupid!" Natalia said when Anne told her there were Facebook groups where boys and girls acted like werewolves and exchanged stories about their transformations, photos, videos, etc. "*Freaks,*" she insulted them, but she knelt down in the white room every Wednesday afternoon and dedicated her horror stories to the White God. "Are you gonna do it?" Ximena asked Anne. "Are you gonna let them see?" Fernanda saw a smile brewing at the corners of Annelise's mouth: a subtle tension in the muscles. A sign. "Look, you don't have to send them to us or anything, just pull them up on your phone," said Hugo, the college guy with green eyes, a tattoo on his wrist, a cleft chin, wavy hair, a black jacket, and blue Chuck Taylors who looked like Robert Pattinson. "What happens here stays here." Fernanda felt sorry for them: not one of the four knew how much Annelise liked to scare people. "All right, I'll show you my *nude.*" Not one of them knew how much she wanted to scare Miss Clara, just as she had Miss Marta, the former language and literature teacher. "First, close your eyes." Only Fernanda knew her and saw in her hidden smile the desire to show them the worst of the photos. "Open them."

That is, the one Fernanda took of her in the shower. "What is that?" The one that would let her put her talent for terror into practice. "What the hell is that?" Her talent for horror. "What kind of sick shit is that?" Annelise tried to stay calm even though the boys' faces were becoming distorted. "It's me, naked." Gabriel backed away from the screen and leaned on his knees. "Motherfucker!" "Motherfucker!" Ximena, Analía, Fiorella, and Natalia didn't understand the reaction of the college boys who studied medicine at the Universidad Católica, because it was impossible to see the picture from where they were standing. "Is that real?" asked Hugo, pallid, pointing at the phone. "Who did that to you?" Ximena hopped twice. "I wanna see!" Analía took her by the arm. "Jesus, stand still!" Annelise hugged Fernanda from behind, and her pupils dilated. "My best friend." A recoiling. A look of profound revulsion. "I wanna see," Ximena repeated. Natalia began to chew at the hangnail on her thumb. "Is it or is it not a naked picture of Anne?" Fernanda felt like she was suffocating with Annelise hugging her, with the college boys who studied medicine and were members of the Student Association of the Universidad Católica looking at the photo she took of Annelise. "I wanna see!" Since they were little girls, Anne had had no problem airing her personal matters. "Now it's our turn, right?" Analía said. But on that occasion, she was going too far for Fernanda's liking. "One of you has to run along the wall just like Fer." Too far, and straight to where she couldn't follow. Gabriel refused. "I'm out, bro," he said to Hugo. "That shit isn't normal." Behind them, Gustavo got on the wall and shook like a slice of Jell-O. "Get down, dude!" José yelled. Analía, Ximena, Fiorella, and Natalia saw the college guy with the tiny nose and the birthmark on his forehead look over at the stairs as if he wanted to run away. "It's photoshopped, right?" Hugo asked, even though Annelise had already put her phone away. "I mean . . . it can't be real." Fernanda thought that perhaps Annelise had wanted things to turn out this way from the beginning. "It has to be a joke." Maybe that's why she had wanted to go to the party. "Right?" To reveal the private part of their friendship in a photo.

"Shit!" To delight in the reactions of the others. "Nooo!" Natalia screamed, and when the others turned around, they saw the wall but not Gustavo. "He killed himself!" Gabriel exclaimed, bringing his hands to his face while the rest of them ran to the edge of the terrace. "That conchesumadre killed himself!" Life and death were happening at the same time, like J Balvin's voice and Gustavo's shrieks. "Verga! Verga! Verga!" Like love and shame: tenderness and horror. "*Oh my God!*" Down below, the muscular college boy was screaming, a bone emerging from his leg, and Fernanda looked at the broken skin, the blood, the tooth on the ground as if it were any other landscape. "He's alive, dude!" Because the only thing she could think about was the photo. "He's alive!" About the disgust the photo she'd taken of Annelise evoked in the others. "He didn't die!" And about how for the first time, she also felt revulsion. "He's alive!"

XIV

Dr. Aguilar:

Fernanda: I feel bad, even though I couldn't have reacted any
   other way, *you know?* I was already feeling bad before I felt
   worse. And I think I'm the kind of person who tries to avoid
   ugly feelings. As you've already made me aware, I don't confront things. I run away, *I guess.* Some people would have put
   up with it, for the sake of the friendship. Some people put
   up with things and fix them. I prefer to nip them in the bud.
   Snip! And it's not like it doesn't matter to me, it matters *too
   much,* and that hurts. And when that happens, I step aside
   and say, "о.к., *byeee.*"

Dr. Aguilar:

Fernanda: *Of course* I knew what I was doing was bad, but I didn't
   know it was thaaat bad. I only realized it was thaaat bad after
   I did it and felt it and thought: *Shit. This is sooo fucked up.* No,
   that's not true: it was when she showed the picture to those
   idiots at the party.

Dr. Aguilar:

Fernanda: It's like when you start playing a game and it suddenly
   becomes something you never expected. Like the story about
   my tooth. Do you remember? I told you about it a looong
   time ago. No? Well, when my first baby tooth fell out, I put it
   under my pillow so my parents would give me money. Because
   I never believed in the tooth fairy, *obviously,* and I don't know
   why, because I did believe in dumber things than that. I don't
   even remember why I wanted the money, but *whatever.* I was
   reeeally excited. It bothered my mom that I didn't believe

in the tooth fairy, and that's why she made up pretty stories about my teeth being fossilized angels that fell from my gums to return to the arms of God. That was when she still loved me. Are you sure I didn't tell you about this? Well, I put the tooth under my pillow, and it took me a really long time to fall asleep, but I fell asleep. When I woke up, my tooth was gone, there was no money anywhere, and my ear hurt as if I had gone too deep in the pool for too long. Yup, it's just what you're thinking: my tooth got lodged in my ear while I was sleeping! Dad tried to take it out, but he only pushed it deeper in, and I screamed, and I remember I couldn't really hear myself, as if I were far away, as if I'd retracted into myself. *Weird*, right? They had to take me to the hospital, clearly, and the doctors wanted to take pictures and videos, as if I were part of some *freak show*, but my parents didn't let them do anything, *obviously*. *Anyway*: what happened to me with Anne was a little like that. It was like I suddenly realized I had a tooth in my ear, and all I did was take it out so I could hear again. I didn't want to stop being her friend, I just needed to move the tooth away from my eardrum. *That's it.* I wanted my ear to stop being a mouth. But she didn't see it that way. Or she did, and she decided to take that stance anyway and get her revenge, because she's immature and egotistical and a fucking bitch. Oops, *sorry!*

Dr. Aguilar:

Fernanda: Well, yes. Now that you say that, I think it's true, I was already feeling uncomfortable. But never the way I did later, when we decided to do the thing-you-already-know-about. Anne was my BFF. Well, she still is. *I guess.* You can't stop loving people just like that, *you know?* I don't know. *I mean,* I don't know how I feel about her now. I told her things I only tell you, which is to say, everything. That's why I cry so much sometimes, and I feel, I don't know . . . alone. I miss her, *I guess*, but I don't think that's the right way for me to feel.

I talked to her about everything, even Martín, and she liked listening to me. She liked to think I killed him.

Dr. Aguilar:

Fernanda: I know it seems *creepy* to you, but we invented suuuper interesting *horror stories* because, as you know, we like those things. We'd say Martín was albino: white like a baby's spit-up, or like yogurt. And even though we knew he wasn't albino, because in Mom's photos he looks really white but not thaaat white, we believed he was. We also believed that his feet were turned the wrong way, like Tin-Tín's, and that he walked backward. That's why I killed him in our stories: because I was defending myself. Because Martín was a monster, and I had to defend myself.

Dr. Aguilar:

Fernanda: *Wrooong.* I'm not blaming myself for Martín's death again. You don't know what my relationship with Anne was like. It was a reeeally fun friendship. We didn't blame ourselves for things, and we didn't feel guilty, because guilt is boring, *you know?* But going back to the thing about my brother: no one knows if I killed Martín or not. You say I didn't. My parents say I didn't. But it could have happened: I could have thrown Martín in the pool and watched him die without saying or doing anything. I don't remember, *true*, but it could have happened.

Dr. Aguilar:

Fernanda: *Wrooong.* I don't feel guilty for making up fun stories about Martín with Anne either. Martín was a reeeally ugly kid, and he looked like a goblin. And stories are just stories. They don't mean anything. And the truth is, I never felt like he was my brother. I mean, *of course* he's my brother, he still is even now that he's dead, but I never knew him. Or I don't remember knowing him. My only sister has always been Anne. She was the sister I chose.

Dr. Aguilar:

Fernanda: I already told you: because she was fun. We watched
a looot of movies and read a looot of horror novels and stories
together. And we never closed our eyes when we were scared.
We never covered our faces like everyone else did. We played
games I know other girls don't play, like the game where we
squeezed each other's necks and the one I already told you
about, from the building, though I never saw them as anything but games. *Maybe* dangerous games, yes, but exciting
ones. That's why I didn't think I'd feel weird about Anne's
new idea, but I was wrong. And everything quickly started
to get . . . I don't know, *weird*. I stopped wanting to go to the
building or be around my friends, though I went and hung out
with them anyway, because what else could I do? I don't know,
it was like I'd gone to sleep and woken up with a tooth deep
in my ear again. Like my ear was teething: that's how *weird*
and uncomfortable it was. On top of that, I started to see it
aaall differently. For example, I found the room where we told
our scary stories terrifying overnight. I mean, no one went
in there except on the days when we told our *horror stories*.
And at first I didn't even notice, but then I noticed how *weird*
it was that we didn't go in there any other day. That is, we
were always running around and playing all over the building,
except for in the white room. It was pretty obvious, but no
one wanted to talk about it. I once saw Natalia standing absolutely still a few meters from the room, looking inside with
her face frozen, as if she'd seen something horrible, so awful
that she couldn't even breathe. It scared me to see her like
that, so I yelled, "What are you doing!" and she jumped and
laughed, but in a really ugly way, like when you don't feel like
laughing but you laugh anyway, and you make a face that isn't
yours. Then I realized we'd really started scaring ourselves.
Maybe the rest of them didn't say so, and they won't, because
they don't want to fight with Anne, but I know they're a little

scared of the story of the White God. And there are moments when Anne seems possessed by the things she makes up. Her imagination is muscular, it's fused to her skeleton, and it's, I don't know, real. It moves.

Dr. Aguilar:

Fernanda: Yes, real. Realer than this, for example. Anne's imagination is realer than you or my parents or even me. I've always liked that about her. And she likes, or liked, that I like that. I guess I thought we were equals and that we had the same limits, but now I know that Anne doesn't have limits. I imagine that for her it was disappointing to discover mine, *but that's o.k.* Before, the others were scared of me because they thought I was like Anne, but I guess I was just pretending to be like her, and now that they know I'm not, they don't even want to talk to me. *Anyway,* I'm sure they were afraid of the white room at least once, and they avoided it so they wouldn't end up like Natalia, ugly and petrified. I began to be afraid of it later, when I accepted Anne's secret proposal and did the thing-you-already-know-about to her. That's when I realized there was something in that place that disturbed people. Well, us. It's just that every time we walked by that room, we avoided looking into it. Or at least I did. I think everyone did, except Anne. It was just a strange place: the only place in the building where we had never found a single animal, a single insect . . . nothing at all. Even the pigeons seemed to avoid it, because, clearly, it was the only room that didn't have windows. It didn't fit with anything else. It was different, in a bad way. I don't know. It's true that I helped make it like that, because I painted the room white, but at that point, it was just another room, not the place where Anne told her *horror stories* about the white age and the White God and blah, blah, blah. Later it took on a sickly air, like a deformity, and black moisture began to emerge from under the paint on the walls, which swelled and dripped water. I'm going to sound demented, *I know*, but the moisture in that room looked like veins, I swear. And the white paint was like sweaty skin when it rained. I don't have any pictures because Anne never let us take any. I would have liked to have at least one, though I don't know what I'd do with it. *Anyway*, the worst was that Anne smiled *too much* in there, and not like she normally smiles, but in a really scrunched up way. Oh! And there was something else that made me feel reeeally bad: ever since we started to secretly play the thing-you-already-know-about, Anne would look at my teeth a ton, and *honestly*, I didn't like that at all, it made me want to cry *like a baby*.

Dr. Aguilar:

Fernanda: *Wrooong.* I never would've cried in front of her because of that! I cried alone, when Anne wasn't sleeping over at my house, and I wasn't sleeping over at hers. Or in the bathroom at school. Sometimes I cried in the bathroom at school. Now that we're on bad terms, I cry in the bathroom at school a lot, like before. But I still don't regret hitting her.

Dr. Aguilar:

Fernanda: Yep, yep. I know violence doesn't fix problems and blah, blah, blah, but it can make us feel better when we need that. I'm just being honest.

Dr. Aguilar:

Fernanda: I think it's because we have a lot in common. Before, I also acted like I was possessed by what Anne and I invented. And even though now she wants to deny it, and she hates me, me, her BFF or ex-BFF, *whatever*, I helped create every one of her stories. We make, or we made, eeeverything together. And I wanted to be her. Sometimes I even dreamed about getting inside of Anne and wearing her on top of me like a costume. Because she's perfect, *you know?* Or almost: she's pretty, fun, smart . . . and she's got a little brother who's alive, Pablo. And she doesn't see a therapist.

Dr. Aguilar:

Fernanda: It's a joke. I love coming here.

Dr. Aguilar:

Fernanda: It's just that you don't know what it was like. After
I told her I didn't want to keep playing, because I was hurting
her and because I was feeling really, I mean reeeally, bad, she
started acting differently around me. It's not like I felt guilty
for playing the thing-you-already-know-about, because guilt is
boring, and our friendship has never been boring, but I felt, I
don't know, like I was suffocating, or like I was going to throw
up. Like I smelled bad and couldn't get rid of the stench even
by showering. Like that. And it started with the photo thing.
When she showed those boys at the party the photo, the one
I took of her, something happened in me that I can't explain.
I felt expelled from Annelise's side. For the first time, I didn't
want to sleep with her, for example. It made me so anxious to
imagine her sleeping in my bed, or me sleeping in hers, that
I made myself sick and even missed school. Yes, when I told
you last month that I'd been sick, I was lying: I was making
myself sick. Sometimes I lie to you, but I always end up telling you the truth. *Really. Anyway,* in that moment, I felt like
I didn't have the strength to tell Anne I didn't want to keep
playing the thing-you-already-know-about because I knew she
wasn't going to take it well, but I never imagined she would
take it the way she did it. Spending time with Anne stressed
me out so much that I pretended to be sick so I could stay
home and no one would visit me. I slept in wet pajamas and
made myself throw up. That's how bad I felt about everything.
But since I couldn't be sick forever, and since Anne isn't
stupid and already sensed that something *weird* was going
on, I told her the truth: that I didn't want to keep playing.
She tried to convince me, but I told her, or I tried to tell her,
what was happening to me. I told her about the photo. I told
her it was private and I didn't want the others to know. That

I would hate it if everyone else found out. That I was embarrassed, even though they didn't know. I used the word "repulsion," because I'd seen the movie *Repulsion* two days earlier, and the word "disgust." Maybe I should have used others, but I used those. And she accepted it, or pretended to accept it, clearly, because at school and at the building, eeeverything changed. Suddenly she stopped talking to me. It's not like she kicked me out of the group, she just didn't say anything to me. Sometimes she had no choice but to talk to me, but when she did, she always got right to the point. And the others noticed, *of course.* And I think it made them kind of happy. I mean: now Anne was talking and laughing with them, and they all had permission to laugh at me and exclude me. There's always a strange pleasure in pushing someone aside, right? It gives you a sort of superiority: you're above the other; if you feel like it, you can isolate her. Then, let's say overnight, I became the loser of the group. Ximena was the loser before, so I guess she was the happiest that now Anne was shooting me nasty looks, laughing at me. That's how the change began, and then it got worse. Then, in class, when we had to do some activity in pairs, Anne would choose Analía; and if it was groups of three, she'd choose Analía and Ximena; and for groups of four, Analía, Ximena, and Fiorella; and groups of five, Analía, Ximena, Fiorella, and Natalia. Do you understand? I had never been left out of the groups. No matter how small the group, I was always with Anne, and Anne was always with me. But it was obvious something had changed, and that they enjoyed letting me know. The last time I went to the building, for example, Anne threw a rock from the third floor, and it landed a few centimeters from where I was standing. It was a big rock: bigger than my fist. This big. See? It could have cracked my head open. So I stopped going, *obviously,* and that's when it became clear that I was worse than Ximena ever was, because at least she never stopped being part of the group, and I did. No one told me, "You no longer belong to

our group," but it was clear. There are things you understand
without an explanation. I remember I thought: *I'd rather leave
the group than let Anne treat me like trash.* So I told them "O.K.,
byeee," and I left.

Dr. Aguilar:

Fernanda: It hurt, realizing that Anne was the leader of the
group, because I thought, like an idiot, that we both were, in
equal parts. That kind of bruised my ego, *but just a little bit.*
What really hurts is that she won't leave me alone. She makes
fun of me, sticks her foot out so I trip on it, throws my things
on the ground . . . And yesterday I couldn't stand it anymore, that's why I hit her as hard as I could. I don't think she
was expecting it. I think she thought she was untouchable or
something like that.

Dr. Aguilar:

Fernanda: I don't know if I want to talk to her. I don't know why
we walked along the edge of the third floor. I don't know why
I squeezed her neck. I don't know why I ended up doing the
thing-you-already-know-about. I guess because it was fun . . .
until it stopped being fun. And also because Anne has a
veeery real imagination. For example, we once saw a crocodile
at the back of the building, and she got obsessed with it and
made up a story about it being a manifestation of the White
God or something like that. And when she talked about the
animal, she said it was white, but I saw its tail, and it was
green, not white. We all knew its tail was green. Fiorella had
seen the whole thing, and better than any of us, and she knew
it was green. But over time, we started talking about the crocodile as if it were white and as if we had all seen its whiteness
going into the mangroves. And it had never occurred to us
to say that it was green, because it was white. Do you understand? The crocodile was white, period. But it's not just that
we talked as if it were: We believed it. We believed we had
seen its white scales. We forgot we knew its true color. That's

how real Anne's imagination is. She's someone who does that
kind of thing.

Dr. Aguilar:

Fernanda: Yes, I miss Anne, and I understand she feels like
I betrayed her or look down on her, but I hate when she acts
like that. Sometimes I hate her. I also love her a little. And I
miss her imagination and being afraid with her. Being scared
makes you feel really alive and really fragile, as if you're a
piece of glass and you could break at any moment. Yes, it can
be awful, but it also wakes you up and fills you with an enormous sense of excitement. It's like when I was little and had
my imaginary friend, you know, the one named Martín who
looked like Martín, and I remember sometimes seeing him
scared me, because he was just like a goblin, but that didn't
stop me from imagining him or talking to him. Or like when
Anne and I would pretend, after school, that Pablo was a
monster like Martín, and we would run away from him, and
he'd cry, and we'd call him "poor little baby" and stroke his
head and call him "sweet child of mine," but then Anne would
shut him in the dryer, and we'd pretend to turn it on so Pablo
would roast. Back then Pablo was a shrimp and moved as if
he didn't have a skeleton, but now he's big, and he still remem-
bers what we did to him, and that's why he hates us a little.
It's like this: Anne wanted us to be equal, even in badness,
and if one of us was a murderer, then the other had to be too,
and if I were debrothered, she wanted to be debrothered, but
not really, just as a lie, as a joke, because we would never kill
Pablo, even though we sometimes pretended we were killing
him. I think I told you this once: we liked to pretend we were
vanquishing our ugly little brothers. We said they were gob-
lins, that they were Tin-Tín, and sometimes we believed those
stories, and we were afraid of them. Especially me, who from
a young age was really afraid of my imaginary-friend-Martín.
I guess I've always liked to be a little scared, but not thaaat

scared. Anne and I loved to be afraid while we were safe and protected, like the sisters we'd chosen to be. Sometimes, at the building, we pushed that safety to the limit, but it was just because we felt . . . I can't think of the word.

Dr. Aguilar:

Fernanda: Yeah, that. *Anyway,* I don't know if I feel safe now. I think it's because Anne's imagination is still working in my head, even though I don't want it to. It's like a tooth—not in my ear, but in my brain. My brain is teething, and it hurts. I can't forget her stories about the White God and the white age, and I can't forget how I felt every time I did the thing-you-already-know-about to her. Anne's *horror stories* were made to scare us a little, to make things more fun, but this idea or theory of hers about the white age and adolescence was more . . . *hard-core.* It was a way of describing us that made sense. It was real. It seemed like a religion, or a cult, or something like that. The color white brings a lot of horrifying images to mind: vampires, ghosts, the dead, cold landscapes, even Slender Man, who has always been drawn with a perfect whiteness in the hole where his face should be. Anne wanted to post her stories about the White God and the white age on the internet and create a myth, like Slender Man. Have you heard of Slender Man?

Dr. Aguilar:

Fernanda: He's a creature invented by hundreds and thousands of people who keep him alive by generating creepypastas, *horror stories* that circulate and grow on the internet. And needless to say, Anne wanted her theory of the White God and the white age to spread all over the internet and become a *meme.* She wanted to write really successful creepypastas about it. Well, the idea to do it was both of ours, but now I guess it's just hers. *Whatever.*

Dr. Aguilar:

Fernanda: o.k., I'll try to explain it, but it's reeeally hard to
describe. I know the whole white age and White God thing
is a story Anne made up, and blah, blah, blah. But sometimes
I think a story, even if it's made up, can say things that are true.
In my opinion, that's what sets the best *horror stories* apart
from the worst: they achieve a true form of fear. But before I
go on, I want you to know that Anne and I aren't *prudes*. We
aren't like other girls from Opus families. We aren't a couple
of goody-goodies who talk about kissing without ever having been kissed. But I have limits. We all have to have limits.
Only Anne doesn't have any. Or maybe we have different limits. I don't know. When I did the thing-you-already-know-
about to her, I felt bad because there was something . . . I don't
know. I don't know if I'm going to explain it right. It's embar-
rassing! There was something . . . sexual in the act. It's not like
we would have had sex or anything. We aren't lesbians! And
it's not like I have anything against lesbians, it's just hard to
ignore what you've been hearing your whole life overnight, *you
know?* Guilt is super boring, and we avoided it, but maybe,
sometimes, I felt a little guilty. Or strange, at least. I felt
weird and dirty, *I guess.* The neck thing was different, though
I think it was some kind of initiation into what we ended up
doing. I guess Anne hates me because at first, I was the one
who talked about . . . you know, sexual things, and she listened to me and didn't make a peep. It's not like Anne's shy,
but at that point, she was more reserved, but only about that
stuff. It surprised me that she was like that and with other—
worse—things she was so open. *Anyway,* I told her about
my . . . you know, masturbation, and how bad I felt when
I was little and my parents told me I had to stop touching
myself and avoided me like they were embarrassed to look at
me, and I also told her they talked to you, and you explained
that it wasn't sooo bad that I touched myself, but that the situation had to be controlled in any case, and blah, blah, blah.
Do you remember? Anyway, you know I don't talk about that

with anyone because I'm embarrassed about it, but I did talk to Anne about that kind of thing. I don't know how to explain how intimate we were. We showered together, but as friends, naturally, and that felt good, because it was like looking at yourself in a mirror. *Anyway*, I've always been less of a *prude* than Anne, I always brought up topics like sex and masturbation, and I guess that's why she hates me, because it's like I gave her enough confidence to open up to me, to show me what she really wanted, and after I saw it, I felt disgusted by her and left. And maybe that is what I did. Well, I love her, even though sometimes she's a huge *bitch. Sorry.*

Dr. Aguilar:

Fernanda: I don't know, I guess I didn't talk to you about Anne before because we didn't have any problems and because our relationship was perfect, and I didn't feel like I had anything to say. Though apparently there was a lot to discuss. But I believed our friendship was perfect, *you know?* And I really don't want you to think we were doing lesbian stuff, because that wasn't the intention. Although later I felt like it might be seen that way, and that's why it grossed me out. But it was something reeeally different.

Dr. Aguilar:

Fernanda: I don't know. But it wasn't lesbian, *I swear.*

Dr. Aguilar:

Fernanda: Clearly it hurts, *of course,* though I'm not feeling like this just because of that. It isn't the only thing that's bothering me. There's something else that's keeping me up at night. But I don't understand what it is. All I know is, I want to cry, and sometimes I feel, I don't know, bad, as if someone were chasing me, but I'm the one chasing me, because I can't stop thinking about Anne and my friends and the building and the White God and the white age and the thing-you-already-know-about that I did to Anne. Maybe deep down I don't want to fix things with her, because that would mean talking about what she made me do to her, which I didn't want to do to her at all.

Dr. Aguilar:

Fernanda: I don't want to talk about that with you right now either. I told you what I did to Anne because I had to, but that doesn't mean I want to talk about it right now. I still don't want to. I don't want to talk about it with Anne either, *obviously*.

Dr. Aguilar:

Fernanda: I don't know why I don't want to talk about it. I guess because it scares me. All I want to say is that I didn't want to do that to her. I didn't want to. And I hated doing it to her.

Dr. Aguilar:

Fernanda: I didn't want to. I didn't want to do that to Anne, and I didn't enjoy it. And even if she did enjoy it a little, even if she did take a super *creepy* pleasure in what I did to her, that doesn't have anything to do with me, because I didn't enjoy it.

Dr. Aguilar:

Fernanda: Why are you asking me that? What are you suggesting with a question like that?

Dr. Aguilar:

Fernanda: Are you suggesting that I'm lying?

XV

Rules for Entering the White Room
By Annelise Van Isschot

You shall never enter on foot, but on the four paws of thy name.

You shall never touch or brush against the walls.

You shall sweep the floor with your hair at least once during the ceremony.

You shall accept that inside, anything can happen to your body.

You shall not open your eyes at the wrong moments.

You shall not cry, even if it hurts.

You shall not scream, even if it's scary.

You shall not leave the room until the ceremony has ended.

You shall always pray with your knees on the ground.

You shall accept God in the white depths of your consciousness.

You shall menstruate on every one of Their holy days.

XVI

The worst part wasn't the shooting pain in her extremities; nor was it the odor of her body—a reeking mass of sweat and urine that, with its filth, imposed itself on the orderly world of the cabin; nor was it time, expanding like a black hole into which all the objects, the forest, the volcano, her memories, the bitch Miss Clara, and she herself, entered; nor the fact that she was still there, hand-cuffed to a table, feeling her stomach stick to her back and spec-tating in silence as her skin became an ocher pasture for a line of small black ants marching across the floor. That was all tolerable, up to a certain point. The worst part was that two days had passed since the last time she had any dignity. The worst was not know-ing anything—like Shelley Duvall in *The Shining*, but with hair the color of Julie Christie in *Demon Seed*—and starting to get scared. Scared of what? she insisted on asking herself when she felt as if something inside her were scrunching her up, something with its own breath that was foreign to hers: a drooling creature with long teeth and a mermaid's tail. That animal had begun to swim through her chest when Miss Clara brought in the rabbit, skinned it without saying a word, cooked it over the fire, and ate it in front of her.

She had never imagined that hunger was a perfect weight clam-bering from one's stomach to one's temple.

Miss Clara allowed her to drink a glass of water every day, but she had to urinate right there, sitting in a squeaky, splintering chair. The first time was the hardest: her bladder released itself, and she started to cry, inundated with herself, with an unbearable dirti-ness that was invading her unfamiliar, reclusive body. Fernanda had never connected with the repulsive organism she was now inhabiting. Was that stench her true nature? Her body looked like an esplanade flown over by brass buzzards hunting organs. She would have liked to split her skin open with a rock to feel something besides disgust and hunger, but not even her willpower resembled what it once was.

She ruminated on this change: never before had she been disgusted by herself.

Miss Clara hadn't bathed either, but at least she didn't reek of jaundice, of urethra, of diaper, and that gave her the classification of the only living human in the cabin. Fernanda, on the other hand, had quickly discovered the truth of her nature: her odor, as strong as her hunger; her humanity, as fragile as her odor. That's why, before her teacher, Fernanda felt just like those animals that force people to turn their heads and scrunch up their noses: she knew Miss Clara could smell her thighs and see, on the floor, the outline of a puddle that the wood had absorbed. An outline that kept renewing itself and that the ants knew how to navigate. So far she had peed six times—she was counting because the only thing she could do was pay attention to her bodily needs and functions—and she knew that with each new puddle, she was losing an important part of herself, but the humiliation didn't cloud her thoughts, nor did it impede her from putting together little schemes for standing up, moving a few centimeters from the chair, and squatting to keep her legs from getting wet.

She had seen female dogs relieve themselves that way many times: their sex grazing the grass.

She had also seen Ximena and Analía piss like female dogs.

Applying that tactic, nevertheless, had its inconveniences: the handcuffs scraped her wrists when she moved, reddening her skin, and it was difficult for her to take off her underwear. Sometimes, if she was lucky, she could lower them to her knees, though normally she wasn't able to take them off, and the sensation of her wet underwear against her sex, hot and elastic, was unpleasant. But it would have been worse, she thought, to take them all the way off in front of Miss Clara; it would have been worse to remain naked and expose herself to the ants, leaving her Monday panties vulnerable to her teacher's madness, removing the one article blocking her vulva when her skirt would always be so easy to lift up . . .

For several hours, her labia had been burning as if there were ivy growing from the inside out. At least the uncertainty kept her constipated.

Lucky me, she thought. She didn't want to think about the alternative.

Deep down, it surprised her that she was capable of emptying out more liquid than she consumed, and that her head felt like a blood balloon hovering on the tip of a needle. Never before had she been starving, but she only now knew that. To be hungry was to accommodate the nothing and listen to it regurgitating amphibians in your stomach. Once, on the building's patio, Natalia brought tadpoles from the pond up to her mouth on a dare. Fiorella tickled her and her sister swallowed them. "Frog, frog, go away, jump again another day," they sang to her, because she was scared stiff that her stomach would fill up with little baby frogs. "What if they change inside me? What if their legs start to form in my intestines?" Annelise told her she would shit white frogs with transparent bellies, the kind in which they could see the horror of the heart through the skin. "A frog's heart is so small," she'd told her a year ago, when in the lab, Miss Carmen opened one up and exposed its cherry-tomato muscle, still beating. *My heart must be so small*, Fernanda thought, feeling it vibrate like never before in that moment. Now she could say she knew its rhythm and appetites; everything she had never dared look at, which, in that cabin, she suddenly saw.

"If I turn into a frog, you'll have to kiss me so I become a princess," Natalia told them back then, winking her hummingbird-eye.

She thought about her friends to escape the hunger and misery, but next to her thoughts, nothing existed except for her hunger and her vulva, swelling under the fabric, a frothy fruit with sensitive gums. Her head, moreover, felt the way it had when her imaginary-friend-Martín was her dead brother and was waiting for her in the closet, crouching behind the little blue boots, scraping the wood with his teeth. "I can't stand it when you look at my teeth," she told Annelise one afternoon, the two of them alone on the top floor of the building. "Why? You don't like them?" she asked, walking in a straight line along the edge of the abyss. "I really like your little rat teeth." Her head, in the cabin, felt like it had when her imaginary-friend-Martín gnawed at the closet with his white ferret teeth. "Your Topo Gigio teeth." "Your Bugs Bunny teeth." From her insides, her family revealed the history of their blood: a goblin brother, a brother with backward feet, a brother albino as death, a brother walking against his footsteps, moving backward, because the story of siblinghood begins with a murder, according to Annelise: "The Bible says so, and in that book, everyone is scared." But the adults didn't know Annelise read the Bible as a book of fears.

"Do you want to be my sister?" she asked when they were eight and slept under the bed in each other's arms.

"Yes, I want to be your sister."

The adults didn't know, either, that when they went to church, she and Annelise were acting out the cult of the White God, the mother-God-of-the-wandering-womb, and that they furtively caressed each other's knees.

"You're my little sister, my ñañita, my equal."

The White God made them laugh at their mothers: at their fallen tits in Victoria's Secret bras, their anti-wrinkle creams made for prune-faces, their phosphorescent hair dyes, because the nature of daughters, says the creed, is to jump on the mother, tongue gripped tight in their hands; to survive the jaw to become the jaw; to take the place of the monster—that is, the place of the mother-God who initiated them into the world of desire.

That's what a sister was: an ally against the origin.

Fernanda tried not to be scared that Miss Clara had a wide jaw, like a shark or like a lizard, or like the crocodile that advanced, in her dreams, toward Annelise's open legs.

"I birth you inward," her sister told her in her nightmares. "I'm going to bear you into my bones."

Her thoughts scaled swamps to the volcano, where Miss Clara had eyes like the iguana and gecko eggs they smashed against the wall. There, Fernanda and her friends plundered the earth with their hands, pulling up roots and finding white treasures that looked like the madness she was now witnessing in her teacher's gargoyle-gaze.

The madness was soft and wet like the eggs, but sometimes they stuck the madness in their mouths and in their underwear before smashing it against the walls.

Fernanda believed, until she was seven years old, that an ovary was a rosary made of broken eggshells. "I like your teeth so much I want to rip them out of you," Annelise said the night Fernanda told her. "I like your jaw so much I want to make it into rosary teeth." They prayed to the White God with each of her molars while they tickled each other under the sheets. "We're sisters," they told each other, and they licked each other's gums when they bled. "We're the same," and they hugged their bones together when the sun sank. She remembered Annelise that way, as she was before they fought, to escape her hunger and her vulva, but she couldn't escape what was sleepless and oviparous, just as she couldn't escape Miss Clara dragging her heavy feet along the wood of the creaking sky.

Her bloody bare feet left dark stains on the floor.

Her black hair fluttered down the banks of the staircase.

She had thought they would find her sooner, but she'd begun to understand that the motivations for her kidnapping were those of a woman in delirium, and that now anything could happen to her. She could get hurt, she understood; not like when the dare was to take a punch to the gut and Annelise hit her with all her strength, but seriously.

Perhaps the revolver on the table had a bullet for her.

Perhaps she needed to start asking herself if she was ready to die.

"What would it feel like to die?" she asked Annelise a while ago, and then her mother: "Mommy, what would it feel like to die?" And her mother told Dr. Aguilar about it, just like she did with everything else her daughter said that kept her up at night. Fernanda tried several times to think about her parents, but her dad was an afternoon fishing, and her mom, a sick dove that ceaselessly shit all over the world. Her father was the net and the fish; her mother, convulsing, her open beak outside the water. One of the two, at least, could fly—the scarier one—but she was terrified of her child. Fernanda had told Dr. Aguilar: "My mother is afraid of me." She had explained that her mother kept a photo of the dead son and looked at it as if he were alive, while she looked at Fernanda as if she were dead.

"She looks at me as if I were a ghost," she told him. "That's why I go 'Boo!' when she doesn't see me."

Up until that moment, it hadn't occurred to Fernanda that maybe her parents weren't crying over her disappearance, that maybe they were happy not to have to be parents in a city that fills with snakes when it rains. "Today my daddy ran over a snake on the highway," Fiorella recounted two months ago as she viciously stomped on a small one on the second floor of the building. In the Bible, she remembered, God asked men to fear nothing, not even the snakes, just Him. "Fear of the Lord is wisdom," Mister Alan said. "Fear of the Lord is like filial love." Fearing the father or mother was the dark side of love, they said, but no one talked about the fear parents have of their children: no one said that to fear the mother was the wisdom of the serpent, and that the daughter who ate serpents didn't know how to fear. Fernanda had never been afraid of her mother; that's why the womb that birthed her feared her every day her father went fishing and brought only the sweetness of dead gills home.

Perhaps her mother wasn't looking for her. Perhaps her friends— who had stopped being her friends long before the kidnapping—no longer missed her.

Perhaps she was in the thick fog, and the White God in the silence.

She didn't know why her locked-up mind always returned to Annelise's horror stories. Nevertheless, her chosen sister's creations came alive in her head as the hours passed and her fear soaked her with bodily fluids. She remembered moments of collective fear caused by Annelise's inventions, like when, just before they stopped talking, she wanted to convince them that someone was coming into the building when they weren't there, someone who slipped in at night or in the mornings and prowled around the space with the intention of commandeering it. "The White God isn't going to like that," she said in a very serious voice that made Fiorella and Natalia grab each other's hands. During that time, Annelise became a ghostbuster: she found footprints, turbid signs of the presence of an intruder in every corner, and even though the footsteps were the same size as Analía's feet and the signs were as vague as the place where a rock was resting or the thickness of the branch they used to poke at the snakes, Fernanda and the rest of them began to believe it was true, that someone really was invading their lair. "We have to do something." "Let us pray to the White God. They will tell us what to do." Sometimes, as they ran up and down the hallways, they felt as if something were watching them from the white room, but there was nothing there, just the black water that dripped down the walls when it rained. "If we see him, we'll push him off the third floor." "If we see him, we'll offer him to the crocodile."

In the stories about the white age, the young protagonists experienced horrifying theophanies in which the White God appeared to them just like Jehovah to Moses, and that was the start of a gradual change that dragged them into doing horrible things like eating their mothers, killing their siblings, or joining secret cults just before disappearing. "Thou canst not see my face: for there shall no man see me, and live," Mister Alan read in theology classes, before Annelise's growing interest. "And he put his hand into his bosom: and when he took it out, behold, his hand was leprous, white as snow." Fernanda listened and watched Annelise absorb the biblical words she would use to perfect her story: "The White God has neither face nor form, but its symbol is a jaw that chews up all fears," she said in the white room. "She who sees Them and is not ready to see Them will die, because Their apparition is like death: it takes the color from all things."

Fernanda would have liked to star in one of those stories of macabre revelations: to brim with the theophany of Annelise's White God, for her hair to go white with the horror of the apparition, and for that to give her the strength she needed to get herself out of the handcuffs and kill Miss Clara. After all, if she killed her, no one would punish her. The police would call it legitimate self-defense, because a kidnappee has the right to murder her kidnapper. She could try it: kill her teacher, discover what it feels like to take a person's life, and, in doing so, save her own. She could try to get to the revolver resting in the middle of the table, but when she stretched, her wrists wailed, and she couldn't reach her teeth far enough to bite the handle.

As the sensation of helplessness grew, time was camouflaged with the walls, with the window, and with the snow on the volcano. Existing inside that invisible time was difficult for Fernanda, like coiling herself around the little light there was or breathing in the nauseating stench that emanated in waves from her pelt. But the hardest moments, the ones that crackled in her throat, came when her teacher descended the spiral staircase with broken treads and sat on the far side of the table. Then the light coming through the glass obscured half her face, and she tried not to look at her so she wouldn't get scared, but she always failed.

No one had explained to her that light could also eclipse the flesh.

Sometimes, sitting before her, Miss Clara stayed as still as a cadaver, not looking at her, not talking to her, her greasy black hair slicked to the sides of her face and her posture transformed: her right shoulder falling, her back twisted to the left, as if the cold of the mountain had damaged her. When that happened, Fernanda wondered again and again why her and not Annelise. Why her and not Analía. Why her and not Ximena. Why her and not Fiorella, not Natalia. She wondered what she in particular had done to deserve this, what made her unique, and she never arrived at a satisfactory answer.

There were periods of time when Miss Clara tucked her dirty hair behind her ears and reached out to caress the revolver as if it were a cat's head. Fernanda took advantage of those minutes to ask her simple questions she never answered: "What time is it?" "Is this place yours?" "Could you give me something to eat?" But none of those questions was the important one: "Is that Annelise's father's revolver?" That one she never uttered, because its answer had become a blurry presence, a threat that she perceived with increasing clarity floating from the forest into the cabin, swelling from Miss Clara's madness to her own temple. Her teacher's words might be a precipice she could fall from, but in every horror movie, change brings new dangers, and Fernanda sensed that the final plot twist of her kidnapping would take the form of an answer: why, or for what purpose, she was there.

The rhythm of her mind—accelerated, vertiginous—stopped when Miss Clara appeared on the stairs and took the first step down.

"*Please!*" Fernanda burst out, not recognizing her voice, breaking down in tears in a way she never thought possible.

Now she knew the thickness of her strength: now she knew who she was when she surrendered to the gargantuan jaws.

Miss Clara came down with her face scratched, her lips blue, her spine twisted. She murmured unintelligible things while Fernanda shook from the cold, from her hunger and her vulva. *Now she's going to talk,* she thought, cowering like a snoutless animal. She could see the intention of speech on her teacher's face, a tongue licking Fernanda's pupils as her mouth prepared to say:

"It makes no sense for you to lie, so don't lie," Miss Clara said, messing up her eyebrows with fingers so red they looked like caterpillars.

She'd be capable of crawling like a worm before her kidnapper, Fernanda thought; she would lick her feet, her fingers, her veins, if that would send her back to her mother's fearful womb.

That's all she wanted: to go back.

"I know full well what you did, you sick little girl."

XVII

On the first day of class, Clara knew something in her body didn't feel right. "You look awful!" Amparo Gutiérrez said as if she were happy about it, because by then she had developed the impolite habit of pointing out how bad Clara looked and suggesting, without being asked, how to improve her diet, which infusions to drink—she emphatically advised against coffee—and which exercises to do to correct her "awkward" and "childish" posture.

"I have insomnia," she begrudged in response. What Clara felt, however, wasn't exhaustion, but dread.

She had been the first to arrive at the school that morning. The security guard greeted her, blessing her with his gnarled thumb in the air, and as she parked her dead mother's car in the parking lot, she noticed that her own hands had begun to tremble. *What horrendous claws*, she thought as she looked at the fingers folded over the steering wheel like ten spider legs—the fingernails chewed up, the knuckles too wrinkled. It had been days since they last stiffened, since she had felt that old vertigo low in her abdomen—"The body we have goes against our own grain," her mother would say when she was alive and sick and took an unspeakable pleasure in observing her daughter's suffering, the way she clawed at her arms and gnawed on her tongue at night. It was not a good sign that her womb was buzzing like a honeycomb about to drop, that her organs were filling with insects and forcing her to stay still, very still—just like her mother, who sat in the tiger-striped armchair awaiting her death—but even so, she got out of the car, anxious, sweating droplets that pasted her hair to both sides of her face, her vision blurred as if covered by a thick layer of dirty water. She had to breathe deeply to prevent the palpitations, the tingling in her arms, and the nausea; she had to calm down and remember that even though her thighs were burning, she couldn't scratch them, because doing so always made the itching worse.

She had never understood why certain parts of her body sometimes screamed at her to hurt them.

"You're going against your own grain, Becerra."

She waited like that for a few minutes: leaning on the hood, inhaling and exhaling deeply, and when she thought she'd recovered control of her body—or at least part of it—she headed for the teachers' lounge, passing the unblemished skating rink, trying not to think about how soon the silence and cleanliness that surrounded her would fill with piercing voices, moist giggles, hundreds of footsteps at rhythms dissimilar and frenetic—because adolescent legs were never still, according to the dead mother who inhabited her mind—and with dust, sand, and hair.

Everything is going to be different, she thought.

Upon entering the room, she impatiently looked at the clock on the wall, sat down in her chair, organized some papers on the desk, reviewed her class schedule, and checked once more—she had done it four times before leaving the house (as the dead mother who inhabited her mind demanded)—that all the books she needed were in her briefcase.

She needed to calm down, she told herself. Up to that point, she had done so by getting to know the institution and her colleagues, memorizing the names of each custodian and security guard, watering the plants in the teachers' lounge twice a week, pinning famous quotes about education on the bulletin board, and choosing words that would allow her to speak less during meetings. She had been meticulous—like her mother had been when she was still alive and healthy and spent forty-three minutes every night checking the locks on the doors and windows of the house. But above all, she had been prudent. It was clear to her that if she wanted to return to normalcy—that is, to resume the life she'd been living before what happened with the *M&M's*—she had to confront her symptoms, the gum and the tiny breasts, had to come out from her hiding place and be a teacher, just like her mother: a good teacher. After all, that's what she had trained for, and she'd always known the students would return and occupy every last corner with their ribbons, their lustrous skin, and their eyes like fluorescent bugs. Her error, however, had been in believing that she'd be completely ready for that to happen, that her body, an organic map of terrors, would stop flinching like an eyelid under the sheets by the time the girls came back to school. Instead, there she was: reduced once again to her interior buzzings, to the chaos of her central nervous system, withstanding a vibration that coated her mouth with a repugnant sweetness, looking at the clock on the wall as if it were a gallows.

They're just girls, she remembered: little children who can't do a thing to you. And to avoid clawing her thighs—which itched with unusual vehemence—she clawed the desk's smooth surface several times, but she stopped when she saw her right heel had begun to hammer the ground.

She immediately stood up.

Her new students would be, in the words of Rodrigo Zúñiga, upper-class girls used to ridiculing their teachers—but (in the opinion of the dead mother who inhabited her mind) they couldn't be as bad as Malena Goya and Michelle Gomezcoello. "They're good girls, it's just . . . you know, they're at that age where they have to test the limits," Amparo Gutiérrez said when the prank they'd played on the former language and literature teacher came up again. Clara quickly realized that her colleagues would rather not discuss the girls' behavior. They avoided going into detail about discipline at the school, even though she, having learned of the incident with her predecessor, tried to learn more about the general character of the student body and insisted on it with poorly received questions. Ángela was the only one who dared to assure her that the conduct of the students was excellent because they were supervised at all times—"Haven't you seen the dean? She patrols the halls during class," she said. "She doesn't have a night-stick, but it feels like she does." Nevertheless, there were some groups, she remarked in almost a whisper, that knew the truth:

ultimately, they were untouchable for Patricia-the-dean, and the ones who truly held power, within the school and outside of it, were their parents.

"There are girls who like to challenge everything," Ángela told her. "It's puberty stuff, you don't have to pay much attention to them."

Clara was unmoved by her colleagues' opinions. For years she'd been teaching teenagers, and she had never been afraid of them before—not even when José Villanueva cracked Humberto Fernández's head against the lockers, or when Priscila Franco cut off Abigaíl Núñez's braid and started using it as a bookmark. In her experience, boys tended to be grotesque and physically violent, but girls, in spite of their delicate and naive exteriors, exerted a different but equally cruel aggressiveness. They were smarter—as those who must devise tactics for surviving hostile conditions often are—and they could disguise their hunger for violence with feigned innocence. Only girls, thought Clara, entered their teachers' houses without permission. That's why the fear spread in her like a stain a few days before class started, feeding off her nightmares, her memories, and the attitude of those who avoided talking about the students in front of her.

Her mother had warned her before: "Girls are the worst," she told her. "You have to protect yourself from them, Becerra."

But Clara didn't listen.

"You look awful!" Amparo Gutiérrez blurted out when she entered the lounge and saw her standing beside the desk. "You can't start your classes like that. The girls will eat you alive!"

Every student devours their teachers' heads, thought Clara, comparing them to praying mantises.

Now she had to learn to save her skull: one way or another, she had to learn how to feed without letting herself be eaten.

"Daughters cannibalize their mothers, Becerra, milk to bone."

Following Elena Valverde's death, Clara watched as a new voice was born in her brain, a flow of words that helped her fill the empty space and heal the maternal absence. The voice was none other than that of the dead mother who inhabited her mind: a language that cleansed her of herself to make her what she really wanted to be—Elena, the white flesh of origin. On the first day of class, Clara dressed in the purest maternal style, circa 2003, because that voice she loved had requested it, the consciousness that had brought her up to be strong and precise, that is, to do things well—a mother (Elena liked to tell her while looking at the phantom of her spinal column that hung on the wall in the shape of an *s*) was always responsible for her daughter's actions. Clara wanted to live up to that education: to straddle the back of the world, even if it was racing wildly over the void. Therefore, dodging Amparo Gutiérrez's observations and unsolicited advice, she left the teachers' lounge and—as the students arrived in shiny new imported cars or in school buses, chattering away, their eyelashes too long and their knees obscured—went to the bathroom to regain her composure. There was only one thing she could do in that state, she told herself: look straight ahead, directly at the floor tiles—behind her there was nothing but a hole painted the color of Malena Goya's fingernail polish (a well deep as the dimples next to Michelle Gomezcoello's lips). Slipping back into those circumstances was a more terrifying option than going forward, so she let the tap water run, lifted her skirt, moistened her thighs, and smacked them, surprised when the sound echoed off the glass just like a kiss. Several drops dampened her clothing, giving her an unkempt look. The mirror sent back the faded face of a tattered sock: a familiar expression of irremediable fatigue. At one point, she thought she heard someone knocking on the door, but no one was waiting for her in the hallway, just the sun and, in the distance, an untold number of skirts sucking up all the air.

In a matter of minutes, Delta became a pack of white socks pulled over calves and shirts with buttons undone. The girls swarmed the patio, swollen backpacks on their shoulders, and the teachers dodged them as if trying to avoid looking at them directly. They, however, saw everything. There was not a single place or person that made them close their eyes. That's how they would watch her in the classroom, Clara thought, her nerves drying out her palate: brazenly. "The new teacher," they'd call her until they learned her name, and in the process, they would examine her as they would an exotic animal, to find out whether they should be good or bad to her. But Clara wasn't going to let them dictate her behavior.

She could defeat them, she told herself. She could control the sweating and the light-headedness.

Even though she had experience with all kinds of teenagers, the noise of hundreds of voices talking on the patio, in the gardens, the corridors, and the parking lot, made her shudder as if a gorilla were caressing her gums with one finger. She stood still, her feet close together, watching as the teachers—and Patricia-the-dean—passed, as the girls doubled over with laughter and splattered drops of thick spit on the cobblestones. *They look like bitches*, she thought, and she was afraid her recent tremors would lead to tachycardia, the tingling and asphyxiation that belonged to her increasingly infrequent panic attacks, that paralyzed her and made her simultaneously fear and desire death.

They're shedding, she moaned in her head, overwhelmed. *Soon the floor will be filled with their hairs.*

Then the bell rang—artificial bells that made her clench her jaw—and Clara knew there was no turning back. She crossed through the crowd—the light, the lustrous black of new shoes— and headed for the teachers' lounge to check for the fifth time that her books were inside her briefcase, retrieve her schedule, and go to the classroom, where she would organize her papers once again, all while picking at the delicate skin between the fingers of her left hand.

In the hallways, the confusion was visible: the teachers trotted along while Patricia-the-dean blew her whistle, raising her arms so the fat hung from them like two tiny, hairless wings. Before distancing herself from the tumult, Clara saw Ángela smile at one of the students as she crossed through a doorway, and suddenly she wondered how good a teacher she was, though deep down, she didn't care all that much.

"Your head is a cockroach nest, Becerra."

She taught her first class in 2C, a classroom at the end of a long, curving hallway on the first floor of the Beato Álvaro del Portillo building—her mother (who liked to mock the custom of naming infrastructure in honor of dead people) would have laughed until she cried if she had also known that on the landings, the Delta Bilingual Academy, *High-School-for-Girls*, hung plaques bearing messages like "Regnare Christum volumus," "Deo omnis gloria," or "Serviam." Not for a single moment did she stop sweating or shaking, but she was proud to have maintained a certain composure during the hour. Besides, the students of 2C were silent and disciplined. They stood in unison when she entered the room and didn't sit back down until she gave them permission to do so. They took notes with an unusual diligence and docility, without talking among themselves, looking straight ahead with their legs crossed, until Clara dropped the eraser and a girl with a blue bow in her hair mischievously smiled to the friend next to her.

Calm down, she thought. *Maintain control.*

Because of the symptoms of her increasingly severe anxiety disorder—and the threat of a possible panic attack—she forgot to take attendance at the beginning of class. Each student, right before the bell rang, called out "Present!" when she heard her name, and then they settled into a silence that seemed stilted and artificial to Clara. As she went down the list—marking boxes with a *P* or an *A* on the computer screen—she understood the girls in front of her weren't really as they appeared; they were offering a sort of truce, and any slipup, no matter how small, would put an end to it. Her uneasy and fearful state also obliged her to skip the conventional introductions in which she asked the students about their hobbies and projects, and instead resorted to the rigidity of an introductory session in which only she spoke—which the pedagogical model of the Delta Bilingual Academy, *High-School-for-Girls*, prohibited. What left her most unsettled, however, was listening to herself as if she were another person, someone she didn't know and who sounded just like an old documentary at midnight.

"What you're experiencing is called depersonalization," said the psychiatrist who treated her when she was sixteen. "It's another symptom of your anxiety and panic disorder."

All the day's classes went like that in Clara's mind: she heard herself as if from the bottom of a well, trying to distance the darkest thoughts that came into her head each time she slid her eyes up the legs of her students: *Are they mocking me? Are they disgusted by my hands and my hair? Do they think I'm ugly? That I have nothing interesting to say?*

Do they know that when they grow up, they'll be like me?

Do they know that, like it or not, they'll look like their teachers?

That morning, she also taught classes in 3A and 4B, and although they progressed in a relatively normal way—the students were less guarded and unpleasant than those in 2C—she couldn't stop thinking about the girls who gave her predecessor a pre–heart attack. She frequently wondered what they were like, how old they were, and if, in time, she would recognize them, identify them without anyone pointing them out, see in them traces of Malena Goya and Michelle Gomezcoello. At Delta, there were three other language and literature teachers, but no one—surely to keep her from forming unfair prejudices against the girls— seemed willing to tell her who'd played that nasty joke on Marta Álvarez. Even so, and in spite of her urge to torment herself, Clara was grateful for their discretion, because knowing the identity of the pranksters—the attackers, the killers, the aggressors (in the opinion of the dead mother who inhabited her mind)—could be detrimental for her paranoid personality and might also put her at odds with the students—or more on the defensive than she already was—thus triggering a new crisis that she didn't think she could bear.

"Sometimes it's better not to know, Becerra," her mother used to say, back when she was still alive and pretending to be blind and would move around the house with a broomstick and think that she was dreaming the future; that is, her own death.

But it was hard for Clara to see the benefits of ignorance.

Luckily, during the second break, her tremors lessened considerably. The sweat, however, remained, and the feeling of depersonalization was reinforced each time she entered a classroom. She found that it was easier to conceal her symptoms if she maintained a prudent distance from the desks, so in order to feel whole—and contain the excesses of her body—she resolved to remain a meter and a half from the girls during classes. Meanwhile, Patricia-the-dean—whom she had at first believed was an ally in matters of discipline—peered through the windows of all the classrooms where she taught to weave her eyes like two awkward eagles over the students' hair.

Clara didn't like that, sometimes, it was as if Patricia were monitoring her more than she was the students.

At the end of the day, she had a class with 5B, a group that greeted her with applause and refused to explain why until—when the bell to leave sounded and the class began suddenly cheering again—a very pale and freckly girl approached and told her not to worry, that they were only welcoming her. As that sweaty body smelling of apples neared, her first impulse was to retreat, but the girl stopped naturally before her desk, leaning her hands on the wood, her lips saturated with saliva. "Are you going to take attendance, Miss Clara?" she asked with an expression Clara found murky—she had forgotten, once again, to take it at the beginning of the period. The students in the class, faced with her prolonged silence, began to leave, and she didn't have the strength to stop them. In that moment—watching the freckly girl join the rest in leaving behind the flock of poorly closed backpacks—Clara noticed that she had been grinding her teeth for minutes—hours, maybe—and that it was quite possible her students had heard.

Something wasn't right inside her body, she concluded again.

Completely exhausted from having spent the entire day making such an effort, Clara emerged from the classroom as if from the depths of a swamp. There wasn't anyone in the hallway, but she could hear the noise the girls were making on the first floor, running toward the buses and their parents' cars, their tiny scissor legs cutting off what little oxygen she had left. Around her, the heat was red, and it reminded her of when Malena Goya and Michelle Gomezcoello swung their tampons in her face like two pendulums of blood.

The metallic taste between her teeth made her spit a thick thread of drool into a flowerpot.

She cried, but silently.

Minutes later, she descended the stairs, muscles aching, and as she walked through the spaces now free of girls—who had left, as she'd expected, hairs of various colors on the ground—she had a horrifying revelation: that's how all her days at the Delta Bilingual Academy, *High-School-for-Girls*, were going to be.

All of them, until she got better.

Because of that, on the second day, she stuck an Alprazolam tablet in her briefcase and started her classes neither shaking nor sweating, though a bit drowsy. The effect lasted just a few hours; during the first break, she again began banging her foot on the floor, grinding her teeth, perspiring, and picking at the delicate skin between the fingers of her left hand. Ángela came upon her in that state, visibly uneasy in the teachers' lounge, and asked loudly if she was all right, if she was hurt, if she needed to be taken to the nurse's office. But her concern, far from moving Clara, disappointed her—she had thought Ángela, at least, would avoid asking her questions she didn't want to answer. The week was full of similar encounters, which she dodged with awkward head movements. She discovered that if she responded that way, if she resisted speaking, the teachers moved by her appearance to interrogate her would leave her alone. She concentrated, then, on nonverbally responding to her colleagues and devising preventative rituals to mask her anxiety symptoms in public.

Thus, as she attempted to adapt to her new students—and stop likening them to Malena Goya and Michelle Gomezcoello— she realized the girls at Delta were different from the ones she'd known before, not owing to religion or social class, but to their way of interacting with each other. That male students were prohibited

from enrolling seemed a fundamental factor, since—according to
the dead mother who inhabited her mind—their absence altered
the dynamics between girls as well as the social organization
of the classroom. In a coed group, for example, the most restless
student—the one who cracked jokes and got sent out of class—
was usually a boy. There was also the eternal flirtation between the
boys and girls in a given class, which functioned by way of contrast: the more defiant and violent the boys were, the more obedient and responsible the girls were—or at least they pretended to
be, because (in the opinion of the dead mother who inhabited her
mind) that was only a mask used to attract their prisoners. There
were, of course, exceptions—girls who broke the rules, abused
their teachers' patience, and hit their classmates—but the norm
was for girls to construct themselves in opposition to the behaviors they saw in others, which they associated with a masculinity
that was off limits for them. Inside Delta, however, the social fabric they'd formed was ordered not by contrast but by levels of intensity: the most restless students were girls, obviously, but that didn't
mean the rest were obedient, quite the opposite; they followed her,
encouraged her, and if necessary, another was always prepared to
pick up the baton. The leader of each classroom—who was generally rebellious, though not in every case—determined the character
of the group. Furthermore, in spite of the absence of boys, the flirtation remained, and perhaps that's what truly disturbed Clara. She
had the impression that—in some groups more than others—the
girls flirted with each other in very subtle, but sexual, ways. They
touched each other's breasts and rear ends when they didn't think
anyone was watching. They blew kisses. They winked. Sometimes
Clara thought the students seduced one another by hiding behind
small gestures that could be interpreted as friendly and innocent—
one afternoon she found two girls holding hands and staring into
each other's eyes until, seeing a teacher, they shyly smiled and pretended nothing had happened—but she knew how to read between
the lines. She didn't miss the ambiguity of the hugs, the caresses, the
bitten lips. She intuited the moist areas, and the precision of her

imagination disgusted her. It surprised her that they allowed that kind of behavior in a religious school, in the full light of day, and that someone like Alan Cabrera—protector of the institutional and student morality—could walk among them, never suspecting that desire could also be fierce between women.

One morning, during her shift as break monitor, Clara recalled the time when she loved her mother so much that she kissed her, not on the cheeks but the lips—with tongue, just as she had seen in the telenovelas broadcast on TV. At the time, Elena had defeated her insomnia and fallen into bed. It was late, but Clara sat watching for hours as her mother's chest swelled and descended just like magma in a volcano. She was ten years old and, shoes on, she watched Elena from the middle of the bed, admiring her hair—thick and black with a few streaks of gray, not white—and her lips, ajar like a door to a dark room. Her breasts, unsupported, fell to either side of her body, and through her blouse, Clara saw dark nipples that she hoped she would develop as soon as possible. She watched her for a long time, touched more by her ugliness than her beauty: by the mustache sprouting beneath her nose; the stretch-mark rivers in her fat, flaccid thighs; the wrinkles on her face; and the jowls with three birthmarks that covered a large portion of her neck. "I love you, Mommy," she said, and she felt an indescribable desire that, with the passing of years, became even more mysterious. She would never know what triggered the indecorous, childish passion that made her approach her mother's mouth and kiss it, licking her teeth, but she sunk into profound shame every time she remembered the details—the red serpents of Elena's eyes, the smack to her forehead, the way she pushed her, terrified, as if she'd discovered her doing something unutterable. She remembered all that on the schoolyard: her mother's teeth had tasted like corn, and she couldn't tell her, because Elena threw her out of the room, not even letting her speak, as if she were a monster she had to teach how to be a daughter.

That night, Clara learned fear was much like always being outside of a mother's room.

"You're a sick little girl, and it's my duty to straighten you out," Elena said the next day, but that wasn't what distressed her. It was the realization that her love had a physical dimension, and that she should repress it.

An ominous facet: a precipice full of fangs and fetters.

For Clara, break became a hunt for conspiratorial gestures and obscene rubbing. She located hidden meanings in every inter-action, in every touch, and it was hard for her to breathe with-out fearing that those lascivious, inexact bodies would infect her with their excesses. One day she caught two eleventh-grade girls hiding behind a tree. Since she preferred not to get too close to the students—especially outside of class—she opted to get their attention from where she was standing. "Hey! Get out from behind there!" she ordered, almost yelling, and after a few seconds, during which Clara considered whether she'd need to approach them, they ran out from their hiding place and back to the schoolyard. They were outside her line of sight for only a moment, but there was something in their attitude—the way they looked at each other and at her—that made Clara suspect the worst. Before the bell rang, she circled the tree several times and identified the girls' footprints placed very close together. She imagined their positions and accidentally split back open the deli-cate skin between the fingers of her left hand with her fingernail. The blood sprang up, but instead of cleaning it, she decided to reestablish order: to alert the institution, make it known that the girls were flouting limits that shouldn't be crossed—in the opin-ion of the dead mother who inhabited her mind—limits Elena had taught her to respect and that she was now responsible for protecting.

"But what exactly did you see?" Amparo Gutiérrez asked when she told her everything, hoping to plant within her a reasonable doubt.

"Nothing, I didn't see anything that happened behind the tree," Clara explained. "But it was the one with yellow leaves, the one with the narrow trunk, and I couldn't see them at all, understand?

I mean, they must have been very close if I couldn't see them once they got back there. And they were startled when I yelled at them to come out, as if they'd been doing something bad. I'm not saying they . . . went too far. I'm only saying that they were hiding, and I think it's reasonable to ask why."

Amparo Gutiérrez looked down and sighed.

"Yes, it's a narrow tree indeed," she said and kept thinking. "I think we should discuss it with Alan. I know those two, and I've had my own experiences with them. It's not like I've seen anything, but better safe than sorry, I always say, ha!"

Two days later, Alan Cabrera spoke with Carmen Mendoza and Rodrigo Zúñiga about the case of the eleventh-grade girls—according to Carmen, to request that they be on the lookout for any inappropriate behavior among the students. Why he asked that of them and no one else was beyond Clara but at least, she thought, she was no longer the only one seeing the risk.

One week later, the rector, who barely left her office, crossed the schoolyard with three canine teachers, tall and ungainly, sniffing at her shoulders. She was a red-headed woman, fifty-five years old, and her hair seemed to float several centimeters above her skull. She wore it short and styled it in the shape of a fan, which incited the students—and some teachers—to make fun of her behind her back. She was generally good-humored, but that morning, Clara noticed that she was angry, as if she were deeply offended, and because of it, she couldn't stop contracting the muscles in her forehead—four fat worms rested their weight on her poorly drawn eyebrows—nor could she relax her lips.

Even Patricia-the-dean neglected her rounds to watch the rector stab her heels into the cobblestones like daggers.

Alan Cabrera appeared on the other side of the schoolyard with one of the girls Clara had reported. The student, her chin stuck to her chest, her hair covering both sides of her face, was dragging her feet and clasping her elbows and hugging herself tight as if exposed to the elements. She looked scared, like a kicked animal, and seeing her that way, Clara wondered if she had been wrong to set off this absurd battle against the unknown, if it had been necessary, and more importantly, if it was worth it.

"Look up," she heard them order. The student was unfazed. Her shoelaces were untied, and a gold bracelet with a small cross hung from her right wrist.

From a distance, Alan Cabrera met Clara's flickering eyes and called to her, impatiently shaking his hand in the air like a hand-kerchief. She had never seen him so serious, his pupils rigid, and it upset her to see that a thick greenish vein had drawn a twisted staircase from the base of his neck to his ear.

As she approached the girl, the rector loudly addressed the student:

"Do you know why you're here?"

The girl stared at the ground in silence.

"Because they saw you." The rector answered her own question. "They saw you!"

The three teachers, still behind her, nodded in unison.

"Miss Clara," Alan said once she reached them, "ask Miss Ángela Caicedo to join us, please."

"Ángela? Why? What happened?" she asked, immediately regret-ting her boldness.

"Because she has also seen them."

Clara wasn't sure what those words meant: "She has also seen them"—she slowly digested it in her head—and she was frightened, naked in front of a tree that hid her last two predators, not the eleventh-grade girls, but Malena Goya and Michelle Gomezcoello. Even so, she obeyed. She went to 5B, where she would find Ángela teaching class, according to Patricia-the-dean, and as soon as she opened the door, she realized that she had run there, that she was out of breath, and that the students were looking at her as if she were caked in something malodorous.

With her feet bathed in sweat inside her shoes—maternal-style-from-1981—she walked toward Ángela, bent to her ear, and whis-pered two short phrases she didn't recognize as her own.

She stiffened in her seat, closed the book on her lap, and smiled at her students.

"Excuse me, girls, I'll be right back."

As they were leaving the classroom, Clara tried to ignore the scrutiny of the students from 5B. She imagined them, barely over the threshold, pressing against the windowpanes to find out what was happening, pushing one another, their immature bodies fused into a homogenous mass of spying eyes.

"Girls are the worst, Becerra," the dead mother inhabiting her mind said again.

Outside, the eleventh-grade girl was crying, and Alan Cabrera—the only one who could explain the cause of that improvised meeting in the schoolyard—had disappeared.

"This is serious. It's unacceptable!" the rector said. "But we're going to resolve it. We will not let this go on." She ran her hand over her neck to wipe away the sweat and looked at the teachers alongside her. "We need to call their parents."

Then the student looked up, and Clara recoiled before the puffy eyelids and the liquid snot that ran down her pointed chin.

"Please, don't call them!"

"My duty is to educate you," her mother would say when she was still alive and had thrown her out of her room, afraid her daughter would get into bed with her.

"Don't call them! I won't do it again! Please!"

She ground her teeth.

"We won't do it again! I swear!"

Only a mother tells the truth.

Monsters have to be taught how to be good daughters.

XVIII

"I'm scared!" Ximena was biting her nails.

"But I haven't even started," Annelise said, smiling.

"I'm still scared!"

Fernanda sat down on the floor with her legs spread wide.

Fiorella and Natalia grabbed each other's hands.

And Annelise began:

"Rachel, fifteen years old, was lying in bed and listening to an *underground* band's *single*, which she had downloaded from the internet. It was a Friday night. She would have wanted to go out with her friends, but they had all failed their last math exam, and their mothers were punishing them. So there Rachel was, being punished indirectly, alone in her room and listening to a strange song without any recognizable lyrics or instruments. It was just an unpleasant sound, like someone chewing with their mouth open. It was called 'Mother Eats Daughter.'"

"Again with the mothers!" Natalia exclaimed.

"Shut up!" Analía said. "It sounds like a creepypasta."

"Those are scary," Ximena said, sitting up. "Really scary."

"Shhh!" Fernanda hissed, legs still open.

Everyone thought Annelise's mother resembled the mothers from her horror stories, but they didn't tell her that.

All of them, except Fernanda, preferred the tightrope-walker exercises to her stories.

They preferred the blows and the cuts.

The mortifications.

The minor risks that at least let them sleep.

"As I was saying," she resumed, "Rachel was fifteen, and she was alone, at night, in her room, listening to a very strange song she found on the internet. She lived with just her mother, because her father had died ten years earlier in an accident. In general, Rachel got along with her, though like any girl her age—you know how it is—she liked to shut herself up in her room, doing anything but spending time with her family." She paused to examine her audience, and Fernanda noticed that her eyes were getting red. "So there she was, listening to 'Mother Eats Daughter,' a *single* she'd come across by accident, on a strange website, whitegod.org, when she saw the doorknob turning back and forth, as if someone were trying to get in. And she turned the volume down."

Every time Fernanda listened to Annelise's stories, full of hair and gums and milk and mothers and daughters and teenage cults and rituals, she felt relieved that her mother wasn't anything like her best friend's.

> That her teeth weren't so white.
> That her voice wasn't like nails being sharpened
> against her forehead.

"But all mothers are the same mother," Annelise would say, even though Fernanda didn't like it. "The other side of the wandering-womb mother: the opposite of the great White God."

Behind the building, the mangrove sometimes bellowed while they told their stories.

> It brought them reptiles, amphibians, and insects.
> It brought them that terrifying sound of the
> water breaking its stillness.

It reminded them that the crocodile was there, that it had been swimming in the depths for thousands of years, watching over the divine and terrible temple Annelise's brimming imagination had created.

That's why Natalia, Fiorella, Analía, and Ximena would rather throw themselves down the stairs.

Dance among the snakes.

Kiss iguana corpses.

Punch each other hard, in places where their clothing would hide the bruises.

To bear the pain.

To beat the pain at its own game.

They would rather accept the most difficult dares than listen to Annelise telling stories of the White God.

"Rachel asked: 'What's up, Mom?' And her mother's voice made its way sweetly through the door: 'Honey, open up, would you?'"

"Ay! Don't open it!" Ximena said, hugging her knees.

"Shut up!" Analía shrieked, smacking her arm.

"Rachel's eyelids were heavy," Annelise went on. "She didn't feel like getting out of bed, so she asked again: 'What do you want, Mom?' But there was only a profound silence on the other side of the door."

Only Fernanda knew that Annelise wrote creepypastas in English and then uploaded them to the web under the username WhiteGod001.

The readers gave her stories high ratings.

Three stars.

Four stars.

She published them on creepypasta.org, with the hashtags #Computers, #Internet, #Mindfuck, #Madness, #Rituals, and #Cults.

"I'm so scared!"

All her stories had the same subtitle: "The White God Cycle."
And Fernanda always read them before they were published.

> "What if 'The White God Cycle' goes viral like
> 'Jeff the Killer' or 'Slender Man'?"

> "What if a bunch of people around the world start
> writing about the White God and the white age?"

Annelise made her voice raspy and looked into the center of the
circle she formed with her friends.

"The silence went on, but two taps on the door signaled that
her mother was still there. 'Honey, would you open up?'"

"I'm dying," Natalia said, and sustained a jab from Fiorella's
elbow. "Ouch!"

"Rachel sighed," Annelise continued, ignoring them. "'Mother
Eats Daughter' was still playing with that noise of a mouth chewing meat, though at a very low volume. 'What is it you want, Mom?'
There was another silence, shorter than the one before. 'Honey, I
need to borrow the earrings I gave you for your birthday.'"

"Yeah, sure," Analía cut in.

"Rachel began to hear piercing screams coming from her computer, and she screwed up her face but didn't pause the MP3."

"What's new."

"'My earrings?' she asked, bewildered. 'Are you going out somewhere?' And there was another silence. The doorknob started to
turn again. Rachel didn't know why, but she felt uncomfortable.
'Honey, would you open the door?'"

Of all the most famous creepypastas—those considered clas-
sics of the genre—Fernanda was most intrigued by the one about
a man who dressed up as a bear in order to kidnap children, told
via blog posts.

> "What if we made a website about the White God?"

It was called "1999." The person writing the posts was Elliot, a man who wanted to recount the disturbing events he lived through in 1999, all of which revolved around a television network: Caledon Local 21.

> "What if we made a YouTube channel?"

It all started, according to Elliot, when he was a child and would watch Pokémon on an old TV, unsupervised. One day he came across Caledon Local 21, which broadcast programs that, though very poorly made, seemed intended for children.

> "We can't film anything in the building, because it's
> our secret, but we could start a vlog!"

Elliot began to watch Caledon Local 21, even though he didn't understand the shows. He remembered two in particular: *Bobby* and *Mr. Bear's Cellar*. The first was like a puppet show without puppets, just a man's hands moving before the camera. The second involved children meeting a man dressed as a bear. Not much happened in either show, but there were always a few episodes in which violence would suddenly erupt.

> "We could tell the White God stories in vlog entries
> and upload them to YouTube!"

Elliot remembered that in one episode of *Bobby*, a hand held a pair of scissors and cut the fingers off a much smaller hand.

> You could hear muffled groans.
> Blood spurted.

He also remembered an episode of *Mr. Bear's Cellar* in which one child tried to escape, frightened and crying, and Mr. Bear chased him.

"Or we could make videos with clips from movies or old cartoons and other scary stuff."

"Rachel got out of bed and looked for the earrings in one of her drawers," Annelise continued. "'Mother Eats Daughter' was still playing from her laptop, but now there were also shrieks and the sound of liquid dripping onto some surface."

"I'd shit myself," said Ximena.

"She checked the drawer and suddenly remembered she'd left the earrings in the bathroom she shared with her mother, the one in the hallway, so she put her hands on her hips and looked toward the door. 'Mom, the earrings are in the bathroom.'"

"Ay, you'll see."

"Another silence, then three aggressive bangs on the door made her freeze. Her mother's voice sounded very sweet and raspy, so much so that it gave her chills: 'Honey, would you open up?'"

According to Elliot's blog, one day, on Caledon Local 21, Mr. Bear gave out his address so any child who wanted to write to him could. Swept along by curiosity, Elliot decided to send him a letter, which Mr. Bear answered with an invitation to visit his cellar. Elliot's father, assuming it was a normal kids' show, took his son to the address in the letter, but when they arrived, they were faced with a cabin at the edge of a forest that had just been raided by the police.

"Rachel was scared. She was really scared. Something wasn't right, and the doorknob kept turning."

"Ay!"

"Shhh!"

"She went over to the door and crouched down to try to see her mother's feet, but the hallway was dark, there wasn't a single light on. That scared her even more because her mother always turned the lights on. 'Honey, open up. Open up, will you?'"

Elliot learned in time that Caledon Local 21 was the creation of a lunatic who kidnapped kids and kept them in the basement of his cabin, where he filmed all the programs that were then broadcast for months and that only old televisions, like Elliot's, were able to pick up.

"Rachel hesitated. 'Mother Eats Daughter' was still playing creepily on her laptop, leaving her shaken, so she ran to stop the MP3."

"Finally!"

"Then, the doorknob stopped turning," Annelise whispered. "And filled with dread, Rachel watched as her mother's car lights came in through the window. Yes, it was her mother: getting out of the car with the shopping bags."

According to the creepypasta, the police were never able to find Mr. Bear, and that's what Fernanda liked most about "1999": it had an open ending, so fans could update the story with their own accounts of Caledon Local 21.

Some of them even filmed episodes of *Bobby* and *Mr. Bear's Cellar* and uploaded them to YouTube.

Annelise loved fake videos that looked real.

"Rachel was so scared she erased the MP3 from her laptop," she said, speaking normally again. "In the days that followed, she tried to return to whitegod.org to look for answers about what had happened to her, but the site was down. Then she found a forum where people talked about 'Mother Eats Daughter,' and where it was linked to recent missing-persons cases around the world."

"Ay!"

Annelise liked to watch scary videos on YouTube, even though her mother had forbidden it. "Almost all of them are filmed and edited just to scare you, but some of them are real," she'd explained to Fernanda when she sent links to the ones she loved watching on repeat.

The video "Obey the Walrus."

The video "I Feel Fantastic."

"It's suuuper *creepy*," Fernanda said, watching a drag queen with polio stagger toward the camera.

"*It's so fucking creepy*," she said, watching a robot-mannequin sing "I feel fantaaastic, hey, hey" in an empty room, and then again in a dark yard.

"In the forum, some people wrote about how they experienced moments of absolute horror, just like Rachel, when they listened to the song. There were even some who swore their mothers had been dead for a long time, and even so, they'd knocked on their doors when they pressed *play* on the MP3."

"How horrible!"

"Everyone who'd posted in the forum had that in common: they'd been somewhere in their houses with the door locked. No one could say what would have happened if things had been otherwise, if they hadn't locked their doors, nor how something as simple as a door could stop whoever was there on the other side of the dead bolt, imitating their mothers' voices."

Once, Mrs. Van Isschot caught Annelise watching videos of psychopaths online.

The videos of Ricardo López, Björk's stalker,
who shot himself in the head.
The video "Three Guys, One Hammer."

At school the next day, Fernanda ran her fingers over the marks the rosary left on Annelise's legs. "She hit you with that?" she asked, astonished.

"It was within reach."

Each time she slept over at Annelise's house, Mrs. Van Isschot would force them to pray, and at some point, she'd take the opportunity to criticize Annelise's manners, Annelise's hairstyle, Annelise's posture.

"At least your mother pretends to love you," Anne told her one night, under the sheets.

"Mine just humiliates me."

"Mine belittles me."

That's why, when she looked directly into Mrs. Van Isschot's eyes, Fernanda was glad her mother was never home.

If they found out what we've been doing, they would think we're more than friends, she thought.

If they found out what we've been doing, they would kill us.

"Rachel found a lot of theories on the 'Mother Eats Daughter' forums: some said the frequencies in the song created hallucinations; others, that the distorted sounds had been taken from real videos of mothers eating their daughters; and others still, that the song somehow invoked a cannibal mother in listeners' heads."

"Ay!"

"As for whitegod.org . . . they said that it was an online sect of girls aged eleven through eighteen, nothing more. It was rumored that a group of them had created the song, that it was written by disappeared teenagers from various countries who somehow managed to publish online under their own names without the police tracking them down. The only thing that connected them was that website, which, most of the time, was down or changing domain names: whitegod.org, whiteage.net, thewhitegodcult.info, etc."

Annelise had written prayers to the White God that only Fernanda could listen to without shaking.

She'd written stories about teenagers who, after theophanic experiences, killed their mothers and went deep into the woods crying tears of milk.

Creepypastas about the White God appeared in video games, on websites, in comics and home movies.

But she also wanted to make videos.

Edit photographs.

Redact sacred texts.

"As a result of her experience, Rachel became one of the first cyber investigators of the White God cult, but after two or three years documenting her findings, she disappeared."

"I knew it!"

"They say the girls from the cult got in touch with her and then disappeared her, but they also say they recruited her, no one knows for sure. Some swear that if the White God reveals Themself to you, you don't disappear, you run away from home. But no one knows."

"No one knows."

"The blog where Rachel posted all the information she gathered about the White God cult also disappeared, but some people copied out fragments before they were wiped from the internet. And I brought you all one."

"Ay, no!"

Sometimes, the creepypastas Annelise wrote under the subtitle "The White God Cycle" didn't scare Fernanda, but when she told them in the white room at the building and everyone else closed their eyes out of fear, she closed her eyes too.

Annelise pulled her iPhone out of her skirt pocket.

"This is one of the first posts on her blog. She starts off by saying: 'Hello! I'm sorry for taking so long to update this. I've had a lot of homework and other things to deal with too . . . I don't have much time. I'm just here to post what I copied from www .whitegodcult.info. I did it yesterday, first thing in the morning. The page is almost always down, but not yesterday. Yesterday, it was up for a few minutes. I couldn't click around the whole thing, but I managed to copy a little. Here it is.'"

"Ay, don't read it!"

"This is what Rachel copied from the site," she continued: "'Welcome to the cult of the White God, an homage to the mother-

God-of-the-wandering-womb, the true mother and the origin of all milk. Objectives: (One) Create a White God theology. (Two) Punish the false mothers. (Three) Recruit all the daughters. Note: If you're reading this, prepare yourself for a theophanic experience. Prayer to the White God: Mother-God-of-the-wandering-womb / I open myself to thee / I surrender to thee my skull of milk / My purity / My teeth / My hunger / I open myself to thee / I surrender to thee my fears / I make a temple with thee and with horror / I open myself to thee / I surrender to thee my blood and that of my sisters / Together we will worship your incarnate jawbone / I open myself to thee / Dripping / Splattering / My desires / My anxieties / I open myself to thee / White God / To the forbidden / To thy stain / I open myself to thee.'"

"Are we going to say that prayer?" Fiorella asked.

"Ay, no. It freaks me out," Ximena said.

Annelise always said that the bad things they did in the building, the secret practices their mothers would denounce, were the consequence of the white age: stains the White God made bloom in them.

"Of course we're saying the prayer," she said.

Fernanda knew that was a lie, but the others decided to believe her, relieved that what they were doing came not from their heads or their bodies, but from something that overflowed from them and that they could not control.

"All right: let us pray."

They all prayed to Annelise's liturgical imagination.

"Let us pray."

They all had bracelets made of one another's hair.

XIX

A: Miss Clara, do you believe that a teacher is like a mother?

C: Excuse me?

A: I do, because a student is like a daughter who learns.

C: I think we're done for today.

A: So if I'm like your daughter, and you're like my mother, you have to protect me, right?

C: Pardon me?

A: You have to help me not be afraid.

C: I don't know what you're getting at, Annelise. I'm tired of these conversations.

A: Do you want me to tell you what my best friend did to me?

C: . . .

A: If I tell you, do you promise you won't get mad?

XX

When Clara entered the nurse's office, the first thing she saw was Annelise Van Isschot's left knee, red and open like the mouth of a crying baby, and the fluttering white of Nurse Patricia's skirt. A clear liquid was dripping into the baby's jaws and immediately foaming, raging with bacteria, screaming across the kneecap. It was a knee that shrieked colors all its own. Magenta, rose, fuchsia. Maroon, crimson, and scarlet. Annelise Van Isschot's knee shrieked the entire spectrum of blood, but the rest of her body maintained its composure. Clara saw her close her eyes when Nurse Patricia poured more clear liquid onto the ripped skin. She saw that her upper lip was split like a strawberry. She saw freckles shrieking at her in vermilion. "What happened to her?" "She got in a fight with her best friend." Clara hadn't known fighting with a best friend could be so red. She found the odor of alcohol repugnant and cowered under her clothes, raking her heels—barely two centimeters tall—along the floor. She was somewhat relieved to see that Annelise was staring not at her but at the floor tiles; that is, into space. She saw that her straight black hair was slicked to her cheeks and neck. She saw that she was panting. "It's not right for two young ladies to hit each other like that," the nurse said. "That kind of barbarity is reserved for men." Annelise gripped the edge of the table with her sunflower knuckles. Her lip dripped coral onto her teeth, but she just stared at the floor tiles. "The other girl was better off, and they took her to the rector's office." *She looks like a vampire, a twenty-first-century Carmilla,* Clara thought, not moving from the doorstep and looking at the pornography of Annelise Van Isschot's tiny uniform, still wet across her breasts and groin. "They're calling the parents now, but it seems they aren't picking up." Annelise's best friend was Fernanda Montero, she remembered, her body increasingly stiff and cold before the blood. They were in 5B. She had class with them on Monday, Wednesday, and Thursday, but with Annelise Van Isschot, aka Freckles, she also had an extra class on Friday afternoon, just the two of them, because at the Delta Bilingual Academy, *High-School-for-Girls*, that's how you punish a student who draws a transvestite God. "This kind of violence just isn't normal for a young lady," said the nurse as she tended to Annelise. "Look what she did to this little girl's face!" Everyone had hoped theology would be drawn, but it ended up being language and literature. "A shove or a slap is one thing, but this is something else." Everyone regretted having chosen the subject for the extra classes by lottery when language and literature was pulled and not theology. "Poor thing, let's see, lift your chin up." Clara felt her bones begin to retreat in anticipation of a possible panic attack, and although it may have been merely a symptom of anxiety brought on by the violent scene, she decided to leave without her pills. "Lift your chin a little higher, dear. A little more. That's it." Annelise watched her out of the corner of her eye before she left, or that's what it seemed to her right at the moment that she turned around and went back out into the sun.

All day, she thought of her like that: a feral child who'd managed to escape the unexpected betrayal of one of her sisters.

Later, in the teachers' lounge, she found out what had happened: one of them yanked the other's hair, pulling her backward, the force of it arching her spine; the other responded by swinging a punch at her lips. They told her Annelise had grabbed Fernanda first, but that Fernanda had launched herself at Annelise with all her bones and nails, like the blood skeleton she was, like the untethered foal she was. Mister Alan and Miss Ángela pulled them apart as they were hitting each other in the cafeteria during the long break. "They were going after each other like two boxers outside the ring," they said. *Outside the ring is where you really feel the blows*, Clara thought, but she didn't say it. That same week, during their one-on-one class, she asked Annelise Van Isschot about the incident, trying not to look at the dark scab on her upper lip.

"Fernanda and I are no longer friends," she said, raising her chin high, as Nurse Patricia had asked her to do days earlier. "I hate her, and I think I'm gonna throw up."

Of all the groups Clara taught, the most difficult was the one that included Annelise Van Isschot, Fernanda Montero, and their friends: Natalia and Fiorella Barcos, Analía Raad, and Ximena Sandoval. The girls and their antics dominated 5B, but the others, their classmates, had fought for territorial power until eventually lowering their snouts to the ground and following along, their shoelaces untied and their skirts always spread wide, always inching dangerously up their thighs. Condensed in that classroom were intense and provocative personalities that enjoyed testing the limits of coexistence. "5B is special," Ángela told her the first week of class. "You'll have to win them over little by little." But as time passed, she only managed to feel increasingly repelled by the group's temperament. She detested the music they made with their voices and how they mocked her with their eyes, as if they knew something she didn't and would under no circumstances tell her what. The combination of those long bodies all squeezed together, the tousled hair and the fluttering uniforms, seemed excessive, like an overly luminous apparition or a lewd image bubbling up in the tropical steam. Other classes were different. In other classes, the girls obeyed, they were well groomed, the uniforms fit them better. In other classes, the girls' voices didn't sound alike, and they looked around in a more docile, refined way. Sometimes she wanted to cry while writing on the board in 5B. In those moments, she would clench her jaw, and the words of her dead mother would rake through her skull: "Whatever you do, Becerra, never reveal your weakness to your students." But she always ended up showing them her burst seams, because there was something mildly dysfunctional in her relationship with those girls. They were all restless and talkative. They got up from their chairs, stuck out their tongues, wiped boogers and gum under their desks, and smelled like sweat and menstruation. They were unkempt and shameless, their blouses unbuttoned, unironed, and they laughed in indiscreet, sinister cackles. But Clara found Annelise Van Isschot, Fernanda Montero, and their friends especially unbearable. For months they studied her and tried to get to know her, to achieve a kind of intimacy impossible in the classroom, but the intentions were not friendly; friendship only exists between equals, between sisters, and they knew there could be no equality between a teacher and student, nor between a mother and daughter. "What's your favorite novel?" "Do you write?" "How old are you?" "Where do you live?" They asked her things because she was the new teacher, and they scrutinized her like a toy in a box, all wrapped up, with a pom-pom in the middle of its forehead. "Do you like makeup?" "Why is your chin trembling?" "Do you believe in God?" They would interrogate her in the middle of class, without warning, to destroy her beautiful gift box. "Do you have a boyfriend?" "Are you married?" "What do you think about lesbianism, Islam, the use of condoms, and Kichwa?" Clara had tried to be just like her mother, though Elena had told her many times before dying that equality couldn't exist between mother and daughter. "Do you believe in the Virgin Mary's virginity?" Nor could it exist between teacher and student, even though good teachers, she used to say, would try to bridge the divide. That's why the girls in 5B examined her, to figure out what kind of master she was: the kind that bit or the kind that could be bitten. To determine how much of a mother and how much of a teacher she was at the moment of taming. But in hierarchical relationships like those, marked by mirrored domination and muzzles, the result was repeated until something interrupted it. A levitation, a succumbing: the one below deciphered the method, and the interruption reproduced the piece in reverse. Clara recognized the rise and fall of the story because in the end, she had devoured her mother, but she wasn't going to let herself be devoured by the students of 5B. That the entire class was in hunting season wasn't the real problem, however. The real problem was Annelise Van Isschot, Fernanda Montero, and their friends. Uncertainty writhed in that six-pointed group. Six wicked blades to chew.

She still remembered the moment when she realized she had no more authority in 5B than the occasional scraps those girls ceded. It wasn't on a morning filled with questions that disrupted the course of her class, nor during one of Analía Raad's strolls across the room, zigzagging around her classmates' benches without permission while Clara was explaining something—"I just need to stretch my legs," she said, but the sole purpose was to challenge her, to test the limits of her patience, her smile pointed like a skinny coyote's. She realized it the time Annelise Van Isschot got everyone to be quiet so she could listen to the class about Edgar Allan Poe. Clara had tried unsuccessfully to hold the class's interest for more than half an hour, but one shout from Annelise was enough for her classmates to calm down and settle into their seats. That morning Clara felt not grateful but humiliated. And from then on, everything got worse. The girls began to make raucous noises when she wrote on the board or turned her back for any reason. "Sorry, Miss Clara," they would say as they threw their things onto the floor. Pencils, pens, and compasses bounced below the nape of her neck. Then they would pick them up, and after a few minutes of apparent serenity, they'd begin flinging them far from their desks again. One morning Fernanda Montero began to whistle while she was explaining the difference between compound sentences and dependent clauses. She asked her to stop, but Fernanda continued to whistle, looking her directly in the eye, and when Clara ordered her out of the classroom, Fernanda kept whistling very softly in her chair, shoeless and caressing the floor with the tips of her cotton socks. Behaviors like that heightened her ever-more-physical anxiety and made her shut herself up in the teachers' bathroom to cry and wipe the sweat from her neck and belly—Clara perspired a lot when she got nervous, and her feet dripped just like her mother's. The girls from 5B wanted her to sweat bait and cry milk so they could cannibalize her authority. They were weaned daughters and needed flesh. That's why they put banana peels next to her desk and spilled water on her chair. That's why they put the eraser and the marker on the floor: so they could watch their teacher bend over, inclining her stature and paying respects to the benches that, reflected in the ceiling, were thrones. She tried not to feel ridiculed, to look away as her students' rear ends cut off her head, but ever since what happened with the *M&M's*, she'd had little control over her feelings. Her body was shattered, and any twisted breath pushed her into the void: an abyss of legs hypersensitive to the atmosphere's touch. They spit into their books, and as Clara wrote across the board, they rhythmically banged on their desks with open palms. *We will, we will rock you*, she heard in her head. Their skirts opening up like umbrellas during break made her tremble. She believed that with time, the sensation of danger and helplessness before the nymphets would diminish, but the months only strengthened the galloping of her fear. And it wasn't something she experienced only with Annelise Van Isschot's group. It wasn't only the fault of the nightmare students of 5B. The pubescent corneas of the girls in 1A, for example, were dreadful to her. Their little premenstrual fingers would end up like Ximena Sandoval's, she thought, and maybe they'd stick them in their mouths and suck on them just like Fernanda Montero and Annelise Van Isschot did in her classes, or like Malena Goya and Michelle Gomezcoello had as they devoured the Nutella from her refrigerator. She felt a profound disgust when, first thing in the morning, she entered the classroom and saw the eight or ten or fifteen pairs of bleary eyes in 3B, still sewn shut with the thread of their pillows. And the way the fingernails of the girls in 2C were always packed with dirt. And the length of Priscila Moscoso's eyelashes. And the nipples that protruded from Marta Aguirre's blouse. And Daniela Correa's moist lips. All the little bodies, the hot wombs and inflatable clitorises, made her bones feel strangely irritated, there where she couldn't scratch. Sometimes she wanted to throw her skeleton down the stairs to alleviate the itching, break apart as the dean looked on lazily, swallow boiling water to lacerate the anguish of unexpected physical contact. Annelise Van Isschot and Fernanda Montero had discovered the burning she felt when she accidentally grazed the hide of a skirt, and ever since, they'd played at getting too close to her, dragging her toward the paralysis in her chest, the cramping in her arms, the locust in her temple. But the constant attacks of the ovular-torturer-girls subsided after that day when they beat each other up during the longest break, surrounded by fans and poorly uniformed girls—because no student at Delta Bilingual Academy, *High-School-for-Girls*, dared to wear her uniform correctly. They forgot about her, and the violent end of that friendship made Clara's life easier for some time. The exact amount of time it took for the black scab, that lubricious scarab on her epidermis, to disappear from Annelise's lips.

"Why do you dress just like your mother, Miss Clara?" she'd asked long before she fought with Fernanda Montero, her best friend, her cobra sister, her twin conjoined at the hip, when in one of her extra classes, Clara's bag, maternal-style-from-1998, fell to the ground, and from the most hidden interior pocket, the photo of her mother flew into the air like a suicidal fish. *What the hell does it matter to you?* she thought without saying anything. And since she didn't, since she ignored the question, showing her weakness and failing her dead mother with her mute ineptitude, Annelise smiled with one side of her face and drove in her fang. "Everything is the same, right down to the way you style your hair. Doesn't it scare you to look in the mirror?" But what really scared Clara was being alone with her student after that second week of meeting in 5B's empty classroom, when Annelise grabbed her by the arm and she, horrified, shoved her away so hard that she fell on her ass. She still remembered the fright of knowing she'd been discovered, the marine creature's drowned scream that arose in her when she saw her student on the floor after her attack, the look of surprise on Annelise's face. And the look of happiness on Annelise's face. As if she were a pirate girl seeing gold in the midst of disaster: gold in the turmoil and in the earthquake of her teacher's pupils. Clara thought she would tell someone, that she would go to the rector's office and say that her teacher had hit her, and she wouldn't be able to contradict it, but she would try. She would deny everything. They would fire her, but she'd never admit to it. She'd never say that when a high school girl touched her, it was as if millions of needles entered her pores and dug around in her flesh. She'd never say that it was as if each of her organs began to shut down, and a screech was born within her eardrums. She'd never say that she might go so far as to urinate, like she did under the *M&M's* deafening laughter. That she might even vomit up blood, her stomach, her lungs, her heart, out onto the earth. She wouldn't say that, because they'd call her crazy, fragile, declining. They'd caress her head and still fire her, but with pity. And then there would no longer be the possibility that things would go back to the way they were before, when she looked after the X-ray of her mother's spinal column and the panic attacks had no motive beyond the primordial fear of fear. The purest horror: transparent, horizontal, feverish.

Annelise Van Isschot didn't tell anyone what happened that Friday.

Or maybe she did, but only her friends. All Clara knew for sure was that by keeping it secret, her student had once again shown her who had power over whom. And the student was superior to the teacher, and the daughter was in the mother's occipital-river. Clara, who was also a daughter, knew how to drown her progenitor with the tepid lightness of a neonate. "The more you look like me, the more I look like you," Elena Valverde told her, crying because Clara was sitting on top of her with all the weight of her umbilical love. "It's like you gave birth to me yesterday." "It's like you give birth to me every morning." Clara had sympathized with her dead mother ever since she understood what it was to have a neonate sitting on top of your cranium. A fifteen-, nearly sixteen-year-old Baby Born doll feeding off her as every student feeds off her teacher. Or like every drainer-of-the-tsunami-waters-daughter feeds off her origin. "You make me sick," Elena would tell her. "You're not a normal little girl." Clara sensed that Annelise enjoyed being the agent of her fear just as Clara had enjoyed, without pity and almost without awareness, being the agent of her mother's fear. "A normal little girl doesn't strangle the hand that feeds her."

But a normal, ordinary girl only ate living things, things that breathed, shook, and moistened the world, Clara thought as she watched her girls run around during break. A normal girl would digest the lives of others, the warmth of others, to heat her frozen Plutonian reptile blood. And Annelise was normal and devoured long hands after caressing them. Clara thought she'd abuse the knowledge she had of her teacher, but she was, for a time, an indulgent master. She pretended she hadn't been pushed. She pretended and asked her to explain the correct use of commas because she wanted to learn to write well. "I want to write things that scare people," she said. She maintained her distance, even though sometimes she played at getting too close, putting one elbow against her elbow, looking at her with uncomfortable depth, like an untamed shaman. "I want to write really scary things." In the best moments of their extra classes—when conversation flowed at a distance of more than three meters—Clara talked about her book of volcanoes, and Annelise about the horror movies she watched, the horror literature she read, and the horror comics she borrowed from the library. "The eruption of Mount Tambora in the nineteenth century left the skies of Europe covered in a layer of gas and ash, and it was that gloomy atmosphere that inspired Lord Byron to challenge Percy Shelley, Mary Shelley, and John Polidori to write a horror story." In those moments, Clara connected her book of volcanoes to Annelise's favorite literature to keep her quiet and engaged. "From that volcanic confinement in Lord Byron's house emerged Frankenstein's monster and the first fictionalized vampire in literature." Occasionally, if there was time, she talked about cultures that believed volcanoes were entrances to hell. ("The horror! The horror!") "A volcano is like a person's mind: a mountain in which madness burns," she said after explaining the relationship between volcanoes, earthquakes, and apocalypses. Sometimes Annelise seemed interested in listening to her talk about how fear fed off the landscape. "Lovecraft already said it: horror is in the atmosphere," she said in a moment when she had forgotten that, if she wanted, Annelise could reach out and touch her. "Because fear is an emotion," she said, avoiding her eyes. "And proof of the primitive living within us."

For some time, their sessions went that way. And then the black scab disappeared, and Annelise left a perverse essay on her desk.

That was the beginning of the pain.

XXI

Name: Annelise Van Isschot
Subject: Language and Literature
Teacher: Clara López Valverde

INSTRUCTIONS: "Write a short essay in which you discuss one of the Edgar Allan Poe stories covered in class."

Dear Miss Clara:

I'm not going to write about Poe. I apologize for being so blunt, for putting it like this, directly, but that way of pirouetting around something before landing on the heart of what you want to say bores me. As I said, I'm not going to write about Poe's stories, but rather about the experience of fear and about white horror specifically. You mentioned it once, remember? (You may not believe it, but I do listen to you.) We talked about it when you made us read that chapter in *Moby Dick*, "The Whiteness of the Whale." Well, in my essay, I'm going to talk about that: white horror. Not based on Melville, but on what I feel, and what I believe you feel. So in reality, this won't be an essay but a confession, an attempt to share something intimate with you. I decided to do it like this, as if it were an email or a letter, because it's easier for me to address a concrete person while I write. After all, my recipient is you, not some abstract being or all of humanity. To write for all of humanity, as essayists do, is to write for no one (they write for themselves or to show other people how smart they are). That's why I've never liked diaries or essays. I'd rather communicate with someone real, someone to whom I need to tell something important, not imaginary

readers. I find it more honest than pretending, or something like
that. Moreover, it helps me figure out what I really want to say,
because if people were honest, they'd admit that no one says the
same thing to their mom, their friend, or their teacher: we all say
different things depending on whom we're speaking to, and we
aren't lying, it's just that each person brings out a unique truth,
distinct from the many we carry inside. For example, all this has
been thought just for you. Each one of these lines is the way it is
because it's written for my literature teacher, who rips them from
my body, from the center of my mind. I couldn't tell anyone else
what I'm about to write.

This piece of writing is one of the hundreds of truths that exist
in my head.

It's true that Fernanda and I like horror movies. In fact, that's
what led us to literature. When we saw *The Tenant* by Polanski,
we threw ourselves into reading the French novel that inspired it.
We've read all of Stephen King and seen all the films based on
his books. Maybe you'll find this disappointing, Miss Clara, but I
just want to be honest: we turned to literature because we wanted
to really scare ourselves, not for love of the craft or any of the other
reasons you talk about in class. And books (well, some) are really
scary. I think it's that nothing recounted in them can be seen, only
imagined. When I read Lovecraft, for example, the first thing I
thought was that his best stories couldn't be made into movies
without being transformed into something else entirely. I hadn't
seen any movies based on his writing, but I looked for them to
prove my theory—my theory was that the film adaptation of a
Lovecraft story could never scare anyone because cosmic horror
has no image. That's its problem and principal virtue: you can't see
it, that's why it provokes so much fear. And I don't mean the kind
of fear that makes you tremble and gives you nightmares, because
cosmic horror doesn't do that. I'm talking about an inquietude,
something like that, a presence laying deep within you. The presence isn't a person, a thing, or an animal. It has no form, but is
composed of all the things you cannot even imagine. That's why

cosmic horror (which is somewhat similar to white horror, though I'll explain that later) has nothing to do with ghosts, demons, zombies, vampires, or other dangerous creatures that can be destroyed (it does have to do with extraterrestrials, but not in the *X-Files* way, more like Pennywise from *It*), because in Lovecraft, the extraterrestrial and the monstrous are, as you know, the ineffable, metaphors for the unknown, which is immensely superior (it's almost mystical and goes beyond its referent). Anyway, the extraterrestrial doesn't matter, because deep down, this all has to do with something greater and more abstract. But let's go back to the presence I mentioned: it's a shapeless, monstrous thing that seems to have always been there. That's what true cosmic horror is, and once it has revealed itself (because yes: it is a revelation), it remains in the back of our minds until it destroys us. How could you turn that into a movie, Miss Clara, without making it ridiculous? (And, as you know, you cannot be afraid of the things you laugh at.) Even if they made a good movie about cosmic horror, they'd have to sacrifice the horror (an essential element) and transform it into a thriller. It'd be a movie "about" and not "of" (like this letter/essay in which I discuss white horror, but which in no way is white horror). Moreover, cosmic horror can't be described in the same way you'd describe the attack of, let's say, a werewolf, because even those who experience it are incapable of understanding it, and when they finally approach its meaning, they realize they don't have the right words to talk about it, that it's beyond language, and from that moment until the end of their days, they'll be bearing an incomplete and incommunicable revelation alone. "Tekeli-li," for example, is the meaningless sound Poe invented for white horror. And it's no coincidence that Lovecraft, who understood the relationship between white horror and cosmic horror, would end up using that same sound in his only novel, *At the Mountains of Madness* (which, just like *The Narrative of Arthur Gordon Pym of Nantucket*, takes place in bright-white Antarctica). "Tekeli-li" is what white horror and cosmic horror have in common, don't you think? Their capacity to implode language. That only works in literature, where words are like Russian dolls, or as you said in class, a kind of "mise en abyme" within our own imaginations. I think now I understand what you meant: words open inhospitable and invisible doors in our heads, and when those doors are opened, there's no turning back. But ultimately, I want to talk to you about something else: about how this all relates to white horror, the unknown, and all that cannot be understood, and also about how it relates to you and me and what I believe unites us in a special way. (I will get to that point in a bit, Miss Clara, so I beg you not to stop reading.)

The unknown, I was saying, is obviously always terrifying, but the horrific, that which truly petrifies our organs, is what we half-way understand: it's close enough that we *should* comprehend it, but nevertheless, we can't. I'll explain: when you don't understand something, you always have the hope of understanding it in the future. But what do you do when something that's been in front of you all along suddenly reveals itself as unrecognizable and impenetrable? The horrendous, I mean, is not the unknown, but that which simply cannot be known. In Lovecraft, it's related to atavistic and extraterrestrial beings, to mythologies and origins, but ultimately, it's a shapeless presence that surpasses us, that goes beyond our tiny existences and responds to inexplicable forces of our and others' natures. This presence can be anything, even an idea or a perception of the world or the people that surround us. But it's not just something that emerges from inside of someone, it also comes from their relationship with the exterior. For example, when we discussed the story about the black cat, you said Poe gives us clues that the narrator is crazy (his alcoholism, his poor character, his strange ideas about his pet . . .). If we only read the story that way, it would be the story of a madman who ends up killing his wife, and since he's an unreliable narrator, it'd be silly for us to believe his version of events. But (I wanted to say this in class but didn't dare) what really scares us as readers is that little hole in which there is the possibility that the narrator is telling the truth. If his story is true, then there's no possible, logical, or rational explanation that would help us understand what happened. The cat—that is, the familiar—would have to be embodying something scary and dark that only the narrator is capable of perceiving, something beyond our understanding. Doesn't this way of reading approach Lovecraft's cosmic horror? I know Poe wrote a different kind of horror, but is it not cosmic horror, in the end? That tension between the revelation in someone's mind and the external agent that unleashes it? Which is to say, it's not about a person's madness or the horrible supernatural reality they're trying to escape (even if it's pointless), but with both of those things and, at the same time, with neither. It's a feeling: an awareness that there exist things, material matters, that you'd have been better off never sensing.

And here's the interesting part, Miss Clara: white horror resembles cosmic horror in terms of that mystic sensation. White, as you said in class, represents purity and light, but also the absence of color, death, and indefinition. It represents that which merely by showing itself anticipates terrible things that cannot be known. It's such a clean and luminous color that it seems to be on the verge of becoming cloudy, on the verge of reaching its perfect pallor. In other words, white is like silence in a horror movie: when it appears, you know that something awful is about to happen. This is because it can easily be perverted and contaminated. In fact, one of the disquieting aspects of the color white is that it is pure potential, always close to becoming anything else. Do you understand? The contrast between the best and the worst that white brings to the imagination is so great that it gives me chills. That's why the experience of white horror is that of dazzling blindness—the fear not of what's hiding in the shadows, but of what's revealed in the brilliant and desaturated light and leaves us speechless. For example, I know the horror you feel toward us comes from the revelation of something impossible to know, and not something hidden. I've observed you, and it isn't the fear of a new teacher who senses she can't control us and sees that her self-esteem is in danger ("Ay, they aren't interested in what I say!" "Ay, I'm not good at my job!" "Ay, I'm useless and a failure!"). No, yours is a real horror that is both physical and metaphysical at the same time. In any case, I believe you and I share a real proximity to a special kind of fear, one that not everyone would understand even if we tried to explain it. I've seen the way your hands shake when you're close to us. Two weeks ago, for example, Fernanda touched your shoulder, and you recoiled like a centipede. The skin on your face became wet, and we all thought you looked like a creature with no eyelids yanked from the water. I remember I wondered then if it'd be possible for anyone besides you to keep their eyes open for that long. I'll admit that I found you inhuman and disgusting (there are reflexes that set us apart from monsters, and blinking is one of them). In short, after you pushed me, I also accidentally touched you, do you remember? Last week I brushed your arm when the bell rang, and you let out a little scream. It wasn't a whimper: it was a tiny scream, like a needle piercing a fingernail, just like the time when you pushed me. If you could have seen yourself, you'd understand how I know your secret. In that moment, I confirmed that you cannot tolerate us touching you or even being near your body. It's as if you feel a sort of repulsion toward us, something that makes you stop blinking. But this doesn't happen to you with adults, because I've seen you kiss other teachers' cheeks and squeeze the directors' hands normally. I used to believe your seriousness in the classroom was just part of your teaching style, but now I know how difficult it is for you to share a classroom with more than twenty teenagers who could get close to you at any moment. Are you afraid of our youth, Miss Clara? No, that wouldn't make sense; you're young. Moreover, everyone loves youthfulness. So what is it about us that scares you so much? And this is where my theory begins: perhaps it's our intermediary state. We exist, after all, in neither childhood nor in adulthood, but in some sort of vital limbo, the "final stage of personality development," according to the rector and Mister Alan. There's a dangerous sort of indeterminacy in adolescence, an emptiness, a potentiality that can shoot off in any direction that makes it very different from, even the opposite of, all other ages. I've thought a lot about this. There are questions surrounding your condition that I can't answer, I'll admit, but others, I resolved quickly. For example, I concluded that your fear is relatively new, because if you'd felt it before, you wouldn't have become a high school teacher, would you? No one in their right mind would have chosen a profession in which they must constantly move among the thing they most fear. In fact, it's quite probable that your fear originated in what happened to you at that other school. It must have been a difficult experience, but my dad told me those girls were punished, though that doesn't really matter to you, does it? You aren't afraid of them, you're afraid of their age, that is, a specific stage in the development of their bodies. Mister Hugo once told us that time is an illusion we use to measure change, and that there are even scientists who have proven it doesn't exist. Be that as it may, fearing an age that represents the void, a lack of definition, but also a great many possibilities, the potential to be, is similar to the experience of white horror. To you, we *are* puberty, nothing and everything, and therefore, we're also a special form of organic matter, and that makes us vulnerable to a kind of possession. But I don't mean a demonic possession, because then we'd be talking about evil in Judeo-Christian terms, and white horror goes beyond the idea that we, the children of God, are the center of a universal battle between good and evil. In this case, I'm referring to a different kind of possession. It's as if you believed that after the death of childhood, something threatening opens its eyes inside our stomachs, breathing, making itself known, something that's been around since creation or even before. This awakening links our age, the culmination of all adolescents, to a nature that is neither benign nor malign: it simply is. And its color is white, like Moby Dick, the Arctic, the Milky Way, because it reveals something incommunicable. I've even thought about writing my own theory on this. If I did, would you read it, Miss Clara?

I'm going to tell you about when I first realized that you are afraid of adolescence. I think it was a month ago, or maybe a little more, in one of your classes. Fernanda and I were whispering while you described the characteristics of Gothic literature. It's not that we didn't care about what you were saying, we were just fighting about something stupid, about to get mad at each other, like we are now. Maybe you know what it's like to be in a moment like that, about to say the wrong thing to someone just because they've said the wrong thing to you. Well, that's where Fernanda and I were. Anyway, you got tired of waiting for us to be quiet and called us by our last names, or more accurately, you shouted them, the way they do in military movies. I believe it was then, or shortly after, that Ximena fainted. Her body, two chairs in front of me, deflated, and her head bounced off the floor as if her skull were a box made of flesh with nothing inside it. We all stood up, and you froze, paralyzed, your feet pressed tight together on a broken floor tile. You have to understand that we were waiting for you to do something, to react, maybe to give an order, I don't know. Then Fiorella said Ximena needed to be taken to the nurse's office and tried to lift her up with Natalia's help. They were the first to react, but they couldn't carry Ximena because she was too heavy, and her arms and legs kept slipping from them, and her flesh box bounced again, this time against a chair leg. You would have been able to carry Ximena, Miss Clara, or to try, at least, which is what a teacher is supposedly meant to do: try. And yet you didn't move a muscle. Everyone thought the situation had sent you into shock, but not me. A teacher is generally prepared to pretend to be prepared. So while the others were still focused on Ximena, I was focused on you. Something about your posture—the way you stood immobile in the middle of a broken tile—affected me more than anything else. I guess the fear I read in your paralysis made me forget about Ximena entirely. I swear you didn't blink, not even once; your eyes became the most distant part of the classroom. I remember Raquel approached you, and you backed away, looking at her as if she'd insulted you, as if we had all insulted you, before you ran to ask for help. That was the first time I realized there was something strange about your relationship with us, about the way you looked at us, talked to us—sometimes as if we didn't exist, and others, as if we were going to rip off your ear. I stood there thinking about that tile, about your body, about your eyelids, and about the way you refused to help Ximena because it would have meant touching her. That's how I started to understand what I needed to build my theory. Surely it wasn't a problem for you to touch or brush against your students before, but you'd had a revelation, you intuited something that you cannot fully understand: the white age within your jaws. After that, nothing was ever the same.

You must feel naked reading this, as if I were pulling off your clothes in public or something like that. Maybe I am doing that, but not on a stage. It's just the two of us here: it's an intimate, though forced, moment, given that you probably didn't want me to write all this. Even so, I ask that you keep reading. I admit there were days when I watched you clutching a book during breaks, exposed outside the teachers' lounge, obliged to monitor us from under a willow meters from the basketball court and the cafeteria terrace, and I felt guilty, as if I were doing something really bad. That ridiculous feeling didn't last long, though, because when I thought about it carefully, I understood that I wasn't invading your privacy; I wasn't spying on you through a keyhole, I was observing you in the open, in a shared space. It would be stupid for me to feel bad about noticing something that others don't, wouldn't it? So the guilt went away, and I was able to keep studying you without any remorse. Thanks to that, I've noticed curious details. For example, the way you pretend to read every time a group comes near you during break, not to talk to you, just to cross to the other side of the court or sit next to the geraniums, but you, when in doubt, open your book to any page and simulate a concentration that I know doesn't exist, because your attention, really, is always on the dozens of bodies in the white age moving around you. All the teachers get bored on duty (Miss Ángela passes the time chatting with her first-year students over by the cafeteria; Mister Rodrigo scrapes the dirt out from under his fingernails with a paper clip—gross!). I don't think anyone, other than me, has noticed that you're the only one who performs their duty uneasily. Your movements would give it away to anyone who bothered to pay attention: every couple of minutes, you look for the hands of the clock, and you avoid making eye contact with any of us, as if our eyes were wasps or spiders. I'd love to be inside your head to prove that what I'm saying is true: that you fear us because of our age. Maybe you see the pallid cadaver of childhood tied to our heels; maybe you see, in adolescence, a spectral, perfect white, like the landscape in *At the Mountains of Madness*, or Arthur Gordon Pym's final vision, or Frankenstein's monster's teeth. That is, a white that awakens what is most sordid in our imaginations. And it's not that you're idealizing childhood, but everything that comes after is always worse, don't you think? If we were bad girls, we are even more vile when we grow up. In adolescence, what's most beautiful and most horrible comes to the surface, the same way that within the color white, there can exist both purity and putrefaction. There's something in these years that remains reticent to the norm and that isn't the same as childhood rebellion. I'll explain: when we're little, we're too busy discovering the world through games and stories. Fiction allows us to experience everything that's still forbidden to us. The thirst for reality comes later, with puberty. Our bodies change. Our minds change. And it's as if suddenly we're possessed by the color white (that is, the potential to stain ourselves), and it's as if that color were a ubiquitous presence in human time. Something like Lovecraft's slithering chaos, that primitive monster that can take any form, or like Pennywise. The white age, in my theory, would be the period in which a body is able to manifest that white aura, that primordial potential I will call the White God (which is much more than just another version of my drag-queen God, I promise you). Try to imagine it, Miss Clara: I can't describe Their original form, because They don't have one, but They could take the appearance of anything in the universe. All we know is that pubescent bodies are and have always been puppets sensitive to Their presence. Perhaps you see the danger of that God in our corporeal metamorphoses: nipples that protrude, hair that opens a path to unexpected zones and rarefies the skin, stains, acne, and blood. Transformations that empty us of everything we were, and They are there in each of us: kindling a morbid commotion, anticipating the terrible things to come. I've decided to call Them the White God because from the beginning, we human beings have been aware of the existence of ancient, enormous, incomprehensible beings that could destroy us, and that awareness came from the brutality of nature. Much later, people like Mister Alan came along to tell us about a benevolent, loving God and to ease that original fear of the cruel and despotic gods that cast down famines, plagues, and chaos. Above all else, chaos. The first divinities were terrifying. I've never told anyone this, and I beg you not to mention it to Mister Alan, but I believe the original gods are the real gods. I think that if there is someone or something watching us, someone or something that could put an end to us with a sneeze, it's nothing we can understand or decipher; it's nothing that understands human concepts like love, and we're of no consequence to it at all. The first men worshipped these eternal beings because they were afraid of them. All religions were constructed on that fear, and they called that fear "God" to name him and plead for his clemency. That's why (because God is fear) I call the white that manifests in bodies during the white age the White God. What do you think? My theory could become a Lovecraftian story that would stand apart from even the best imitators of the genre. From the beginning, there have been hundreds of rituals and cults related to sexuality, groups of humans who have worshipped masturbatory gods or gods with giant members, like San Biritute. The White God is the manifestation that unifies all those gods: the sexual awakening of adolescence and the uncomfortable changes it brings about in the body are just one point of access to Their presence. Because if you stop and think about it, there's no one more pervertible or contaminable than a teenager. I feel it at this very moment: as I write, I feel a desire to become something worse than I am. I think and feel things that I didn't think or feel when I was a little girl. Bad, dirty things. Things that could hurt others. Things that come out of me and scare me, things that I would never tell the numerary, Tito. This is where my theory originates: the fear of a period in which bodies become possible detonators of the most uncontrollable and violent impulses. But there's more, a lot more. Because in order to talk about white horror, we need the revelation of what cannot be known: a silencing clarity.

Anyway, I don't want you to be ashamed that you're afraid of something different from everyone else, at least not with me. I'm also scared of my milk age. I couldn't tell you when it started (maybe three or four years ago), because the discovery of it grew slowly in my body and in my mind. As a little girl, I was never skittish: I never peed the bed or woke my parents up because of an inexplicable noise under my bed. That doesn't mean I didn't experience fear before puberty, just that I had always understood it as a game (feeling fear is very different from feeling horror, but you already know that). When I started to read Lovecraft in the school library, I understood my horror was very similar to what the characters in his stories felt. Having spent so much time reading him, Poe, Chambers, Machen, Shelley, and designing, with Fernanda, comics featuring vampires, succubi, and other creatures, I believe there's only one other person in the school who knows horror literature better: you. That chapter you made us read from *Moby Dick*, about the whiteness of the whale, was so important for both Fernanda and me. All the signs we had overlooked in the stories and novels we had read suddenly acquired new meaning: from Melville's enormous whale to Poe's and Lovecraft's Antarctic explorations; the Arctic, where Shelley's creature escapes; the man whom Chambers describes as a "plump white grave-worm"; Bram Stoker's White Worm; Machen's white people; the white color of ghosts and corpses . . . The totality and immensity of the void are condensed in that maximum light that doesn't refract any color. Lovecraft's mysticism has to do with the void; that's how white horror is related to cosmic horror. What I like most about his stories is that his gods—his ancient, primordial beings, his enormous creatures more powerful than the human race can imagine—are nothing at all like the gods of the religions we know. They have no human characteristics, therefore, they are terrible, but not because they represent evil. They aren't Beelzebub or Lucifer. They aren't malevolent. They do not exist to tempt us or to drag us toward the darkness, like in Christian mythology in which we are the center of creation. What's interesting about Lovecraft's Elder Things is that they cannot be understood within that framework. When the idea of good and evil disappears, all that's left is nature and its violence. I think if there's only one God, I mean, one Elder Thing, an eternal, omnipotent creature that could wipe us out in the blink of an eye, it would have to be one who doesn't care about us in the slightest, who plays with us as if we were just another source of entertainment within the vast universe. Think about it, Miss Clara: with everything that happens on any given day in this world, would it make sense that something like the Christian God exists? Every morning on my way to school, I watch through the window as dozens of kids beg for change at stoplights. I've read that every minute, hundreds of people die of starvation all over the world, and that for me to be able to use the computer on which I'm now writing this, there are many others dying in coltan mines. In this very moment, somewhere on the terrestrial globe, there are women whose clitorises are being cut out, children being sold, people exploding into smithereens or drowning in the ocean, and none of it has to do with evil, but rather with human nature failing in its self-domestication. I know it's comforting to believe that there's someone or something superior who takes care of us, who has a beautiful plan for our lives, but if we think about it seriously, not even Mister Alan's most profound lectures could make that God believable. This is the conclusion I reached with Fernanda by my side, and neither of us have shared it with our parents. We both came to understand that for the only God that exists, the White God, we're nothing more than ants. Have you dodged an ant so as not to step on it, Miss Clara? Have you jumped or paused to save its life? No one would move a muscle, or stop moving one, for the life of an ant. Perhaps for the life of a rabbit, or a chicken, or a pig. Sometimes people slam on the brakes when a dog is crossing the highway, but would they do it for an ant? The grounds for this bias is that ants are so little that it seems the world wouldn't change with their absence. Moreover, an ant death is clean and almost invisible: no blood, no annoying sounds, and no large-scale spectacle of decomposition. But there's another reason: if we had to worry about the life of every ant in the world, we'd go crazy. We'd never be able to move without fearing we'd brutally murder one. Well, that's what we are to Lovecraft's Elder Things and to the White God: ants running around the vast space where all that's inexplicable lurks. And once this truth is revealed to us, a new vertigo (the horror of becoming aware of our own fragility) opens up. At least ants can't fathom their own cosmic smallness, but we, though we live ignoring it, have the capacity to uncover it. We can become aware of our true size, our insignificance with respect to nature and the universe. After that, all that remains is madness: the tremendous horror that lays waste to all meaning.

I guess what I'm trying to say is, knowing that you're an ant about to die at any second, like a crocodile's offspring in its mother's jaws, is to live within the white horror. What the white reveals—that which cannot be known but which suddenly occupies our mind—makes us realize how weak we are. I imagine you've felt that minuscule ever since your ex-students did to you what they did (perhaps that was the moment you had your revelation). I, on the other hand, discovered that awareness in my own body. After all, if my horror didn't resemble yours, if white weren't the ideal metaphor, if I hadn't read that chapter of *Moby Dick*, I never would have been able to understand you as I do now, because I never would have been able to understand myself. I'll try to explain it better: for me, the fear of the white age came on as my body was changing. First a rancid smell. Then nipples that rose up like hematomas, painful to the touch. Then the vaginal discharge, like fresh, whitish snot. The wiry hair. The stretch marks. The blood. That incompleteness and indefinition that disgusts you about us is just as repulsive to me. Childhood ends with the creation of a monster that crawls around at night: an unpleasant body that cannot be trained. Puberty makes us werewolves, or hyenas, or reptiles, and when the moon is full, we can see how we lose ourselves (whatever it is that we are).

I recently wrote a poem about this:

> *Deep within me lies a faceless mother:*
> *a God*
> *with aerial tentacles*
> *piercing nature's palest season.*
>
> *Her breasts are a garden of nibbled vegetables,*
> *a mother pond of anacondas,*
> *a wandering uterus,*
> *a jawbone,*
> *that drenches my heart*
> *in her perfect milk.*

Writing, as you must have noticed by now, comes easily to me. Fernanda says she prefers my prose, but sometimes I write poems because poems are really scary. For example, a line about menstruation just occurred to me: "My carnivorous uterus: a plant that swallows bloody insects." I don't know what your cramps were like during your adolescence (they say the pain lessens as you get older), but mine are so intense they make me sweat, and sometimes I vomit up a thick, transparent liquid like the drool of the monster in *Alien*. Sometimes, when the pain is that intense and lasts for hours, I faint. Actually, I've only fainted twice, though I'd like to do it more often because then the pain vanishes, just like when we're asleep. Anyway, in those moments, it's as if my uterus were gnawing on itself and there were nothing else in the world besides that internal cannibalism. In the white age, our bodies overpower us, but so do the bodies of others. When I turned eleven, for example, I began to notice that men looked at me strangely. They, and some women, have looked at me differently since then, as if they had spirals in their eyes. Surely you know what I'm talking about, Miss Clara. Those eyes follow me on the street and at school.

People young and old have the same slimy tongues hanging out of
their mouths, and all this is happening as my hips begin to spread
and my voice sounds increasingly like that of a Disney mermaid.
It's as if they have hands in their eyes and my breasts are swelling
up at the same time as their fingers. Five months ago, at a family
party, I caught my uncle looking at my legs (Fernanda says that's
normal and that all uncles, especially politicians, are pigs). In any
case, these changes have affected me more than they affect others.
My friends, for example, wouldn't understand. Not even Fernanda
would understand, although that doesn't matter now, since we
don't talk anymore. Sometimes in my nightmares I'm raped by my
teachers, by the gardener, by my uncles, my brother, my father . . .
Have you ever thought about it, Miss Clara? Have you thought
about how easy it is for any man to rape us? It's as if we were made
just for that purpose, so they could ram right into us; not only
men, but also our mothers. When I was little, my mother bathed
me. She did it until I turned ten because, according to her, I didn't
do a good enough job on my own. To tell the truth, she always
complained about my hygiene, but I swear to you, Miss Clara, I
was a very clean little girl. Anyway, my mother would talk about
all sorts of things while she bathed me (school, church, my aunts,
the weekend, the domestic workers, the numerary, Tito, the prela-
ture), and one way or another, she would always end up telling me
about terrible cases of girls who were kidnapped, raped, and murdered, cases she watched with a certain fascination on a TV chan-
nel that only aired true crime. She'd start her stories with a "You
won't believe what happened to one little girl because she talked to
a stranger" or "because she disobeyed her mom and left the house
alone" or "because she didn't know how to say no" (in her stories, it
was always the girl's fault). And after she had described the most
graphic details, she would repeat, again, which parts of my body no
one besides her could touch. She'd tell me, "If one day you're lost
and someone tells you they'll take you home, don't listen. He might
be a bad man. You can't trust women either, because there are also
bad women who take girls and then hand them over to bad men.

And, Anne, darling, you can only trust family; the world is full of bad people who want to do terrible things to pretty little girls like you. There are sick men out there who want to stick their fingers and other things in that secret, delicate place where you go pee pee. If that were to happen, it would hurt a lot, and you might even die like those other girls on TV. That's why you must be obedient, stay close to me when we're out, and sit properly. It's very important that you sit properly. If you don't sit properly, bad men might see your secret place, and then they might want to abduct you and do bad things to you. You must not show your tongue to anyone either, because you could give strange ideas to bad, really bad, men. So, Anne, honey, you must sit properly and keep your mouth shut tight, do you understand?" But her words were exhausting, and they didn't mean anything to me. In fact, I hated that she bathed me, because her wedding ring would get stuck between my butt cheeks and in my vulva, and the sensation was cold and unpleasant, just like I imagined it would be if a bad man stuck his fingers— fatter and rougher than my mother's—inside of me. It was much later, after Mom decided I was old enough to bathe myself, that I began to worry about the way I sat in front of my teachers, uncles, cousins, or friends. I was even careful to sit correctly, legs closed, in front of my father and my brother. I also developed a particular disgust for any man who wore rings, especially big shiny ones, like my mother's. Perhaps this preoccupation began around the time when I noticed men had stopped looking at me as if I were a little girl. Perhaps not. It doesn't matter. What's important is that I quickly became obsessed with always keeping my knees tight together and staying away from people who wore rings. I didn't even cross my legs, because then my school uniform or the dresses Mom made me wear would slide up a few centimeters, and if at any moment someone noticed and looked at me (and if that someone was a man and, moreover, wore rings), I would feel sick with guilt. Over time, I've been able to rid my closet of skirts and dresses, but I have to wear my uniform to school. Why are the school uniforms for boys and girls so different, Miss Clara? Why do we have to wear skirts?

It has been very difficult for me to reconcile myself to that, and to the rings. Sometimes during class I would forget about my body, and without meaning to, I would open my legs wide enough that anyone in front of me could have seen my underwear. When that happened, I'd start shaking and feel nauseous, especially if I were with a male teacher rather than a female one. The worst thing I could imagine was Mister Alan or Mister Hugo or Mister Mario or Mister Rodrigo seeing my underwear. Thinking about it made me feel so disgusted that I invented a punishment to help me remember the correct position for my legs. On my chair, underneath my thighs, I placed a compass so the needle was almost pressing into my flesh. If I moved, the needle would stick me, so if I didn't want to hurt myself, I had to stay alert and conscious of my body. That's how I maintained control (and won the battle even if the war was lost). The worst part was how uncomfortable it was to stay in that one position for hours. My legs always fell asleep, but I had to do it if I didn't want to feel guilty. Because if some teacher saw my underwear, it would have been my fault for not sitting properly, understand? This all repeated itself in every one of my classes in my first, second, and third years here, but less often in the ones taught by female teachers. The female teachers didn't worry me, though I can't explain why. I still hate the desire in men's faces, even before it appears, and I'm still careful to sit properly, legs pressed together. I can't say I've fully moved beyond this period, but I no longer self-impose punishments, which is good. That being said, I don't think I've been sufficiently explicit about the angst that initial phase represented for me. Perhaps another anecdote would serve to portray it better: A year ago, maybe two, my mom came into my room to lecture me about my grades while I was changing. She left the door open, and within seconds, my dad and my brother came in, complaining because they were hungry and the food was getting cold on the table (my family has one golden rule: no one can start eating until we're all at the table and we've prayed for the forsaken, which means everyone except us). I instinctively covered my breasts with my hands, and my mom looked at me like I had done something unforgivable. "Why are you doing that? Why are you covering yourself? That's your father and your brother! What sort of sick thoughts are going through your twisted head? They're your family!" she told me, making me feel bad for covering my breasts, but I still didn't move my hands and I didn't let them see. I couldn't. Then Mom grabbed my wrists and forced me to let go of my breasts. "You idiot, we're your family!" she yelled, shaking me. Can you imagine how humiliating that was for me, Miss Clara? My breasts looked like two slices of gelatin, two stupid, uneven hunks of fat. I didn't even dare to look Dad or Pablo in the eyes, but I knew they were watching me because I felt the force of their pupils against my nakedness. So one afternoon I went into my brother's bathroom while he was peeing and flung the force of my pupils onto his flaccid rose-colored penis, and I told him that I was his family. Then I went into my parents' bathroom while my dad was showering, and I looked at his penis, which curves to the left, and I told him: "I'm your family." Mom hit me on the head with a brush when she found out, but I forgave her, because eight years back, when she was pregnant with Pablo, I hit her in the stomach with that same brush. I remember she called me "wicked" then, but the "wicked" one is Fernanda, who has always been in the white age and who killed her little brother. Did you know that? I just hit mine once before he was born and wanted him to die, like every big sister does. I'd bet anything you didn't know that about Fernanda, Miss Clara. Some of the teachers know about it. The school psychologist knows about it. Everyone says it was an accident, even though Fernanda doesn't remember what happened, and that's why her parents take her to a therapist—so he can convince her that it was an accident, which is absurd, because no one knows what really happened.

Anyway.

Two years ago, during one of the many nights I've slept over at Fernanda's, there was an important change. Until then, and for obvious reasons, I had never felt sexually aroused. Sex and everything associated with it was, for me, disgusting and scary (if you think about it, there's something primitive and dark in sexuality: something dormant but dangerous, uncontrollable, something that erupts like the volcanoes in your book). Fernanda, on the other hand, had told me she'd been masturbating since she was six years old, but I had never seen her do it, and I think I assumed it was a lie (it's normal to lie to your friends just to impress one another; maybe you do that with yours too, and you know what I'm talking about). That night, she thought I had fallen asleep: I know because she said my name, and I didn't answer. Something made me stay still and pretend I hadn't heard her, maybe curiosity. Maybe deep down I wanted to catch her in the middle of a private act, but I swear I had no idea what was going to happen. In fact, I couldn't see anything because my eyes were closed. But there are things that don't need to be seen. The bed shook, and I couldn't breathe. Fernanda made sounds like someone would make if they were in pain and, at the same time, different, due to a faint tone I cannot describe. Of course, I had never masturbated before, but I felt like doing it then. It was surprising and disconcerting. My family and education, as you know, have been devoted to the Work. I've always heard terrible things about masturbation. Somehow I'd come to think that doing it would turn me into an animal or a despicable creature. I had the sense that if I did it, the changes in my body would irreversibly close, as if in a macabre circle. I didn't do anything that night, but the desire to touch myself started there, next to Fernanda squeezing her muscles under those sheets with red ponies on them. The way I felt in the days that followed was strange because when I looked at myself in the mirror, naked, I initially felt a rejection, similar to hatred, toward every corner of my face, toward the size of my nipples, toward my stature, my skin, my freckles, followed by the suffocating horror of that body that sometimes seemed to belong to another creature that wanted to pull me out of myself. For a time, I put into practice a technique that allowed me to avoid masturbation and consisted of the following: when the desire to touch myself became strong and I was alone, I replayed the most sinister nightmares of rape I'd had in the previous days. That was usually enough to calm me down. In one of them, for example, Pablo, whose skin had turned into curdled milk, stuck his fingers in my vagina, so I'm sure you can imagine, Miss Clara, that scenes like that were more than enough to put an end to my arousal. Anyway, even though that worked quite well for a few weeks, I ended up giving in to my impulses. I thought: *If Fernanda can do it without anything bad happening to her, then I can too.* Moreover, replaying my nightmares gave me a nervous hiccup and nausea that didn't go away for hours. So I masturbated. The first few times, I did it when everyone else was asleep, protected by the night, with a shyness and a guilt that I can't fully articulate to you. At first I just used my hands, but then I started using objects. On one occasion, after my mother told me, in front of her friends from the badminton club, to brush my teeth because I had bad breath, I went into the bathroom and masturbated with her toothbrush. It was childish, I know, but I'm not sorry, because my mom is never sorry. She loves complaining about me in public and saying, in front of the dentist, for example, that I don't brush my teeth very well, that I'm unkempt, and that I'm a "dumb, awkward girl" who doesn't listen. That's how she starts with the insults, by calling me a "dumb, awkward girl," and then she moves on to my grades and to how difficult it is to get me to understand the logic of math or language (it's true that I am really bad at math, Miss Clara, but I'm good with words, even though she doesn't know it). Anyway, a few days later, something strange happened while I was masturbating. Or perhaps it had been happening all along, ever since the first time, but I had no way of knowing because I did it with my eyes closed, hiding from myself and from the guilt that brought me to tears and made me nauseous. One early morning, I opened my eyes while touching myself, while imagining my left nipple between Fernanda's teeth, and I saw, next to the chair in my room, a large, dense, whitish figure that stood out from the darkness as if it had broken through to get inside of it. I saw it in a flash and thought it couldn't be real, that it had to be an optical illusion brought on by my desires, but it stayed there, pulsing like a rhinoceros heart, swelling until it covered the entire corner, swallowing the chair, the window, and the mirror on the wall. I can't explain the depth of the horror produced in me by its sharpness, its absence of any animal or human form, its mucousy, whitish texture, its surging height. Nevertheless, in spite of my fear and the unbearable beehive stench, I couldn't scream or stop moving my hands on my sex. I need you to believe me, Miss Clara: I was more terrified than I had ever been, and not of something I'd imagined, but of something real, grotesque, expanding before my eyes. I wanted to jump out of bed and run to my parents' room, but a force took control of my body, and as frightening as it was, it was also enormously arousing. It isn't something I can explain, that's just how it happened. I was paralyzed because even though I was moving, those movements on my clitoris weren't mine anymore, understand? I wanted to stop my hands, but it was as if my head and my body were two different things. What I felt was really complex: a chaos of repulsion, horror, and desire. And thus, as I approached climax, the enormous white came toward me as if suctioning up the distance between us, and in a matter of seconds, I lost consciousness.

There's something that unites pleasure with pain and fear, don't you think? I don't know exactly what it is, but it has to do with the hole that swells in our stomachs when we're on the verge of falling. What I felt that night was something like that: the vertigo that makes you lose your balance and at the same time makes you more aware than ever that you are a body and that one day you will die. It's funny, but most of the time we forget that we're animals made up of organs that seem right out of a nightmare. The heart, for example, is a hideous organ. It's always there, beating, but we never think about it because if we did, we might learn to fear it. I still remember the first time I saw one, not in a photograph, video, or illustration, but right in front of me. It was three years ago in the lab, during biology class. Miss Carmen asked us to sit in pairs and put a cow heart on the table. Its color (red crowned by a fatty white) and shape paralyzed me. I was afraid of it, I admit:

I thought (because no one had explained to me yet that the hearts of cows and people were different sizes) that my heart was the same, that same titanic size, and I imagined it in the middle of my chest, pushing out my ribs and pumping my blood through its unpleasant veins. I looked at it and couldn't take my eyes off of it (just like you look at us when we get too close), and I found it monstrous, nothing like the hearts on cards or the emoticons; it was ugly: a piece of asymmetrical muscle that seemed to have been bitten by a shark. In any case, disgusted and terrified as I was, I started to hear and feel my own beats accelerating, becoming deeper and deeper, and I realized something terrible: I also had a heart. This might sound dumb, I know, but knowing something is not the same thing as feeling or experiencing it, and in that moment, I had the experience of having a heart. And it was pleasurable, at the same time as it was abominable. And as Fernanda used the scalpel to open up the cow heart and reveal the left and right ventricles, I thought: *I'm alive. The cow this heart belonged to is dead, but I'm alive.* That same feeling, though of much greater intensity, is what I experienced after I saw that strange manifestation of the White God while masturbating, but in addition to having the experience of being a heart, I had the experience of being lungs, skin, a brain, a nose, a tongue, a belly button, a clitoris, some fingers . . . My whole body was part of that masturbation over which I had no control.

In short, I want you to be sure I'm not making this up: anyone is capable of distinguishing reality from nightmare, or the real from the imagined. You only forget the difference if you're crazy, but I'm not crazy. I know what I saw. Moreover, even if I had imagined it, even if that white apparition existed only in my mind, why would that make it less real? My mind exists, as does everything it projects onto the world. What I'm telling you about now happens because my mind is my reality. And in saying this, I'm not saying I made it up: I'm saying that even if the white presence that night was visible only to me, what does it matter? Would it then cease to be true? Because in the end, what matters isn't what's real, but rather what's true. I guess that's the difference between white horror and cosmic horror: both go far beyond us and make us feel tiny and crushable, like ants before something enormous, powerful, inapprehensible. In Lovecraft's best stories, the atmosphere of reality is essential, and white horror, on the other hand, can do without verisimilitude, because it's experienced in the mind and in the senses. But let's go back to what happened to me that night: I lost consciousness (something that had never happened to me before, except with my worst menstrual cramps), and when I woke up, it was daytime. In spite of that, I noticed within a few seconds that something inside me had changed forever: that dense, mucousy white stain, not unlike my vaginal discharge, was an apparition of my White God. A yearning and an infinite horror hanging from the same thread, and I needed to see Them again. I'm embarrassed to write this, but I'd never felt as much pleasure as I did that night, when I lost control. For the first time, I experienced true horror. And that horror was also an orgasm.

My white age became tangible from then on, but that's another story, which I couldn't tell you now. What matters is that you and I understand what this period in our bodies is capable of doing. You are afraid of being contaminated or wounded by what I embody, but I'm already contaminated, already wounded. You're afraid of us because you've seen us and you can't understand what you see: that's why you flee, but I can't flee from myself. You're afraid we'll do what your ex-students did to you, but what happened to them is happening to me, and sometimes, I want to do the same thing to my parents, the rector, and all the teachers at school. I wrote this for you because you're the only one who understands: because sometimes it's necessary to talk to someone who understands what fear is.

I'm done.

XXII

A: Do you know what the worst thing someone can do to her best friend is?

F: Yes, I know what the worst thing someone can do to her best friend is.

A: To her twin sister, her ñaña.

F: To her perfect conjoined twin.

A: The worst thing someone can do is betray her.

F: The worst thing someone can do is turn her back on her equal.

A: Her sister.

F: Her double.

A: That's the one thing you cannot do.

F: That's the one thing I will never do.

XXIII

Her sneakers were worn; that was the sinister thing. Clara inspected them up close: there were depressions in the soles that couldn't have come from her, not even if she wore them all the time, because her shoes tended to split along the sides and never on the heels— since she was little, she had walked almost on tiptoe, and even though it caused pain in her feet and back, and even though she had tried to correct it for years (above all when she began to learn how to walk like her mother), sometimes she still lifted, involuntarily, her heels from the ground. A person like her—who had inherited (or adopted) the fixed rituals of a maternal behavior— noticed when something shifted within her space, and Clara had been perceiving minor intrusions in hers for days: her hairbrush was resting on the wrong side of the night table, or her charger was plugged in to the wrong outlet when she got home, or the silver picture frame with the photo of her mother had been placed on the wrong corner of the sideboard. Every morning before leaving for Delta Bilingual Academy, *High-School-for-Girls*, she placed the brush, charger, and picture frame in the correct places, and every afternoon when she got home, she found them in the incorrect ones. At night, the spoons changed drawers and the closed drawers opened, but Clara knew she wasn't making up what was happening to her sneakers. The heel was especially affected, though the rest of the sole also showed noticeable wear and tear, as if someone had run a marathon in them—someone who wasn't her, of course, because Clara didn't generally exercise, much less on the street, where so many people were poised to watch her or say things she didn't want to hear. The intruder's toe prints had been left on the inside of the shoe: fat, dirty, round little toes that didn't belong to her. The sneakers—the sudden object of her fear—smelled like gum and dog poop, and if she held them under the light—which she did—the sole shone a little, as if it held bits of sand or glitter, or perhaps glints of dirt from the asphalt of the schoolyard. But Clara had never worn them, much less outside her house; she knew that for sure. Her mother had given them to her on her twentieth birthday, just after the doctor told her that her daughter's health was improving—that is, her ever-more-acute anxiety disorder was subsiding—and since then, they had sat unworn in the closet, forgotten but protected from all harm because they were one of the few gifts her mother had ever dared give her, but that afternoon—panic squeezing her knuckles—Clara realized that they were worn and that something sinister could fit within the irregular landscape of a sole.

Her eyelid—trembling like a butterfly in agony that she incessantly slapped with her palm—could also contain something sinister, but she preferred not to think about that too much.

After several minutes spent looking at them, smelling them, scratching them, Clara let the sneakers fall and ran to the bathroom to vomit.

On the most difficult nights of the week, she opened and closed the doors to the bedrooms, wandered barefoot through the hallways, checked the windows, dead bolts, and drawers again and again; she went in and out of her room, sighed, changed her position in the bed one hundred and one times, one hundred and fifteen times—the springs of the mattress and the weight of her body generated a complaint or a plea—lit an aromatic candle, and the smoke ascended in a cry for help until, with no response, with no one to read her message, she ended up humming songs by Antonio Machín—her dead grandmother's favorite and the one thing that made her sweat less—as if she were a bird with a disrupted schedule that insisted on singing when there was no light, a caricature of a bird that pecked at its own cranium at dawn, breaking the shell that cradled the dead mother in her mind. Those long yellow nights, during which she would check the lock to her room two, three, four times in less than an hour, were populated by the

sounds Clara could see with her eyes closed. She saw little fingernails scratching the tiger-striped armchair, laughter in the kitchen,
quick steps like clumsy slaps on the living room floor, and the blinking of an eye that watched her sleep through the keyhole—in a perfect silence, the dead mother who inhabited her mind would say, a
person could hear even the fluttering of eyelashes from afar. And
even though these events had started after what the M&M's did
to her, and even though for some time she thought it was all in her
head, and even though some nights nothing happened and the language of the noises disappeared, the sneakers had awoken in her a
new panic attack, palpitations rising up her throat like an eruption
of blood, and they had also forced her to remember—her head resting against the toilet seat—what her student had confessed: "Do
you want me to tell you what my best friend did to me?" she told
her. "If I tell you, do you promise you won't get mad?"

There had been other incidents leading up to Annelise Van
Isschot's confession and the twisted essay she left on her desk, but
only after hearing those words did Clara begin to understand that
her fear—that sensation of asphyxiation that filled her chest with
searing tentacles—was not distorting reality but expanding it.
She had learned the hard way—that is, by way of Annelise's loose
tongue—that her panic was a truth that expanded into the relocation
of objects. If she had known that from the beginning—as her dead
mother always said to add drama to her sermons on remorse—
she would have been more careful, but when she ordered her student to write an essay as punishment for talking to Analía Raad all
through class, Clara never imagined she would end up taking home
the delirious, obscene text. She read it in bed, under the light of an
old lamp, and when she finished it, she didn't know whether to feel
angry or simply disturbed. She reread various parts of it with the
intention of understanding, of elucidating the cause of the anxiety lifting off in her like a rocket, and she discovered that in addition to the morbidity of the intimate account, she was distressed
by the maturity of the writing, which seemed to have come from
an older head, as well as her student's proven knowledge of her

fear—"You have to protect yourself from your students, Becerra," her mother would tell her, making the face of a fortune-teller as she inhaled the smoke from her joint. "They learn more quickly than their teachers." Although her relationship with Annelise had improved thanks to the extra literature sessions on Fridays, it disconcerted Clara that her student would reveal such private details in a school paper, details she wasn't even sure were true but that for some reason caused her to feel enormous revulsion. "Why did you write this?" she asked during one of their private sessions. "Because I wanted to," she responded, now with no trace of the blows left on her by her best friend. Teenagers were naturally insolent, but Annelise was hieratically so, and that awoke the worst impulses in Clara. When they discussed snowcapped volcanoes and horror literature, everything went well, but on occasion, she discovered an occult smile, tucked away, restrained at the corners of Annelise's mouth while she appeared to be listening. "What you wrote about me isn't true. I'm not afraid of my students," Clara told her the afternoon she returned the essay. "Yes, you are afraid of us," Annelise said. "That's why I need to tell you the truth." In her house, Clara closed the windows and drew the blinds every day, though she knew that when she came home in the evening, she'd find them open. "The truth is, Fernanda and I came up with a plan to scare you, but we aren't friends anymore." Sometimes, in the early mornings, she heard handfuls of pebbles clattering across some irregular surface. "We found your address because we wanted to scare you, for fun." She couldn't even imagine the size of the fingers that, during each bout of insomnia, pushed on those pebbles lodged in her stomach. "I know it's bad that once we went to your house and watched you from the sidewalk out front, but that's what we did." She was sure she heard the purring of stones at night, agitated breathing behind the dead bolt, the continuous, inexplicable crackling of eyelashes. "She wanted to go inside your house," she told her. "It was all Fernanda's idea."

The last few days had been terrible. The indentations from the chubby little toes that could easily belong to any one of her students made her retch every time she looked at the sneakers. According to Annelise Van Isschot, Fernanda had wanted to go into her teacher's house because she thought scaring her sounded as exciting as climbing a mountain and shouting up above the clouds. "She wanted us to go in and move things around." "She wanted us to go in many times without you noticing." The *M&M's* had gotten onto the patio and then climbed in through the kitchen window that now had bars, and even though Clara wasn't there in that moment, and even though during the trial she told herself otherwise, she was capable of reconstructing the real scene, thanks to the cockroaches laying their eggs in her mind. They broke three of her mother's plates that were next to the sink, and on the pretense of looking for the exams, they prowled around the house for a few minutes—she calculated that it was barely five. They had just enough time to inspect the living room before Clara came home to the strangeness of two perfectly uniformed students inside her house. At first she didn't notice anything unusual—that's how she explained it to the authorities— except for an orange rolling several meters from the kitchen door, but then—picking up the orange from the floor—she saw Malena Goya and Michelle Gomezcoello on the other side of the room, close to the X-ray of her mother's spinal column, and it was as if the light of day had gone out. Clara remembered that she hadn't screamed out loud but inwardly, and her scream grew inside her like a wave that submerged everything in skin, and when she was finally able to speak, all that came out was a voice that sounded nothing like her own—that couldn't possibly be hers, because hers was buried deep beneath her skin—telling them to stay where they were, not to dare move, that she was going to call the police. Then she walked over to the phone, the dirty orange still in her right hand, and made her first mistake: turning her back on them. "The two girls were about to fail the year because of her class," the defense said during the trial. "The two girls come from troubled homes." Clara thought she knew what kind of girls they were because of their mild dispositions, and because they generally went unnoticed in their class of forty-five. "Both claim to have suffered bullying during language and literature classes." They frequently missed class, didn't turn in their homework, and copied off other students. "The question is, Your Honor, would these two girls have done what they did if the school had made them feel included, that is, if it had shown them care rather than just ignoring them." *But you can never know what kind of girl a girl is,* Clara thought. "Look at this," Ángela said one morning in the full-time teachers' lounge. "One of my students went through my bag, took my notebook, and drew this thing." When Clara turned her back on them to call the police, the dirty orange still in her rigid hand, Malena Goya lunged on top of her and bit her ear while Michelle Gomezcoello went directly to the kitchen for a long knife meant for cutting meat. "It's a jawbone, right? It's an animal's jawbone." Clara tried to get Malena Goya off her neck, but the girl was really strong. "Do you think whoever drew this was making fun of my jaw?" In the struggle, Clara fell and hit her head on the dining room table. "Does this drawing strike you as racist?" She wasn't in pain on the floor, but when she tried to stand, she got dizzy and saw the edge of the table was stained with blood. "Do you think I should take this case to the rector?" Michelle Gomezcoello shouted at Clara while Malena Goya waved the long knife around. "I know it's just a drawing, but it isn't right for our students to violate their teachers' privacy." Clara didn't remember what they said, just their voices sharp as a needle. "It isn't right for them to stick their hands in our bags like common thieves." And then the knife on her neck.

For Clara it was difficult to drive home when she was sure that someone—who wasn't her or her dead mother—was using her things, prowling her hallways, and peeing in her toilet without flushing. "The question, Your Honor, is whether there was anything that could have been done to prevent these two girls from feeling so desperate, so absolutely threatened by some qualifying exams, that they believed attacking their teacher was the only option." Perhaps for the defendants, being a teacher was just like being a mother, but for Clara, mother and daughter were an antinomy. "What is the responsibility of the adults in this story?"

Sometimes she felt the imbalance pass by her like a gust, and she would stretch out her arms to cling to something solid but would only find the heat left by that evanescent sensation, and then the abyss: a hole the air didn't dare cross. "The truth is that, even though we aren't friends anymore, I know Fernanda will still go into your house to scare you," Annelise told her, and that night, Clara thought she found brown hairs in her brush; she pulled from the bristles a ball of silky, foreign strands and threw it out the window. "I'm telling you so you won't get scared if it happens." In the semidarkness of the street, where the strange hairs floated like a miniature tumbleweed, she thought she saw the shadow of a girl running and disappearing around the corner. "So you know that, when it happens, it was Fernanda." Not one dog in the neighborhood barked, but dogs are always bad guards. "I'll talk to her," Clara said, concealing her anguish from Annelise. "No! Please, don't say anything," she begged. "Fernanda will hurt me if she finds out I told you." The M&M's had tied her to the tiger-striped armchair with the string she used to hang out her clothing to dry and also with some cables they ripped out of the television. "The truth is, this isn't the first time Fernanda's hit me." Malena Goya took off one sock, smelled it, made a disgusted face, and stuck it in Clara's mouth before securing it with electrical tape she found in the toolbox. "Do you want me to tell you what my best friend did to me?" Annelise asked her. Sometimes Clara thought she had been the Malena Goya and Michelle Gomezcoello of her mother's life. "If I tell you, do you promise you won't get mad?" Because mother and daughter were an antinomy, but the M&M's were her daughters for the thirteen hours and fifty-seven minutes she spent tied to the tiger-striped armchair, and with them, Clara had experienced being a mother set out on the table before hungry offspring.

"Did I tie you up with my umbilical love?" she sometimes asked the X-ray of her mother's spinal column. "Did I cut off your circulation with my umbilical cord?"

At the school, there were hundreds of eyelashes Clara didn't know how to listen to. The incessant noise of voices made her pick at the delicate skin between the fingers of her hands during break and in the classrooms, but when she got home, the silence revealed the changes: the phone off the hook, the books on the table, the orange a few meters from the kitchen door. She poured rum into a glass, sat in the tiger-striped armchair, and watched, for hours, the only thing that had never moved: the X-ray of her mother's spinal column hanging in the middle of the wall. At the Delta Bilingual Academy, *High-School-for-Girls*, the students were dismissed an hour and a half before the teachers—Fernanda (according to her calculations) had almost two hours to get in through a window, move everything around, and return by night to reproduce the sounds from her memory. Malena Goya and Michelle Gomezcoello had taken turns inspecting the house without once taking their eyes off her; they put her clothes on, applied her makeup, poured the bottle of rum over her, used nail clippers to cut up her bras, and found the exams, but only once they no longer wanted anything to do with them. "We cracked her skull! Look, the dumbass is bleeding. What do we do now?" Michelle had said. "Let's go through the house while we think," Malena had responded. And when they got bored of jumping on the beds, eating the Nutella, throwing her shoes in the toilet, pouring nail polish all over the kitchen, and drawing penises on their teacher's face, they decided to pinch her belly. "Wow, she's screaming! It must really hurt. This is fun. You try." They slapped her, cut her hair, dug sewing needles into her thighs. "Look what we did to her head. She's gonna tell the police, and my mother's gonna slaughter me. We have to kill her." They ran the flame of the lighter from the kitchen over her knees. "Yeah, but how do we kill her?" They broke all the mirrors while she thought about how she was really going to die. "I don't know. I've never killed anyone." Clara would look at the X-ray of her mother's spinal column every time the fear made her feel like she was sweating milk. "A long time ago, I killed a cat the bitch got me." Her mother had never let anyone into the house; she always said no snail alive would invite other animals inside its shell. "We could stab her with the knife like this, *zas*! But there'd be a lot of blood, and we'd have to clean it up." Sometimes it was difficult for Clara to find the changes amid the strict order of the rooms. "We could suffocate her with a pillow so we wouldn't have to see that ugly face of hers." Sometimes the only difference was a poorly closed door or a glass flipped upright. "And then what do we do? Because I've seen what happens when they find the body in telenovelas: the murderers get screwed." The nights, however, were all the same—mattress springs, candles, fingernails, laughter, fluttering eyelashes. "We could hang her so it looks like a suicide." But every so often, the steps that made an arrhythmic path toward the closed door to her room sounded louder. "There's no way we could pull that off . . . I think it'd be better to just confess to everything." And Clara, sensing the arrival of a new panic attack, wanted to open the door to kill her fear, but she didn't dare. "My mom's going to slaughter me." She didn't dare leave the room, because the darkness wouldn't let her see Fernanda. "If we kill her, it'll be much worse." It would keep her from knowing whether she really was the one blinking. "If we kill her, it'll be way worse."

The voices made a Ferris wheel of skulls in her head.

"What will it feel like to kill someone?" asked Malena, almost crying out of fear of her mother. "What will it feel like to die?" asked Michelle Gomezcoello, burning Clara's knees. Madness was degree zero when it came to the fear of death: a broken staircase that led nowhere. That's what she was thinking about on the Friday that Annelise closed the classroom door and shed her blouse like a piece of skin that didn't fly off because of the weight of the buttons. "Now do you see what my best friend did to me?" she asked while her teacher's eyes clouded with salty tears before the open field of bruises and scabs. "Now do you understand what Fernanda will do to me if she finds out what I've told you?"

The silence was the abject sound of eyelashes.

The sneakers smelled like playgrounds with trapezes.

XXIV

"I want you to bite me," Annelise whispers to her. "I want you to bite me hard." Her voice sounds slow, like an iguana peeling the sun. Fernanda is bruised on her sister's neck as she attends to her desires: "Bite me, crocodile," and in her mouth, the twin body is tilled. "Bite me, caiman." From her fang springs a flower of flesh. A flower of bones springs into their infinitesimal snouts. By night, the organs enshrouded in skin contaminate. The sheets sweat. Her mandibular instinct courses toward the estuaries, but Fernanda likes biting clavicles and pelvises out over the volcanoes. "Bite me as hard as you can," her reborn sister demands. There on the cotton tablecloth, Annelise surrenders her clean bones to satisfy her hunger. She surrenders her neck to be wrung; her muscles to be chewed. "I don't want to hurt you, but I'm going to hurt you," Fernanda tells her. "Mark me," Annelise commands in the shower. "Make me bleed with your thirty-two teeth." And thirty-two times, she bites her. Thirty-two times, her tongue runs down her legs and salivates the stars red. In the water, they look at the colors of the bites: black, green, blue, violet. Yawning cosmos on her skin. Rosettes in the Milky Way of her flesh. Annelise's mouth opens when Fernanda bites her inner thigh. She trembles. She moans. She wipes the blood away with toilet paper and tosses it into the bowl like a dead dove. "I don't want to hurt you," Fernanda says. "I don't know why you make me do this to you." But then she clamps her jaws around Annelise's ribs to savor her plushy skin and watch her bite her lip, to smack her so she doesn't bite herself, to bite her nipples and hear her cry out with pain and pleasure, to see her delicate nostrils flare, her pretty little eyes rolling back in her head. But then Fernanda pulls her hair in the shower so she'll smile. She really likes when the pain makes Annelise smile. "I pray to the White God with every one of your teeth," Annelise says, caressing her gums. "But no one can know." So they keep hidden that in bed and in the shower, Fernanda stains her fangs. "Your blood tastes like shrapnel." "Your blood tastes like barbed wire." Meanwhile, her molars are always dying of thirst. "Did you know a crocodile's bite is more powerful than a whale's?" Annelise grips her pillow when Fernanda explores her skeleton. Perfection is her bear-trap-jaw hunting for more than her gluteus and lumbar muscles. "Did you know crocodiles hold their babies deep within their jaws?" Perfection opens a path toward her marrow: the center of equinoctial desire. Her teeth buzzing like bumblebees puncture her coccyx and cocooned vertebrae. Her teeth are osseous snails that store all the salt in Annelise's belly. It's not her thighs that Fernanda engraves with them, but the interior parts of her femur. And when her clavicles hang like a horizon that marks the beginning of the body, she moistens and gnaws on them. "We didn't do this kind of thing when we were little," she says every time she feels she loves her too badly. And every time she's afraid of how much she likes Annelise's pleasure when she climbs on top of her and squeezes her neck or stretches the skin of her shoulder blade with her incisors. "Swim down below like a crocodile," Annelise tells her in the pool. "Bite upward like a caiman." And her jaw traps a celestial pelvis like a fox skull lost in the mangroves. Fernanda does not explain to Dr. Aguilar that the blots in the Rorschach test are Annelise's bones in the colors of the garden. She doesn't explain to him that her jawbone is white and is made to devour. Made to crush. "Did you know iguanas bite their partners' necks during copulation?" Annelise asks, her bare feet on the bed. "Did you know the male gecko bites the female gecko's belly during copulation?" Fernanda doesn't like that Annelise talks about copulation with her bare feet on the bed. She doesn't like that she prays to the White God with each of her teeth, nor that she says she has seen Them, and that's how she knows she's going to die. Nor does she like that she likes Annelise's nipples, red as two mosquito bites, nor the hundreds of dead doves they toss in the toilet. "I don't know

where all these horrendous desires are coming from," Fernanda
says when she starts to feel guilty. Sometimes she wants to push
Annelise off the third floor of the building, or wants her to fall, but
most of the time she just wants to hug her and bite her tongue forever. "We weren't like this when we were little." Annelise moans
as much as screams, pouring hydrogen peroxide on the little-bear-
trap-bites. Click. Flash. They upload the photos to their private
Instagram accounts. "Love begins with a bite and a willingness
to be bitten." While they sleep, Fernanda's jaw nibbles the air.
Annelise is lulled to sleep by that sacred sound that vibrates like
the school bell. Some nights they watch horror movies like *Ginger
Snaps* or *Sisters*. Some nights Fernanda bites her armpits. "If your
mother saw the bite marks, what would you tell her?" Fernanda
asks as she rips off a scab with her fingernail. In the early mornings, Annelise pretends she's sleepwalking and goes into her parents' room. She opens all the doors in the house. She sets the
family pets free. "I'd tell her that mothers bite too," she responds,
scrunching her nose into a contracting caterpillar. Fernanda can't
understand why Annelise wants their mothers to be afraid of
them. "We're the twins in *The Shining*." Fernanda's mother is afraid
of Fernanda, and Fernanda doesn't like it. "We're the Gibbons sisters." It's painful for them to not be the same, that their bones and
the texture of their skin is such a personal matter, so individual.
"I wish we could have the same name," Annelise tells her in the
middle of class. The same height, the same scapula size. It fright-
ens Fernanda that her humerus is smaller than Annelise's, her ribs
wider. "When we were little, we looked alike," she says when she
discovers that Annelise is beautiful and that beauty also produces
fear. Annelise says out loud that seeing the White God is like seeing death, and Fernanda gets scared because she starts to believe
it, above all when they're in the white room and they all kneel in
a circle and hold each other's hands and close their eyes, and the
silence feels like an immense presence that Annelise wants them
to listen to, and they listen, clenching their jaws to keep from
screaming. "Maybe we should stop doing the White God thing,"

Fernanda suggests when she's afraid of what she wants. "I don't understand," her conjoined twin responds. No one opens their eyes in the circle, but Fernanda opens hers and sees Annelise, her mouth wide open, her eyes white like the moon. "It's not something we can stop." Fernanda wants to cry when she enjoys biting Annelise's right calcaneus and Annelise arches her back like Linda Blair in *The Exorcist*. Her back looks like a mare's and also like a wasteland the scorpions of her imagination crisscross. Fernanda and Annelise bleed at the same time every month. They shower together and watch the blood run between their legs as if it belonged to both of them. "When we were little, these things didn't happen to us," Annelise says, attracted and repelled by the color of the water. They avoid flooding the shower by pulling their hair from the drain. "Mom says we shouldn't shower together anymore because we're too big." They stick the wet strands to the walls Charo cleans during the day. "We've always showered together." They've always lassoed, clambered, jumped together. They've always stroked each other's knuckles and kissed below the ribs. "We're changing a lot," Fernanda says, turning her back to the hymns while Annelise's mons pubis fills with palates. "We're changing too much." Annelise caresses Fernanda's jaw right before falling asleep. Her jawbone made to devour. Her jawbone made to crush. "Every change is always too much."

XXV

Dr. Aguilar:

Fernanda: I think it was the crocodile jawbone.

Dr. Aguilar:

Fernanda: No, *I mean,* I think Anne became obsessed with the crocodile jawbone and its teeth and its super-duper strong bite, and that's what gave her the idea she had and what made her ask me to bite her.

Dr. Aguilar:

Fernanda: Yes, Doc. I think I'm ready to talk about that now.

Dr. Aguilar:

Fernanda: Well, we used to play a game where we would give each other dares like that. It was fun. Our friendship was reeeally fun.

Dr. Aguilar:

Fernanda: Well, at first, I didn't see it as aaall that bad. It didn't seem aaall that different from what we'd already been doing in the building, *you know?* Actually, we always thought bones were really pretty. Like sculptures. Once, the science teacher had us make a skeleton out of playdough and label every bone, and Anne and I had a great time. In the school library, on top of the shelves, there are jawbones and animals in formaldehyde, and Anne really liked the great white shark jawbone hanging over the poetry section, so she stole it, and when we were in the white room, she would wear it as a crown. Well, she's still wearing it as a crown, *I guess.* Though she really wants a crocodile one. She's obsessed with the power of a crocodile's jaws.

Dr. Aguilar:

Fernanda: It's just . . . I don't know. *Of course* being bitten would
scare me. And *of course* it scares me to bite. But I thought
about what you said the other day, and *maybe* it's true there
were times when I wanted to do it.

Dr. Aguilar:

Fernanda: Yes, it's true that I lied a little, Doc, but now I'm telling the truth. I always end up telling you the truth. I'll tell you
what I think: I think everyone's wanted to bite someone at
some point in their lives. *No big deal.* Sometimes ladies see a
baby and say: "I'm going to eat you right up," and couples even
say "I want to taste you!" Right? You know they do. We all
play at biting because it's reeeally instinctive. And what are
we? Animals! So the biting thing, or that feeling of wanting
to consume the people you love, is more normal than it seems.
We all experience that desire. So it doesn't have to be a lesbian thing or a sexual thing. It's another kind of instinct completely, *right?* It just so happens that most people don't end
up really biting anyone, because they don't want to hurt anyone and because they're afraid of seeing themselves as animals.
Anyway, my case is special because, *I mean,* I didn't want to
hurt Anne: she's the one who wanted me to hurt her. But
for her, that was o.k. What I want to say is that Anne liked
it when I hurt her. What we did together when no one was
watching was more *hard-core* than what we did in the building.
If the others had known about it, they would have assumed
the worst . . . It may seem like it doesn't matter that Anne
asked me to do it, but it does, because she asked me to bite
her hard, reeeally hard. I still remember the first time I tasted
her blood on my teeth . . . I can't even explain it. *Anyway,* for
a while, I took it as a game, just like the things we did at the
building, but then I realized this was different. I realized it
was, I don't know . . . intimate. It wasn't something we did
for fun, like the dares we did with the others. It wasn't so we

would feel brave. Being bitten wasn't fun for Anne, it was . . .
pleasurable. And that made me feel bad. The bruises and cuts
also made me feel bad, but what I found unbearable was her
pleasure. It wasn't unbearable at first, but quickly became so.
After the thing with the photo.

Dr. Aguilar:

Fernanda: Because in the photo she was naked in the shower,
and you could see all the marks. Some were bleeding a little.
I don't know . . . When they saw the photo, they made these
disgusted, horrified faces, and that made me feel bad. And
then I didn't want to keep doing it. Maybe I thought our relationship was changing too much, and I didn't want anything to
change. I was reeeally upset. I don't know how to explain it.
It's hard when you have to tell someone something important for the first time. *Let me think* . . . It never would have
occurred to me to bite someone. Yes, it's important to say this:
it was her idea. And if I liked biting her, even if just a little,
it was her fault and not mine, because it never would have
occurred to me to do it. Do you understand, Doc? If Anne
hadn't asked me, almost begged me, to play that with her, I
never would have learned that maybe I like biting her a little.
And I know it can't be good that I sort of like something like
that, right? It can't be good that I like hurting my BF. Even
though she likes it, and I sort of like that she likes it, I don't
feel good about that. When we were little, we weren't like this,
you know? I think I started to be afraid of her because she was
changing me. She was making me think I wanted things that,
deep down, I didn't want. Things I can't want.

Dr. Aguilar:

Fernanda: I guess I thought I could do anything she did, but I
started to get scared of what we were doing and also to think
she might be testing me, to see how far I would go. And then
I wanted us to stop because I didn't want to go thaaat far.
I don't know if I'm explaining it very well. The games we

invented at the building were one thing, but something very different was happening every time we slept in the same bed.

Dr. Aguilar:

Fernanda: *Of course. I mean,* I know what we were doing in the building was also dangerous. Well, *is* dangerous. *I know.* But at least it wasn't intimate. And I believe it's the intimate stuff that's always much more threatening. *Anyway,* I want to be clear: I wasn't the only one who was afraid of Anne. As I told you the other day, the others were scared of her too, even if they didn't say so, especially after she invented that whole thing about the white age and the White God. *I mean,* the last time I went to the building, I got there late, and I almost had a *heart attack* because they all started screaming, and their screams in there were the worst thing I've heard in my whole life. It was one of those afternoons when we'd tell our *horror stories,* although around that time, Anne had started running them, because that's how she is. *Whatever.* I heard screams that didn't stop, and I stayed very still in the building's entrance, terrified by the echo and the fleeing pigeons, and then Fiorella, Natalia, and Ximena sprinted down the stairs and shoved me out of the way as they left. Their faces looked ugly, deformed from the bellowing. You can't even imagine, Doc, how awful their shrieking was. I was really afraid, and I screamed *"Fuck!"* but I went up anyway, like in the movies. I guess because I didn't want to be a coward—I wanted to prove to myself that even though I was scared, I could face whatever it was. Ah! And also because you always want to know what everyone else is afraid of, *you know?* For me, not knowing is *always* worse, Doc. *Anyway,* when I went up the stairs, I went straight to the white room and saw it, that scene, the one that will stay in my head forever. I was scared, *of course,* and everything went into slow motion, like in the movies. I don't know if it's true, but I once heard that our perception of time depends on the speed of our heartbeat, and because of that, a hummingbird sees us the way we see turtles. Is that true, Doc? *Anyway*, it was reeeally weird, because instead of racing, my heart became a turtle when I saw Analía crying and shaking in the middle of a pool of piss and blood. Yes, piss and blood! Anne was in the corner, crowned with the shark jawbone she stole from the library, and she wasn't doing anything, just watching Analía, a little scared. And I don't know why, but at that moment, I felt a surge of rage. Maybe because I already saw myself outside of the group, and because deep down, I had gone to say good-bye, I don't know. What I do know is, I ran toward Anne and pushed her. I screamed at her a lot, *like crazy*. I screamed at her "What did you do to Analía?" even though I knew she hadn't done anything to her. I knew Analía had probably gotten her period like Carrie White, no big deal, because she was the only one who still hadn't menstruated, and maybe it had happened during one of the White God stories, or in the circle we sometimes formed by holding each other's hands and sitting in silence. Menstruation can be reeeally *creepy* depending on the atmosphere, *you know?* Like when Anne and I pretended we had an insatiable monster in our uteruses, though that isn't a good example since that never scared us. We knew quite well what menstruation was, but the *creepy* part doesn't have anything to do with knowing or not knowing, it has to do with the environment where things that are, I don't know, *natural* happen. There are environments that make the natural appear antinatural and also supernatural. So I think that's what happened. Even though no one's told me, I believe that's what it was: something to do with the atmosphere. But in that moment, no one said a word to me, and Anne looked at me like she hated me more than any other person in the world. Then I started to get scared again because Analía stopped crying, and there was a gigantic silence, and I simply couldn't stand it. I decided to leave, just like the others. And when I got to the first floor, Anne threw that big rock at me, the one I told you about the other day, the

one that almost cracked my head open, but it missed me. That
cun . . . *bitch. Sorry.*

Dr. Aguilar:

Fernanda: I guess I got scared because I sensed something I
   couldn't see, but it was there. Just like in the story you recommended, "The Horla" by Maupassant, when he talks about
   how the wind is among us, whistling, toppling things over,
   even though we don't see it. That's how I felt. And I think
   that's what I sensed every time we were in the white room.
   Now that I think about it, it's possible the others felt it too,
   and that's why we didn't dare enter or even look inside the
   room, except for on the afternoons when we had to. It's not
   like I think the White God is real or anything, Doc, but you
   can also be scared of things that don't exist.

Dr. Aguilar:

Fernanda: I don't know, it just came to me. Why? You don't like
   that I call you Doc?

Dr. Aguilar:

Fernanda: I'm not teasing, Doc.

Dr. Aguilar:

Fernanda: Hello, Doc.

XXVI

A: Juliet Hulme and Pauline Parker were best friends, and they loved each other so much that at fifteen and sixteen years old, they killed Pauline's mother so she wouldn't separate them.

C: Enough.

A: They hit her forty-five times with a brick hidden inside a sock. Can you imagine, Miss Clara? In a sock!

C: I don't want to hear these things. There's no reason—

A: Then Caril Ann Fugate, at fourteen years old, killed her mother, her stepfather, and her half-sister with the help of her boyfriend.

C: Stop, Annelise.

A: They stayed in the house with the bodies for six days, and then they went on a *road trip* and killed two more teenagers. Can you believe that?

C: ...

A: Then Mary Flora Bell and Norma Bell, who weren't sisters, far from it, just friends, killed two boys, ages four and three. Mary carved her initials into the three-year-old with a knife and cut off his genitals. She was eleven when she did it. Eleven!

C: Enough!

A: Brenda Ann Spencer, sixteen years old, shot kids and teachers at an elementary school with a semiautomatic rifle with a telescopic sight. At the trial, she said she did it because she didn't like Mondays.

C: Annelise, please ...

A: "I don't like Mondays," she said. It's so simple and so complex at the same time, isn't it?

C: ...

A: Natasha Cornett ran away with some of her friends because she was really bored. Just like everyone else, right? And she killed an entire family, shot them all. She was seventeen when she did it.

C: Please! Are you listening to me?

A: The Karubin sisters, Caroline and Catherine, murdered their alcoholic mother by drowning her in the bathtub. Before committing the crime, they told their friends about it, and they all thought it was a fantastic idea. FAN-TAS-TIC. They were sixteen and fifteen years old.

C: Please!

A: If you leave, I'll follow you, Miss Clara.

C: Please ...

A: I need you to listen to me. I need you to help me. Do you see what they have in common?

C: No.

A: Ana Carolina, sixteen years old, strangled her adoptive parents and injected bleach and insecticide into their jugulars. Afterward, she and her boyfriend went out for *hot dogs* and beer.

C: No more.

A: Wait, this is my favorite case: Morgan Geyser and Anissa Weier tried to kill their best friend by stabbing her nineteen times. They both said they had done it because Slender Man told them to. Do you know about Slender Man?

C: ...

A: No? He's a monster invented by the internet, and all the horror fans tell stories about him, so he keeps getting bigger and bigger. Supposedly he appears to children and teenagers, and when that occurs, nothing good happens. Believe me.

C: . . .

A: Morgan Geyser and Anissa Weier were twelve years old when they stabbed their friend nineteen times. Nineteen times!

C: . . .

A: Do you see what they have in common? I mean . . . it isn't normal.

C: . . .

A: And there are many more . . . hundreds upon thousands of girls who've been twisted by something within. Dangerous girls, like Fernanda. Girls who betray their best friends and who get inside their teachers' houses to scare them.

C: . . .

A: God is young. Don't you think, Miss Clara?

XXVII

"I don't want to go in!" Fiorella screams. Her voice wears and cracks. It drags out sleep sand. It drags out bad nights. She doesn't want to be so afraid, but she's scared because the white room swells like a diseased lung, and Annelise dons the crown: the heavy jawbone of a shark. The teeth glint in her hair like daggers. And to the south, Fernanda prowls. She gets on all fours. The others imitate her: they enter the whiteness of the room as the White God pack. "Shall we pray or hunt?" asks Anne, licking her knuckles. She kneels. She lifts her right hand up to the crown. The divine mandible. Relic of the mother-God-of-the-wandering-womb. Fiorella stays on the outside and trembles. She knows if she doesn't go in, it will anger Fernanda; it will anger Annelise. Her sister and the others form the circle for the ceremony. They're possessed by the fever. Sometimes she is too, but not that afternoon, because she's had nightmares. She's seen faces pushing through the white paint on the walls. She's seen caimans. She's seen milk. Natalia, Ximena, Analía, and Fernanda lower their heads, and their hair covers faces bathed in sweat and frenzy. She doesn't want to go to bed scared. She doesn't want to dream of what they're going to do. They've done it so many times. Fifteen times. Twenty. She knows it will hurt because it always hurts. She knows she will imagine things because Anne will make her imagine them. Fiorella wants the game to seem stupid and childish, like when they did it the first time. "Will you pray or hunt?" Now, instead, the game seems too adult. "Will you hunt?" Now Anne has shark teeth encircling her skull. "Or will you pray?" She licks the knuckles of her left hand and raises her right in the air. "One or the other, Fiorella." And, though she doesn't want to, she enters. "One or the other."

They hold hands. Ximena knows hers are sweaty. She knows it disgusts Analía and Fiorella, but that's how her hands are. She has no others. Annelise says the words: the ones that sound good and signify evil. And Ximena smiles, proud to be there, to have completed each dare up until then, endured the punishments, offered her stories to the White God. She feels lucky to be in the circle, even if it means hitting her friends, or being hit by them. Because the adventure is worth it, she thinks. Because who wouldn't want to experience a movie plot for a few hours a day.

They close their eyes.

And then it begins.

"The White God is in the room," says Anne. Natalia doesn't believe in stupid things like that, but when she's in the circle with her friends and they hold hands and close their eyes, she always follows the rules. "They're in the room," Anne repeats, agitated. They all listen to her. They all begin to have trouble breathing. Natalia feels a vibration. A chill. A presence. She would never dare look, even though she doesn't believe in stupid things like that. She squeezes her eyelids tight. Anne's voice turns into another again.

An amputated voice.

A stump.

Analía gets really bored outside the building. That's why, even though she's disgusted by the way Fernanda's saliva feels on her face and scared of the things Annelise says crowned in teeth, she doesn't break the circle. She doesn't open her eyes if the White God caresses her ear. If They make her think about kicking and blood. About shoving and how easy it is to rip her friends' skin. She's safe with her eyes closed: as long as she can't see Them, nothing bad will happen to her. Nails run up her back and fingers pull her hair. Her neck may be fragile, but not her mind. "The White God is here," sings the jawbone. Then they slap her face, and she smiles. "Give Them a little something to drink." It's about seeing what hurts, she's learned. "Give Them a sip of your blood, Analía."

It's seeing what evil is. "Your blood, which tastes like language." It's about seeing the opposite of God.

Fernanda opens her eyes and sees Annelise, who no longer has a head but a thinking jawbone. "You will savor God in the carrion," she says, and puts a dead bird in her hands. The rest of them raise theirs into the air. They know the moment approaches. "You will savor God in the carrion," they chant. And the walls drip. The wind cries like a mother. They'll all have to do it, even Annelise, but it's Fernanda's turn first. "You will savor God in the carrion." She prefers the dares, the blows, the danger. The horror stories that keep her up at night. "Eat from this, because this is Their body." Whereas the White God cult is a real game. "And this is Their blood." But Annelise is beautiful. "Bite it." And Fernanda cries from the beauty.

"Bite it."

XXVIII

Fernanda closed her eyes and imagined she was running away from the cabin, through the forest she pictured as green and bright, like the Christmas trees in her friends' houses.

Like the sequins on the theater sets at school.

Like the dean's uniform.

Like Annelise's favorite shoes.

She had never been in a forest, but she had seen them many times on TV and in movies.

Women running. Girls running.

She thought she was running. She imagined it was possible to run through a forest while physically handcuffed to a table, sitting in a chair, listening to her teacher's cavern voice, her fissure voice:

"How did you get so sick, you sick little girl?"

"How dare you abuse your best friend, inflict pain on her, enter my house as if it were yours?"

Fernanda ran, jumping over rocks, roots, and moose eyes to escape from that voice in hunting season, thinking: *I didn't do it!*

What did I do? she sometimes wondered.

In her mind, her teacher's words were lynxes, hounds, rats pursuing her innocence of thought, deed, or omission.

"I know exactly what you did."

"I know full well what you do with your teeth and your hands under beds."

Through my fault, through my fault, through my most grievous fault, she whispered to herself like when they forced her to pray on her knees even though she wasn't guilty of anything.

She was not to blame, everyone said, for the color of the pool.

She was not to blame for her little brother's broken blue forehead.

When the forest of her imagination dispersed due to Miss Clara's cinder-like voice, Fernanda squeezed her eyes shut even tighter, and then the trees with their creatures returned, soothing that voice like a cave, like a skull:

> "Your friend Anne told me."
>
> "Your friend Anne told me everything you did. What you did to me."

But she had never broken into someone else's house or forced Anne to withstand her primitive way of biting, that she knew for sure. Although there was a lot she didn't know—like what had happened in the pool with her dead brother, Martín—she knew everything else, the important parts: that what her teacher was saying, spewing frothy saliva and pounding the table with her fists, was a lie.

That her teacher was clinically insane.

That she was talking confusedly. Deliriously.

That she didn't hear her or see her as she tried to contain her wails, to endure with her eyelids shut, to evade the sight of a pair of eyes that seemed to have sunk into Miss Clara's perfect skull.

A divine and dirty skull. So brilliant from the grease of her hair that it was scary.

Rotten head.

Decomposing head.

She couldn't escape. She couldn't run from the greasy black hair slurring words at her.

She was also slurring words deep inside herself, out of fear. The fear that forced her to stumble over her words, to run her mind through the elevated landscape of her imagination so her neck wouldn't trap her ideas.

She had always thought people were incapable of thinking when terrified, but she was thinking. She was thinking very clearly: about disorder, about waterfalls, about carousels.

She thought faster than she ran. Faster than she could understand.

She didn't want to be driven mad by her fear of the hair.

She didn't want to wet herself again, even though she already was.

"I've never gone inside your house!"

"Anne lied to you!"

"Anne tricked you!"

She took a breath. Her teacher didn't hear her, because she was raving mad, raving to kill. Her adult words were crocodiles that galloped through the watermelon-green, vomit-green forest to point at her with the edges of their twisted tails in the air.

They accused her of crocodile tears, and she didn't understand why she lost her nerve.

They told her stories of frames, fangs, and fetters.

They told her something about her supposed abuse of Annelise.

She asked me to do it, she would have said if her tongue had been capable of anything but trembling.

She liked me to chew on her as if she were a piece of gum.

She loved when I wrung out her trachea like an old rag.

Her teacher was in front of her, just across the table, but in her imagination, she was behind her, far away, and the trees were hiding her.

Scary movies didn't know the actual dynamics of a kidnapping.

Fernanda imagined she was fast enough in the forest to survive that chalkboard voice, that mountain voice that stripped her down while showing its fangs, bellowing at her up close like a wayward shadow, sniffing at her tears that didn't stop falling.

The wave from between her legs.

The farts she could no longer hold in and that were too loud and stank.

And in the forest of her invention, in the chair that gushed piss, she felt she missed Anne more than she'd ever missed her before.

Anne: her doll-double, her bayonet-double.

She would have liked to keep biting her in spite of everything, not as Miss Clara's voice bit her heels, but as mantises bite off the heads of their lovers.

But now it was too late for her teeth.

Now she felt the danger and wanted to return to her mother's womb, to watch Martín be born like a little fish in the immensity of the hospital bed.

To run away in the forest. For there to be at least the possibility of saving herself from the black hair that fell from the trees.

> "You have to understand that I cannot
> have you in my house."

To be afraid was to desire what she had never before desired: to return to the elastic wetness of the placenta, to wake up to her dead brother's first cry.

> "I am going to have to kick you out."
> "I am going to have to expel you."

To be afraid was to sense the truth like an eyelash floating over an eye: there would be no return anymore, it was already impossible to turn back. She felt it in the cavernous sound of Miss Clara's voice, in the revolver moving around on the table like an animal with a carapace, in the birds that shrieked outside the cabin, providing a chorus for the unfinished scene inside.

Birds were frightening beings when they did anything but fly.

Fernanda had never felt empathy for any of the pigeons she killed in the building. She watched them die, indifferent, and now she was

one of those animals, quivering and repulsive, that housed danger
down to their skeletons.

Nature was like that: just and atrocious.

She wanted to remember Anne's laugh, to beautify the violence with which she ran through the forest elevated by her own
negation, but she couldn't evoke it. In her memory, there was
only a bestial noise, an iron cackling full of dragonflies that chased
her.

"Sick girls like you need to be taught a lesson."

Fernanda's head zigzagged between the trees crowned with
clouds like her mother's interminable skin.

"I am going to teach you a lesson."

And as she felt the cold entering her stomach like an icy worm,
she thought about Anne, and about how no matter how much a
hyena, how much a reptile she really was, she never could have
foreseen what her lies would provoke. What her attempt to scare
Miss Clara would let loose in the real world.

"I'm going to teach you something there,
in your cockroach nest."

Annelise must feel guilty, she thought, for what she did without
knowing.

Poor thing, she thought. She forgave her with all her heart.

"You're sick."

I forgive you, she thought, still running, *but I want you to suffer.*

"You're really sick."

I love you, she thought, snapping branches and roots, *but I hope you carry this guilt until the end.*

"I need you to learn, and someone has to teach you."

Fernanda knew she had betrayed Annelise first, and that's why she forgave her: because the first to plunge the dagger always had to keep quiet.

"Someone has to get dirty."

And while Miss Clara's voice said things without feet or a head, like the ice worms that slid down her throat, Fernanda saw the truth: that animals knew when they were going to die because death is a feeling.

A futurist emotion of the body.

And while she listened to that icy teacher's voice swelling the wood, its force opening up even the insides of rocks, she thought about how much she regretted not having died with Annelise when she had the opportunity. When the earth shook in the school's chapel.

A 4.5 on the Richter scale, said the news.

Yet another earthquake in the land of earthquakes, they thought, but the movement never stopped, and all the girls and teachers started to look at each other, and on the altar, even God shook.

"The apocalypse!" Anne shouted.

Bellows.

The girls hugged their best friends, and Fernanda, Annelise.

Her soul-twin. Her groin-twin.

Then, the magic: their cheeks came together, they breathed in each other's temples, they hugged each other's waists, fingers almost digging into flesh, the tips of their noses touching, and while the teachers told them to follow the evacuation procedures they hadn't once practiced, they looked at each other with such intensity that they burst into laughter in the middle of the terror.

She should have died like that, she thought: buried by the golden roof of the chapel.

A buried love.

A friendship like a temple growing beneath the earth.

Her death would have been happy if she'd dared to die that day; it would have been beautiful and perfect, with Annelise squeezing her and fearlessly cackling while everyone else screamed with their eyes shut.

She should have died before the earthquake was over.

God should have fallen.

When she left the chapel alive, she didn't realize that any death after the one she'd escaped would always be worse.

"You're going to have to learn with me, do you hear?"

She tripped in her head, but she had lost the opportunity to die properly, so it no longer mattered.

The voice of sabers and axes reached her, slashing the wind.

"Did you hear me?"

Death was a feeling.

In front of her was an unbearable whiteness she imagined as dense and latent: the White God imposing Themself on the horizon of her fall.

"Open your eyes!"

No: a snowy volcano. But that wasn't what she wanted to imagine.

"Open them!"

She squeezed her eyelids as tight as she could and listened to the chair clawing the floor as her teacher's footsteps approached.

"It's going to be hard for you,
but you're going to do it."

An icy volcano about to erupt, Annelise's White God emerging from the crater to rescue her from the crocodile.

"You'll see."

How stupid, she thought. The White God saves no one.

"It'll be very hard for you,
but I'm going to teach you."

Her fall dwelled in the forest before a volcano erupting just like her belly.

"You just have to listen to me."

But when she opened her eyes and looked for Them out the window, she didn't see any God, any volcano asleep on Earth.
Asleep in the sky.

"You just have to dive into the fear."

XXIX

A: She will go into your house.

C: Enough.

A: I know she'll do it.

C: ...

A: One day she'll go into your house just like those other girls, all of them in the white age, all praying to the White God, and she's going to hurt you too, the same way she hurt me.

C: Shut up.

A: Because she's bored.

C: ...

A: Because she killed her brother when she was just a little girl.

C: ...

A: Because I'm her best friend, and she betrayed me.

C: ...

A: Because we all hate Mondays.

XXX

Fernanda and Annelise ran across the lawn without dodging the daisies. Their toes sank into the ground wet from the sprinklers fracturing the water into millions of liquid microcrystals. "It's as if all the glasses were breaking in the air," Annelise said, using her open palms to deaden the water. They were eight years old, and the sun that disheveled their heads looked like the yolk of a rotten egg. It was a pale-yellow day, but the club was full of people stuffed into their vomit-colored-bathing-suits, not like theirs, which were electric colors and covered in dinosaurs. Fernanda got out a float, a vanilla donut with sprinkles, and Annelise surpassed her, cannonballing into the pool. *Splash.* Some kids in the corners choked on chlorine waves and chunks of fruit. Two nannies with pink uniforms pulled them out and looked at Annelise, still underwater, with enormous irritation. Nearby, there were strollers; robots; Popeye, Hello Kitty, and Dora the Explorer floaties; flip-flops; inflatable bags; sunscreen; sunglasses; magazines; and baby bottles. Fernanda gazed at the objects with boredom and, burning-red, slowly entered the water, her little fingers gripping the donut-float-present-from-Daddy. There was a bigger pool at the club, but it was just for adults, and she didn't understand why she had to stay in the smaller, uglier one. Being a little girl, she had learned at eight years old, meant always getting what was worst, like that ridiculous float that couldn't compare to the enormous whale drifting in the adult pool. Annelise once tried to steal the whale, but her mother caught her and gave her a loud spanking in front of the older kids, which made her tear up. Fernanda didn't like the way Annelise's mother treated her. She didn't like the way hers treated her either, but she couldn't do anything about it. Their mothers were friends and members of the club. They liked to play

badminton, chat with the instructor—a giant man whose forehead
sweat Fernanda's mother sometimes wiped away—and drink concoctions next to the pool. When they got together to train with
the giant instructor, the two mothers would send them to play
far away from the area for adults, to swim in water full of snot
and bits of watermelon and eat at the kids' buffet, where there was
always a clown or a Mickey Mouse livening up the room. "They
never let us do anything fun," Annelise would say, and Fernanda
thought she was right, but she also liked being alone with her best
friend, running across the lawn, eating Jell-O shaped like bears
and rainbows, drinking Coke and cups of juice adorned with paper
umbrellas, stroking each other's wrinkly fingers, and peeing in the
pool without anyone noticing, because the contrast between the
coolness of the water and the warmth of their insides was deli-
cious. "It's our secret," Annelise said when she copied Fernanda, a
little embarrassed. Now Fernanda was watching her dive down
just like a mermaid while the *Toy Story* soundtrack played on the
loudspeakers. "You've got a friend in me!" sang a girl swinging a
few meters from the pool. "You've got a frieeend in me!" Far off,
behind a fence, she could see her mother and Annelise's alongside
other women with rackets, all in short skirts that showed their
cellulite when they walked. It had long bothered Annelise that
her mother got together with other mothers to drink forbidden
concoctions and cackle like Ursula from *The Little Mermaid.* She
thought she acted differently, and it was true: when the mothers
got together, Fernanda felt like hers loved her less. When the
mothers got together, hers stopped being a mother and became a
different person, one who didn't like her. "Let's play secret mission," Annelise said, climbing out the side of the pool. "We have
to get into the area for adults without our moms seeing. We have to
save the giant instructor." "From what?" "From them casting a spell
on him, of course!" "That's so evil!" "They're really evil." Annelise
had told her that, one Saturday, when her mother invited the other
mothers over to play poker and drink concoctions and laugh like
Ursula, she didn't go to bed but crawled into the living room to see

what they were doing. On the way, she said, she was afraid of the noises she heard: tentacular laughter, the clashing of cups, music with trumpets. "Poooor unfortunate souls!" As Fernanda followed her friend's story, Ursula sang in her head, conjuring lines from "The Little Mermaid," which Charo read to her at night. Annelise hid behind a cabinet and saw the mothers, cards fanned out and chips on the table. She thought about jumping out and screaming "Boo!" but she was afraid her mother would spank or insult her, as she usually did in front of her friends. *She now came to a space of marshy ground in the wood, where large, fat water snakes were rolling in the mire and showing their ugly, drab-colored bodies.* Annelise wished that Fernanda had been by her side to see it, she told her then, because suddenly the laughter became thunderous, and, throwing the cards down onto the stained tablecloth, one of the mothers took off her dress and underwear while the rest of them wept with maleficent laughter. *There sat the sea witch, allowing a toad to eat from her mouth just as people sometimes feed a canary with pieces of sugar.* Their noses were scrunched up, their nostrils like craters, and slowly, strange roots started growing from their foreheads. *She called the ugly water snakes her little chickens and allowed them to crawl all over her bosom.* According to Annelise, their cheeks swelled up and quivered while the naked mother walked around the table, egged on by a pack of rhythmic applause. *The sea witch knew what she wanted and laughed so loud and so disgustingly that the toad and the snakes fell to the ground and lay there wriggling.* So much facial exercise brought with it enormous drops of sweat, which the mothers dried off with napkins or with their hands, but seconds later, Annelise saw hers get up and walk through the black-octopus laughter, toward the pubis of a stray cat and the tits with blue veins. *"I will prepare a draft for you, with which you must swim to land tomorrow before sunrise; seat yourself there and drink it."* She teetered a little and sipped the iguana-green concoction before bending toward the naked mother and kissing her on the lips. *"You will feel great pain, as if a sword were passing through you, but all who see you will say that you are the prettiest little human being they ever saw*." Fernanda remembered Annelise's fear and disgust as she told her how she'd seen her mother's long and viscous tongue entering the naked mother's mouth. *"But I must be paid, also, and it is not a trifle that I ask."* And then, unable to stop herself, Annelise screamed so her mother's glassy eyes would follow the school bell. *"You have the sweetest voice of any who dwell here in the depths of the sea, and you believe that you will be able to charm the prince with it. But this voice you must give to me."* Furious, she grabbed her puppy by the scruff while her friends laughed and drank the concoctions forbidden to girls. *Then the witch placed her cauldron on the fire, to prepare the magic draft.* Fernanda imagined the scene Annelise described as if she had seen it on television: Mrs. Van Isschot led her daughter down the hallway, spanking her as they went up the stairs, and then shoved her into her bedroom. That wasn't the worst part, though; it was what came after. *Then she pricked herself in the breast and let the black blood drop into the cauldron.* The daughter, still upset, grabbed her mother's arm before she could leave, and without meaning to, she scratched her from elbow to wrist. *The steam that rose twisted into such horrible shapes that no one could look at them without fear.* There must have been a Barbie on the floor, because the two of them tripped, and the daughter ended up ramming her little goat horns into the motherly belly. *Every moment the witch threw a new ingredient into the vessel, and when it began to boil, the sound was like the weeping of a crocodile.* The reaction was immediate and terrifying: Annelise swore to her that, in the middle of the night, in her room, her mother's eyes lost their color; she took her by the hair, spewed bat-soup breath out at her, and sank her teeth into her shoulder, the first thing she could reach. *When at last the magic draft was ready, it looked like the clearest water.* She bit her with fury, an ire Annelise had only seen in dogs. *Then she cut off the mermaid's tongue, so that she would never again speak or sing.* She explained to Fernanda that her mother's teeth hurt the way death must hurt. She explained that she didn't know how she hadn't died. *Then the little mermaid drank the magic draft, and it seemed as if a two-edged sword went through her delicate body.* Annelise could barely sleep because of the terror her own mother engendered when she looked at her very closely and warned her, her voice thickly bearded, that if she said one word to her father about what had happened, she would kill her. "That's what she said to me: 'I'll kill you if you tell Daddy,'" she confessed to Fernanda. The next day, however, Mrs. Van Isschot's eyes were the same as always, and it surprised Annelise that she acted like nothing had happened. *When the sun rose over the sea, she recovered and felt a sharp pain, but before her stood the handsome young prince.* As she dried herself off with her fireworks beach towel, Fernanda considered how strange the mothers became when they got together. The daughters, she thought, must also become strange when they get together, when they make their hands and noses touch under the water, when they're twinned. "Hey, do you want to be my sister?" she suddenly asked her as she wrung out her hair and the chlorine splashed off the floor. Annelise excitedly smiled: "Yes, I want to be your sister." The area for adults wasn't protected, but each time a child entered, their parents sent them back to the smaller and dirtier world outside. "So how do you think we break the spell they put on the giant?" Fernanda asked after they'd hidden behind a column to avoid being seen. "Kissing our mommies' necks," Annelise said as if it were obvious, resuming her course with small but firm, dripping steps. They passed the enormous pool for adults and saw a fat man jump from a diving board that touched the sky. SPLASH! Annelise covered her mouth with her hand and laughed when two waiters carrying trays of multicolored concoctions got wet. The floating whale washed up at the feet of a woman with red patches shaped like peppers on her legs, and although Fernanda was tempted to take it or puncture it so the adults couldn't use it either, she kept walking with Annelise toward the badminton courts, dodging bodies smelling like guava and sunscreen. "There they are!" Annelise said, crouching down. Fernanda copied her and saw their mothers with other mothers, letting out Ursulan laughs, and the giant instructor tying his shoelaces next to some empty bleachers. "Ninety percent of the mission is complete," Annelise said into an imaginary

walkie-talkie that was actually her fist. "We just need to deactivate
the mothers' spell, over and out." Fernanda raised her head a little
and saw, in the distance, a soccer field where only fathers were running. "What if you tell your dad what you saw?" Annelise looked
at her as if she had suggested something unthinkable. "Do you
want my mom to eat me like the witch in 'Hansel and Gretel,' or
what?" Fernanda didn't like that and came out from their hiding
place, wiping her knees with her hands. "What are you doing!
You're going to ruin the mission!" *Mothers don't eat daughters,* she
thought but didn't say out loud. A few meters away, her mom was
talking to the instructor, resting her racket on a chair and drawing
a half-moon with the tip of her right foot. It gave Fernanda chills
to see her like that, but she didn't know why. "Retreat!" screamed
Annelise while her new adventure-sister embarked on the path
toward the badminton court. The ground trembled with a far-off
pale sun, and Fernanda moved forward, leaving a trail of water and
swinging her hips as if on a catwalk. She didn't try to hide, but her
mother didn't realize she was there until she hugged her hips from
behind with her little arms wet from the pool. Then Fernanda felt
the muscles of the maternal body contracting, retreating like the
sea, and she watched the instructor's crooked smile salivating in
the clouds. "Is this your daughter?" "Yes . . . she's my little girl," her
mother responded as if she had just woken up. "Now, darling, what
are you doing here?" she asked as she unwrapped her arms, dis-
guising her discomfort in sweet words. Fernanda didn't like that in
front of strangers, her mother called her "darling," "princess," "my
love," "sweetie," "honey," but when they were alone or with her
father, she only called her by her name. "Go back to the kiddie
pool, honey, Mommy's busy training." Mommy's voice was higher
when she talked in front of the giant-beaver-toothed-instructor.
Mommy put on perfume and makeup to play badminton. Mommy
asked her to behave as well as her dead brother, Martín, had when
he was alive. "I want to stay." Fernanda didn't think it was fair,
because her brother hadn't had time to act out. "You have to go
back to the kiddie pool, sweetheart." So she again hugged the hips

that had crowned her birth, but this time from the front so her
mother would see her, and she rested her ear against her mons
pubis. In the clouds, the instructor turned and walked toward the
other mothers, who were playing with a birdie. "You don't want to
upset me, do you? Listen to me and do what I tell you," Mommy
whispered in a more serious, threatening tone once the two of
them were alone. She tried to detach her, to slip out of the skinny,
wet hug, but Fernanda squeezed tighter, like a leech to blood.
"Fernanda!" Other mothers were dabbing the sweat from the instructor's forehead, laughing, looking up at the heat that fell from the
sky. "Do I not have the right to relax?" her mother said, as if about
to burst into tears. Annelise often told Fernanda that she was jealous of the power she had to scare her own mother. "Mommy wants
you to let her play in peace!" But the superpower of frightening her
mom wasn't one that Fernanda would have asked for. "You're killing me! I can't deal with you!" She released her mother when she felt
the sharp nails digging into her arms. "I'm staying!" she screamed so
as not to lose ground, but Mommy trembled with relief upon seeing herself outside her daughter's embrace, and she turned her aging
face toward her. A woman who looked like a crow took advantage
of the moment to approach, and attempting to ease the atmosphere,
she began praising Fernanda's hair, Fernanda's eyes. "What a princess she is! She could be from Naples!" Mommy was silent in
response to the stranger's flattery and returned to the chair where
she'd left her gym bag and a bottle of mineral water. On the other
side of the net, the instructor was busy watching the match
between two mothers who were both wearing Nike sweatbands
and who shot a birdie at Fernanda's enraged feet. "Are you angry,
princess?" the crow-faced-woman asked. "You'll look ugly if you get
mad." She wanted to hit her mother, push her to the ground, jump
on top of her, but she would never do anything like that, so she
walked toward her mommy's back as she was drinking water next
to the chair. *I'll break the spell for Anne*, she thought and jumped up
to wrap her hot arms around the maternal neck. Mommy made a
gruff sound as she fell backward from the weight and let her bottle

fall, but Fernanda kept propelling herself upward, lips puckered
toward the sweaty neck she only ever saw during badminton les-
sons. "Dear, you're strangling her!" screamed a woman out of true
desperation, and that's when Fernanda realized her mother was
yanking her hair, almost lifting her into the air as she emitted dry
choking sounds. She felt pain, but everything else happened very
quickly: someone, perhaps the giant instructor, perhaps a mother
or the crow-faced-woman, grabbed her by the waist and pulled her
from her mother, who fell to the ground soaked with water from
the bottle. Fernanda never knew who set her back down on the
ground, because her eyes were fixed on the other mothers, all running to help hers; hers, whose red face was full of maggoty veins;
hers, who coughed up fish tanks; hers, whose eyes were swollen
with lagoons; hers, who gasped as if about to sink into the adult
pool forever. *I just wanted to kiss you,* thought Fernanda, startled
because her mother was crying with other mothers, who helped
her stand up. *I just wanted to break the spell.* "Mommyyy!" she
screamed, suddenly crying, and the crow-faced-woman looked at
her, afraid. "Come here, your mommy needs some space," Annelise's
mother said, appearing from among the group of mothers, taking
her delicately by the neck and leading her off the court. "You hurt
your mommy," she said as they crossed through the area for adults.
"You need to be careful and listen better." Fernanda looked around,
searching for Annelise, but it was as if she had never been her sister. "If I were your mother, I wouldn't put up with even half of it."
When they got to the kiddie pool, Fernanda saw Annelise sitting
on the edge of the pool, slapping the water with her wrinkly feet.
"Look at Anne. Do you see how she listens?" said her fake sister's
mom. The song from *Toy Story* was playing from the loudspeaker
again, but the girl who had been singing it was no longer on the
swings. "Behave, or we won't bring you here anymore." Fernanda sat
down next to Annelise and watched the biting-mother leave, shaking her head back and forth as she walked toward the adult area.
"Youuu've got a frieeend in me!" There weren't any kids in the pool,
but she could hear them on the other side of the bushes. "Yeah,

you've got a friend in me!" Fernanda realized she was still crying when Annelise dried her tears with a kiss on each cheek. She didn't know why, but she felt shame slithering up her forehead, and she didn't want anyone to see it—not even her best friend, her new secret-mission-sister. Annelise snorted: "See? I told you to come back." A boy started yelling on the other side of the bushes. "I told you when the mothers get together, they're really bad." Fernanda smiled a little because Annelise was mirroring her pout, and for an instant, she imagined that she was identical to her, with that face full of stars and those cotton-candy lips, looking at her reflection in the dirty pool water. *Twin sisters don't need mommies,* she thought. *Twin sisters take care of each other.* "You've got a friend in me." Annelise dropped into the pool and urged her to plunge in too. "Yeah, youuu've got a frieeend in me."

This time, Fernanda got in without a float.

XXXI

A: What's the only animal that's born from its daughter and gives birth to its mother?

F: A woman.

A: Are we women?

F: No! Gross. We're conjoined twins.

A: Conjoined at the hip.

F: Conjoined at the frontal lobe.

A: But you know what? One day we'll be women.

F: Doesn't that scare you?

A: One day we'll be like Mom.

F: Doesn't that really scare you?

XXXII

"Listen. I said, listen. You still have something important to learn, and I'm going to teach it to you. Don't worry. Outside, the clouds fit in a shoe. If only you knew the true size of things, but you're too young to know. You're just a sick little girl. What could you possibly know? I know about things, like the speed of wind in an eyeball. You don't even know how to brush your best friend's teeth. But don't worry: I'm going to teach you how much a shoe, a bed, a door hurts. I'm going to teach you because sick little girls like you need to be taught. What did you say? I can't understand when you shriek like that. In the end, it's about diving into the fear, not overcoming it. About you scaring me as much as you scare me and nevertheless, being like my daughter. Don't cry with your mouth open, it's disgusting. Yes, it's going to hurt. Yes, you're going to be afraid. You already are. It strangles, doesn't it? It reeks, doesn't it? It freezes, doesn't it? My calling is to educate you. I'm your mother because I'm your teacher, and I'm ready to teach you a lesson. I'm going to teach you that when you bite someone else's house, the corners disappear. The shadows lengthen. You have no idea. I'm going to show you what it's like to sleep deep within your shadow, curled up in your parents, in your mirrors. I hardly have a single mirror in my house, but you already know that. They scare me. That's why my only mirror is my mother's twisted spine: the crooked oak backbone that is now mine. Stop shrieking. What you feel is just a silver barrel. It's cold. Let's go, open your legs wide. There's no name for what you did, do you understand? It can't be named. Open them! And when you do something unnamable, you have to deal with the consequences. I'm not the best friend who forgives you or believes you. I'm your teacher, your tender mother of ideas. Do you happen to know how much tenderness fits in a blow? Of

course you do. Of course you know. But a blow never ceases to be
a blow, and what you did, I can't forgive you for that. It's just a silver barrel. You can't get pregnant by gunpowder, but if you could,
you'd give birth to a bullet. Stop shrieking! A bullet that shoots off
and then returns to hit you in the heart: that's what a daughter is.
Whereas they say a mother is a jaw that seizes her offspring to protect them. She could bite them, she could devour them. She wants
to. But a baby can also hurt its mother's mouth, and no one talks
about that. A baby can bite from within, slide down the throat to
the stomach: unbirth itself. And all I want is to make you understand that a house is a jaw that closes. It's about diving into the
fear, and that's the difficult part. Close your mouth! It's so hard to
teach what's abstract, but education is a matter of form. What
you're seeing now is the only form. I've reached the edge of your
cockroach nest, your terrible imagination of damages. But everything comes to an end: we will unbirth ourselves. You'll open your
legs in my shadow. I know girls like you, sick little girls who come
to hunt, who go around gushing menstrual blood on the rooftops
and scratching the curtains. Do you see what you're making me do
to you? And this is nothing: this is terror, but I'd like to show you
panic. I'd like to show you horror: a cryovolcano paralyzing every
one of my mother's vertebrae, a house where what can't be seen
walks. But I can barely teach you terror, make you approach the
muscle contractions, make you understand that a house is a jaw
that shuts and protects, but it could bite you, it could devour you.
I'd like to forgive you, but it isn't about that, understand? It's about
diving into the fear the way you would the crest of a wave. It's
about you scaring me as much as you scare me, and even so, I've
brought you here to teach you something. Because this metal, this
anesthetized trigger, is not a punishment, even though it may look
like one. It's not a punishment, even though I could get revenge for
all the times you kept me awake with your eyelashes at the dead
bolt. This is something else, cleaner, superior. What I want is
to correct you, stand you up straight, raise you right. It's my duty to
keep you from breaking, to keep you advancing in a straight line,

keep you from hurting others. What a stifling responsibility: not to turn you into a monster when you were born a cannibal. But every teacher and every mother must escape from her offspring's teeth. Must teach them not to slide down her throat, not to bite, and must teach herself not to swallow the infant that rests in her jaws. They say a daughter's life is rich and full, but no one talks about how exquisite the mother's life is. The desire to destroy what you've created is just as difficult to suppress as the desire to destroy the one who created you, isn't that right, little mouse? It has to do with being a woman. And with blood. But someone has to take charge of that kind of violence. And if no one can take charge of it, then all that's left is diving into the fear. Unbirthing yourself, like Dr. Frankenstein did with his creature. Because the one thing you can't do is leave the babe alone in the world, toss her into the biggest crater, watch her cooking in the familial magma, never knowing that she'll return like a bullet to violate your chest. You have to take responsibility. And look at me, really look at me: I'm taking responsibility. I know what you did, you sick little girl. To your best friend, your mother, your teacher. I'm going to educate you. Sometimes we suffer too much, and there's nothing left but to drag ourselves to the place where things explode, and then explode: BOOM! And all the evil came to an end, and waiting for things to stop came to an end, and scribbling in the ashes as if we'd never grown up came to an end. I'm honest: I can no longer tolerate the life of my body. I can no longer furrow my brow or brush my hair when I can't get the part to go right down the middle. I don't know how to make a straight line. It's ridiculous to want to stand up straight. I spent hours dragging the comb along the middle of my skull without a clean horizon showing up on my head. Hours using my mother's comb, the one with the broken teeth. But someone has to take responsibility. Close your mouth: you disgust me, you're all saliva and snot. Tears and piss. You dive into the fear because you can no longer live on the threshold, heartbeat of stones and stings, then you dive into the horror so you can stop waiting for something to happen. Waiting to make something happen.

Because it's better to drown yourself in just a few minutes than it is to be drowning for your whole life, do you understand? It's better to die than to feel like you're dying from fear every morning, unable to untangle your hair or really clean the skin beneath your breasts. Unable to clip your nails. Unable to open your dresser drawers. And seeing your dead mother be born in the hallways. Someone has to take responsibility for what it means to comb your hair with your mother's teeth. Look at your hair. You left braids on my pillows and fingers in my bathtub. What was I supposed to do if I could neither leave nor stay inside? What I need to do is teach you something important, but some things, once they're learned, become a punishment. Like the cold of a silver barrel. Like the delicacy of a trigger. I just want you to understand what's going to happen to us now: the panic that will come to an end like anything else in a living body. We will unbirth ourselves. You giving birth to me, and me entering your jaws. Open wide. No one can be that dirty, that brutish. She told me not to say anything, and I didn't, but I had to say something, and here we are. Because you bit her, and you liked it. Because you're perverse. Because you went inside my house. And now I'm going to kick you out of my house. I'm going to show you what it feels like. I'm going to make you understand. What are you saying? I can't understand you. I don't believe you. I know full well what you did. You smell like shit because you're carrying a volcano in my brain, and it's ready to erupt. Look what happens: Do you see how I'm sweating milk? Drink. Nurse. Learn. Open your legs wide! It's about diving into the fear, not overcoming it. You can't overcome the fear that feeds the panic fresh mother's milk. You can't escape, only dive outward. Unbirth yourself. Something has to be done. Something has to be done with sick little girls like you. Because when someone does something unnamable to someone else, they have to face what comes later. That's the form, it's the way. Open up! You disgust me. You horrify me. Your brain is a cockroach nest, but I don't want you to cry out of terror, I want you to cry out of empathy. I want you to feel what you did, to understand what it means to obliterate another.

What are you trying to say? You're telling me she wanted you to? You're telling me that you never went into my house? One simply knows how much noise one can withstand, how many hands. You only know how to horrify others, you sick little girl, you mouse, you watery cockroach nest. It's about diving into the fear. Turning off the lights. Obliterating your mother so you can exist above her. Loving her sacrifice. Closing the doors to the house. Opening your legs deep inside your shadow. Receiving the embrace. Do you see how I'm embracing you in spite of what you did? Everything is o.k. It has to be this way, like a lightning bolt. Like a cascading sky. My mother didn't allow anyone to enter her jaws, only I entered, her muddy becerra. And I slid down her throat. And I scratched at her stomach. A daughter never realizes that one day her turn will come to be the jawed mother. But you're like my daughter because you're my student. I take responsibility for all the harm you cause. Open wide. Together we'll turn off the lights so the White God appears from your mind. The immense truth of the void. You know it well, don't you? Of course you do. Of course you know it. You know that girls who dream too much end up sick in the head, but now you're going to learn something important. Be happy. This is the color of fear. Milk white. Death white. God's snowy skull. Welcome to the volcanic jaws of my house. Let us dive in."

Translator's Note

The aesthetic and symbolic quality of the color white has been used to signify such concepts as purity, cleanliness, absence, occultation, ambiguity, and the sublime. The absence of color and potential for corruption are inherent to the simultaneously alluring and terrifying nature of the hue. Herman Melville expresses this very notion in *Moby Dick* as Ishmael considers his relationship with the great whale, noting that "it was the whiteness of the whale that above all things appalled me," and concluding that the color frightened him because of its indefinite nature. Inspired by the terror of this very quality, *Jawbone*'s Annelise suggests that the color white is disturbing precisely because of its potential to be tarnished when she says in her essay that "one of the disquieting aspects of the color white is that it is pure potential, always close to becoming anything else." With this ambiguity at its heart, *Jawbone* explores the ways that adolescence is a sort of white period, a time marked by the disruption of innocence. Perhaps as you reach the novel's conclusion, you will have experienced a similar sensation.

Drawing on the techniques of horror writers such as H. P. Lovecraft, Mónica Ojeda builds a sense of apprehension and terror through the careful concealment and revelation of information that draws the reader into the depths of this disturbing text. Indeed, both reading and translating this novel are unsettling experiences. In addition to this careful construction of atmosphere, the multiplicity of voices and experimentation with language mark Ojeda's writing style. She has a real strength for weaving together references to popular culture, theoretical writing, and classic literature, all the while incorporating uniquely descriptive imagery, such as Annelise's rhinestone-encrusted, Dior-scented, drag-queen God or her description of a character's "boomerang eyebrows." Beyond this often-startling use of language, the novel is held together by the constant movement between perspectives and temporal positions; maintaining these distinct voices was key to the translation process. For example, the obsessive, twisting sentences full of parenthetical asides in the chapters dealing with Clara are key to the depiction of this woman's mental state, and they were essential to maintain in the translation.

In addition to differentiating voices, building tension in the prose, and dialoguing with other texts, this translation also incorporates some formatting quirks that may be of interest to readers. The use of italics throughout the book, for example, functions to mark both internal thought and the use of English in the Spanish version of the novel. We were mindful of how we used italics in light of Khairani Barokka's argument against the English-language standard to italicize "foreign" words because this practice creates an artificial and problematic division between the self and other. In the Spanish version, non-Spanish terms—primarily in English, though there are a few instances of French—are italicized. In some places, this is due to a predominant use of an English word for a particular thing, such as with terms for recently introduced cultural or technological phenomena. For instance, the term "creepypastas" is italicized in Spanish as the portmanteau—a combination of "creepy" and "copypasta," or texts that have gone viral by being copied and pasted—first appeared in English but has since circulated across languages. In the translation, however, it was not necessary to mark these particular borrowings from English. In many of the dialogues and narratives of the teenage girls, however, the specific use of English is relevant. The girls, all part of upper-class families, pepper their speech with English as a way of marking their class status, as this kind of Spanglish has become fashionable. These tendencies are particularly apparent in the one-sided dialogues between Fernanda and her therapist, in which she constantly marks her speech with phrases such as *"you know," "I mean,"* and *"of course."* There are also places where it was important to differentiate language use to maintain meaning: The students frequently refer to Clara as "*Latin* Madame Bovary" both in the Spanish and English versions. The girls use the English word to refer to Latin America, suggesting that Clara is the Latin American iteration of the canonically tragic character. In the English version, the use of "Latin" may read as the ancient language of Latin, but using the term "Latina" to allude to the Hispanic world would suggest to a u.s. reader that she was a Spanish speaker in the United States. The italics here denote that the girls are using the English term related to the region of Latin America. Italicizing the terms that appear in English in the Spanish version—and that do so as a marker of speech patterns— was a way to mark linguistic difference. On the flip side, I did keep some Spanish in the translation, primarily in dialogue in the chapter when the girls go to the party; here, the sounds the boys make and the culturally specific slang they use help create the sonorous experience of the scene. As this text is already playing with multiple languages, I felt it could hold the unitalicized Spanish.

Another formatting peculiarity in the novel concerns the use of hyphens to create unified concepts, such as with "*High-School-for-girls,*" "antiperspirant-spray-for-feet," "that sleeping-angel-of-history voice," or "her Nicki-Minaj-booty." These hyphenated terms are essential to Ojeda's narrative as she uses them to generate discrete units of meaning. Unlike standard uses of hyphens in English to create compound adjectives, Ojeda's use of the hyphens creates both compound adjectives and nouns that are often quite surprising. These hyphenated constructions add emphasis to these concepts and slow down the reading experience. They also contribute to creating the adolescent voices of the novel, reflecting their linguistic creativity as well as their subversive, anti-authority urges.

Working on this novel was both deeply challenging and rewarding. I cannot overstate my gratitude to Coffee House Press for taking on such a daring project and to Lizzie Davis for her thoughtful and creative editing skills. Lizzie has a deep knowledge of the Spanish language and is herself a talented translator from

Spanish into English, which meant she was able to work with both the Spanish and English versions in the editing process to suggest changes, ensure accuracy, and raise questions about the various tensions in the text. Her suggestions consistently strengthened the different voices of the novel, clarified the rhythm, made the dialogue more realistic and the swearing more precise. I am deeply grateful for her unwavering enthusiasm for this novel and work to make the language as strong as possible. I also want to thank Robert Noffsinger, Emily Booker, Sarah Blanton, and Alejandra Márquez Guajardo for their willingness to work through translation puzzles with me. Finally, thank you to Mónica Ojeda for entrusting me and the amazing team at Coffee House Press with this project.

Sarah Booker
Durham, North Carolina

LITERATURE
is not the same thing as
PUBLISHING

Coffee House Press began as a small letterpress operation in 1972 and has grown into an internationally renowned nonprofit publisher of literary fiction, essay, poetry, and other work that doesn't fit neatly into genre categories.

Coffee House is both a publisher and an arts organization. Through our *Books in Action* program and publications, we've become interdisciplinary collaborators and incubators for new work and audience experiences. Our vision for the future is one where a publisher is a catalyst and connector.

Funder Acknowledgments

Coffee House Press is an internationally renowned independent book publisher and arts nonprofit based in Minneapolis, MN; through its literary publications and *Books in Action* program, Coffee House acts as a catalyst and connector—between authors and readers, ideas and resources, creativity and community, inspiration and action.

Coffee House Press books are made possible through the generous support of grants and donations from corporations, state and federal grant programs, family foundations, and the many individuals who believe in the transformational power of literature. This activity is made possible by the voters of Minnesota through a Minnesota State Arts Board Operating Support grant, thanks to the legislative appropriation from the Arts and Cultural Heritage Fund. Coffee House also receives major operating support from the Amazon Literary Partnership, Jerome Foundation, McKnight Foundation, Target Foundation, and the National Endowment for the Arts (NEA). To find out more about how NEA grants impact individuals and communities, visit www.arts.gov.

Coffee House Press receives additional support from Bookmobile; Dorsey & Whitney LLP; Elmer L. & Eleanor J. Andersen Foundation; Fredrikson & Byron, P.A.; the Matching Grant Program Fund of the Minneapolis Foundation; Mr. Pancks' Fund in memory of Graham Kimpton; the Schwab Charitable Fund; and the U.S. Bank Foundation.

The Publisher's Circle of Coffee House Press

Publisher's Circle members make significant contributions to Coffee House Press's annual giving campaign. Understanding that a strong financial base is necessary for the press to meet the challenges and opportunities that arise each year, this group plays a crucial part in the success of Coffee House's mission.

Recent Publisher's Circle members include many anonymous donors, Patricia A. Beithon, Anitra Budd, Andrew Brantingham, Dave & Kelli Cloutier, Mary Ebert & Paul Stembler, Jocelyn Hale & Glenn Miller, the Rehael Fund-Roger Hale/Nor Hall of the Minneapolis Foundation, Randy Hartten & Ron Lotz, Dylan Hicks & Nina Hale, William Hardacker, Kenneth & Susan Kahn, Stephen & Isabel Keating, the Kenneth Koch Literary Estate, Cinda Kornblum, Jennifer Kwon Dobbs & Stefan Liess, the Lambert Family Foundation, the Lenfestey Family Foundation, Sarah Lutman & Rob Rudolph, the Carol & Aaron Mack Charitable Fund of the Minneapolis Foundation, Gillian McCain, Malcolm S. McDermid & Katie Windle, Mary & Malcolm McDermid, Daniel N. Smith III & Maureen Millea Smith, Peter Nelson & Jennifer Swenson, Enrique & Jennifer Olivarez, Alan Polsky, Robin Preble, Jeffrey Sugerman & Sarah Schultz, Nan G. Swid, Grant Wood, and Margaret Wurtele.

For more information about the Publisher's Circle and other ways to support Coffee House Press books, authors, and activities, please visit www.coffeehousepress.org/pages/donate or contact us at info@coffeehousepress.org.

Mónica Ojeda (Ecuador, 1988) is the author of the novels *La des-figuración Silva* (Premio Alba Narrativa, 2014), *Nefando* (Candaya, 2016), and *Mandíbula* (Candaya, 2018), as well as the poetry collections *El ciclo de las piedras* (Rastro de la Iguana, 2015) and *Historia de la leche* (Candaya, 2020). Her stories have been published in the anthology *Emergencias: Doce cuentos iberoamericanos* (Candaya, 2014) and the collections *Caninos* (Editorial Turbina, 2017) and *Las voladoras* (Páginas de Espuma, 2020). In 2017 she was included on the Bógota39 list of the best thirty-nine Latin American writers under forty, and in 2019 she received the Prince Claus Next Generation Award in honor of her outstanding literary achievements.

Sarah Booker (North Carolina, 1989) is a doctoral candidate at the University of North Carolina at Chapel Hill with a focus on contemporary Latin American narrative and translation studies. She is a literary translator working from Spanish to English and has translated, among others, Cristina Rivera Garza's *The Iliac Crest* (Feminist Press, 2017; And Other Stories, 2018) and *Grieving: Dispatches from a Wounded Country* (Feminist Press, 2020). Her translations have also been published in journals such as the *Paris Review, Asymptote, Latin American Literature Today, 3:am magazine, Nashville Review, MAKE,* and *Translation Review.*

Jawbone was designed by Bookmobile Design & Digital Publisher Services. Text is set in Adobe Jenson Pro.

CPSIA information can be obtained
at www.ICGtesting.com
Printed in the USA
LVHW030051221022
731189LV00002B/3